Tallyho, Tallulah!

a novel

Douglas McEwan

Electric Noggin

ORANGE COUNTY, CALIFORNIA • 2012

AN ELECTRIC NOGGIN BOOK
This is an original publication of Electric Noggin.
Electric Noggin, 1431 Madison Street, Tustin, CA 92782.

The dialogue quoted from *Whatever Happened to Baby Jane* on epigraph page, and quoted for *BJ!* in Chapter 12 come from the motion picture *Whatever Happened to Baby Jane,* screenplay by Lukas Heller, copyright © 1962, renewed 1990, Warner Brothers Entertainment Inc.

Dialogue quoted from *The Boys in the Band* on epigraph page and in chapter 16 is from *The Boys in the Band* by Mart Crowley, copyright © 1968, Mart Crowley.

Quotation from *The Music Man* on the epigraph page, and quotations and paraphrases-for-satiric-purposes in Chapters 1 and 16 are from *The Music Man* by Meredith Wilson, copyright © 1957, Meredith Wilson.

Description of the teaching exercise/game "Fish Families" in chapter 6 is from *Auntie Mame: An Irreverent Escapade* by Patrick Dennis, copyright © 1955, Patrick Dennis.

Quotation from *7 Faces of Dr. Lao* on epigraph page is from *7 Faces of Dr.Lao,* screenplay by Charles Beaumont, © 1963, Turner Entertainment Company, a Time Warner Company, Galaxy Productions Inc., and Scarus Inc.

Quotation from *Sunset Boulevard* is from *Sunset Boulevard,* screenplay by Charles Brackett, Billy Wilder and D. M. Marshman Jr., copyright © 1950, Paramount Pictures, renewed 1978.

Quotation from Gore Vidal on epigraph page is from the essay *Sex is Politics* by Gore Vidal originally published in *Playboy Magazine,* copyright © 1979, Gore Vidal, reprinted in *United States: Essays 1952 - 1992* by Gore Vidal, copyright © 1993, Gore Vidal.

Cover art photography by hyku

ISBN 978-0-9858463-0-5

Print-On-Demand version printed in the United States of America.

10 9 8 7 6 5 4 3 2 1

Contents

A Note on Sources

11

Prologue
The G.O.D. Dam Story

14

Part One
Something Sottish This Way Staggers (June)

21

Part Two
Suddenly, This Summer (July)

89

Part Three
Village of the Darned (August)

167

Acknowledgements

212

This book is dedicated to the radio comedy legend,
Karl "Sweet Dick" Whittington,
my first mentor; the man who first told me I was funny,
that I was a writer, and who began the task
of teaching me what the hell I was doing.
He even paid my A.F.T.R.A. initiation fee.
These things are not forgotten.
And to
Rosemary Stevens,
my own high school drama teacher, whose wisdom, courage,
kindness, taste, knowledge, and love
have been with me for almost half a century.
I'm sure this book will make her giggle.
DM.

"Trouble, oh we got trouble, right here in River City, with a capital 'T', that rhymes with 'P', and that stands for Pool. We've surely got trouble right here in River City; gotta figger out a way to keep the young ones moral after school!"
-*The Music Man,* Meredith Wilson.

"Your 'very sensitive girl' guzzled her way through six cases of Scotch, and slugged two studio cops, not to mention one or two other less savory items of publicity before we got that so-called epic in the can."
-*Whatever Happened to Baby Jane,* Screenplay by Lukas Heller from a novel by Henry Farrell.

"It was all very queer; but queerer things were yet to come."
-*Sunset Boulevard,* Charles Brackett & Billy Wilder.

People have got to know whether or not their President is a crook. Well, I'm not a crook."
-Richard M. Nixon, November 17, 1973, lying, as usual.

"Sex is politics."
-Gore Vidal.

"The city's name was Woldercan. It existed beyond the edge of the world, some years before the beginning of history. There are no records of Woldercan, no artifacts, no descendants of its people. In fact, there is no real proof that there ever was such a place. Yet it was as real as pain. ... And because He had been angered, God pointed His finger and visited upon the city of Woldercan the greatest plague of all: Oblivion."
-*Seven Faces of Dr. Lao,* Charles Beaumont.

"Who do you have to fuck to get a drink around here?"
-*The Boys in the Band,* Mart Crowley.

A Note On Sources

Readers of my previous book, *My Lush Life,* the autobiography of Miss Tallulah Morehead, The Nearly-Living Legend, may be hard pressed to believe that, after exhaustively recounting 103 years of her remarkable life and adventures as one of Hollywood's most regarded movie stars, there could be anything left to tell from her amazing life. Certainly Tallulah had spilled every secret she could remember. However, when a brain is as well-lubricated as Miss Morehead's, sometimes bits and pieces slip through it, sometimes entire decades.

Readers of *My Lush Life* will recall, for instance, Chapter 41, *The Seventies,* consisted of a single blank page. Miss Morehead retains no memories whatever of what occurred between the night of the premiere of her final film, a hardcore lesbian-porn picture titled *The Carpetmunchers,* which she co-wrote and directed in 1969, and her waking up in her lavish and well-stained bedroom in *Morehead Heights,* her opulent and decaying mansion, mounted ever-less-firmly astride massive Tumescent Tor on the California coast, just north of Malibu, eleven years later, in 1980. For all she knows, she never stirred out of doors for that decade, remaining in seclusion, without so much as adding a single husband to the string of nine spouses she recounts in the book's other chapters.

However, in researching another book, *My Gruesome Life,* the autobiography of Tallulah's great friend, horror icon Guy Thanatos, I discovered evidence that Tallulah had not spent the entire 1970s moldering away in her house. At times she was quite active indeed, but recalls nothing of her adventures during that time span. Indeed, Guy himself recalls being best man at one of her subsequent weddings, to a man whose name and face no longer ring any chimes in Tallulah's notoriously slippery memory. This led me to suspect that there were as-yet unmined riches to be discovered, if only one knew where to dig.

Since 2006, I have been employed, among other tasks, in helping Miss Morehead maintain her unique and unusual blog, *The Morehead the Merrier* (http://tallulahmorehead.blogspot.com/), which has brought me into her home again, on an almost daily basis, and allowed me the freedom to poke around in its forgotten nooks and neglected crannies. And it was deep in a trunk in her bat-infested attic that I found a box of bound papers bearing the title *The Personal Journal of Miss Tallulah Morehead's Excursion to Alta Caca, California, June to August, 1974.*

What I found in this box was a first-person narrative, dictated in Miss Morehead's own distinctive oral style, apparently taken down and typed up each day by her then-personal assistant Iris Cole, of a summer Tallulah spent in the once-idyllic mid-California beach resort town of Alta Caca, starring in a local summer stock stage musical, and sharing her expertise with young thespians by teaching an acting workshop. As I read the account, I was riveted by her never before told adventures.

But I also knew that there must be more to the story than just what her pages related. A glance at the rise and demise of Alta Caca amazed me so much that I sought out the handful of survivors of that historic summer, whom now, thirty-eight years on, are fewer *on* the ground than *under* it. I endeavored to hear their sides of the tale, and put together the missing pieces of the story, a story that was as new to Tallulah when I read her the finished manuscript (Tallulah never reads if she can avoid it. Too much focusing), as it will be to you.

So while most of what follows will be in her own words, here and there throughout I have inserted third-person narrative written by myself, distilled from the reminiscences of the handful of survivors who would and could speak of it. Some of the survivors, once they learned what I was asking about, refused to speak at all, pleading a desperate desire not to provoke again: "The nightmares, the screaming, the horror, the horror!"

Of particular help was Merle Mirkin of San Francisco. The charming Mr. Mirkin had just turned fifty when I sat down with him in his tastefully furnished living room, with its beautiful panoramic view of the Bay City visible through the enormous sliding glass doors leading out to his sundeck. Unlike many of the other former-Alta Cacans with whom I had attempted to speak, he did not blanch with terror at the mention of Tallulah's name, nor curl up in a fetal ball, replying to my queries only with whimpers. Rather, he smiled, and said, "Ah yes, I remember The Summer of Morehead so extremely well. It was the summer I found myself, so to speak, and was freed from the baggage of my past. She freed me. I would like to tell the story, yes. And to tell her at long last how grateful I am for what she gave me. Well, that is, for *most* of what she gave me. And as for that one little gift that I did not appreciate, a few injections cleared it up anyway, while the good I got from her has lasted me my entire life. And you should speak to my sister Fanny as well. She loves to talk about Tallulah – on her good days."

So here, constant reader, is the full, never-before-told story of Tallulah Morehead and the township of Alta Caca. But it seems that, before I can tell you the main story, I must first preface it by telling you The G.O.D. Dam Story. May I suggest you engage in Australian Foreplay, that is to say, **Brace yourself!**

Prologue
The G.O.D. Dam Story

Millions of years ago, back even before the birth of Miss Tallulah Morehead, (hard as such a prehistoric time is to imagine), what would, millions of years later, become known as the North American Continental Plate, careening westward at a rash, foolhardy speed of a few millimeters a year, collided with a smaller land mass that was similarly dashing heedlessly eastward at a hair-raising velocity of an inch or two per decade in a desperate attempt to crest the churning Pacific Ocean's surface and breathe the air of freedom. These two massive geologic titans were each an irresistible force, yet each met the other as an immovable object. The results of this low-speed collision, for all of the millennia that have followed, have been the fault lines which crack the foundations of California, the raising of the Pacific Coast Mountain Range, and across the Central Valley, the even-greater Sierra Nevada Mountains, and of course, the frequent earthquakes that have long troubled the residents.

Bits of the California coast even continue to crumble and fall into the sea from time to time. I spent my childhood living on the Palos Verdes Peninsula at the southwest corner of Los Angeles County. The southeastern coast of that peninsula, where Rancho Palos Verdes meets San Pedro, has been sinking into the sea all my life. The section of Palos Verdes Drive South along which we used to traverse when heading into Long Beach can now be glimpsed from the current stretch of that highway, lying far below in cracked segments, as the land which supported it was washed away from beneath it. One morning when I was in college, a friend of mine who lived two blocks from the cliffs overlooking the sea in San Pedro, was awakened by a loud roaring to discover that he now lived only half a block from the sea.

Long before man evolved, less than two hundred miles north of what would become the idyllic community of Santa Barbara, a triangular shard of the land mass moving ever eastward up from under the sea, rammed its way into the coastal mountain range, like a randy drunken sailor coupling with a street slattern in the cramped back seat of a steamed-up Chevy sedan. It forced apart two great legs of that majestic range, and cracked a fresh fault line deep into the mountains. The result was a flat triangle of land some seven miles wide at the coast, which reached back some five miles, and terminated at the base of a sharp cliff only one fifth of a mile wide, isolating this acreage so that it was inaccessible except by sea. Behind the cliff, the mountains formerly joined were thrust apart by the new fault, creating a steep, deep gorge, two miles across at its widest point, and edged with nearly perpendicular walls, which extended back inland some fifteen miles. A river soon roared through this gorge, tumbling over the cliff in a proud waterfall, and turning the triangular flat land below into a marshy delta.

The inaccessibility of this piece of land, and the swampy marshland you found if you somehow managed to get there, discouraged the state's aboriginal occupants from ever settling there. Nor did the European invaders who usurped the state find this land worth the tremendous amount of trouble it took to get there, and it remained unsettled until the 20th century. Up to then its primary residents had been beavers, who found the fertile delta and its abundant trees a prime dam-building locale, which in turn, only made the land marshier. Its flat-tailed rodent residents inspired the occasional mariners who put in there to name this triangle of land Beaver Valley. The perilous chasm behind it, which claimed the lives of many who approached its sheer rims too closely, became known simply as The Gorge of Death, and the river running through it became called the Verdes River. Eventually the fault line lying deep beneath all of it, when finally detected in the 1960s, was christened after a favorite California son, as Richard Nixon's Fault.

In 1919, Republican California Governor William Stephens decided that by harnessing the Verdes River with a dam across the one-fifth-mile mouth of the Gorge of Death, thereby creating a reservoir in the Gorge, and building a modest hydroelectric plant below the dam, his state's always-growing need for water and power could be further fed, as well as providing employment for veterans home from the newly-concluded First World War.

The job of building The Gorge of Death Dam, quickly popularly abbreviated to The G.O.D. Dam, and then, inevitably, The God Dam, was awarded to Damfino Construction, a contracting company owned by the Damfino Crime Family. As "Contractors" they were as likely to put out a contract on a person as on a house, hotel, or any other dam project. The exact means by which Don Lorenzo Damfino obtained the God Dam contract remains unclear, although there was one memo unearthed which vaguely mentioned the contract being awarded in part to benefit the "health" of Lt. Mayor Clement C. Young. Don Lorenzo in turn, assigned the job of overseeing the God Dam construction job to his son-in-law, Russell Zygote.

However, around the time the God Dam construction got underway in 1920, Damfino Construction was also hired to build the swimming pool and massive hedge labyrinth, *The Befuddlement,* for Morehead Heights, Miss Tallulah Morehead's movie star mansion, then being built on Tumescent Tor.

As it happened, and as chronicled in *My Lush Life,* Russell Zygote had gone to high school with Tallulah back on Long Island, where he had been among the select few dozen boys who had had affairs with the sexually precocious movie legend-in-embryo. Indeed, Tallulah in her memoirs listed Russell as one of her two favorite teenage lovers. Despite being married to the pathologically jealous daughter of a ravingly homicidal mob crime boss, Russell found himself unable to resist the siren call of his former paramour who, in the intervening years, had become one of the most famous and glamorous women on earth. Absenting himself from the God Dam construction site in Beaver Valley, to tarry in the backyard of Morehead Heights, nearly 300 miles south, Zygote personally gunited the swimming pool until the day he was able to "accidentally" encounter Tallulah, at which time they almost instantly reignited their long-dormant affair.

For the next few months, with an almost suicidal recklessness, Russell Zygote pursued an extremely ill-advised, and wildly uninhibited, sexual relationship with Tallulah, often remaining absent from the God Dam construction site for weeks at a time. Meanwhile, showing the integrity and ethics synonymous with organized crime and Republican administrations, certain cost-cutting, profit-increasing measures that were perhaps poor ideas to employ when constructing a dam intended to hold back billions of tons of water were submitted to Russell for his approval. Russell, intoxicated by non-stop, intense sexual encounters with one of Hollywood's greatest beauties, and exacerbated by the erotic danger of cuckolding the daughter of a man who had killed people for "Looking Funny," Zygote probably glanced at no more than the cost-savings highlighted on the bottom line before signing off on measures that would have terrible consequences later on.

By the time the God Dam was completed, not only had Russell's affair blown up in his wife's face, resulting, through the loving intervention of his still-adoring wife (by all accounts, Russell Zygote was one hell of a lay) in Russell losing only his toes, but also the bullet-riddled bodies of Don Lorenzo Damfino, his son, Guido "The Sadist" Damfino, and their business associate, Luca "The Sodomite" Cristillo, had washed up onto Santa Monica Beach. Their murders remain officially unsolved today. Fearing that he might be the next target of the never-identified killers, Russell Zygote altered his last name and went underground, reemerging only decades later as "Russell Zee," co-producer of soft (and hard) -core porn movies and cheap drive-in exploitation features, several starring Tallulah Morehead, with whom he had one last fling.

Whatever the mistakes that may have been made during its construction, when finished, the God Dam held, and the reservoir, soon named Swan Song Lake, swiftly filled the former Gorge of Death. A four-lane highway had been blasted out with dynamite along the south rim of the Gorge of Death, from Pacific Coast Highway twenty miles inland, to the God Dam site. It then descended in a series of sharp turns into Beaver Valley spread out below, where a group of buildings had been hastily erected to house and feed the construction crews. When the God Dam was completed the marshes dried up, since the Verdes River was now more of a creek through the center of the valley. The beavers might have been annoyed, had there been any left, but they had all been eaten by the work crews who erected the God Dam architectural wonder that dried up their former homes anyway.

Many of the workmen took a liking to the new beachfront valley, and wanted to stay after the God Dam project was finished. A number were hired to man the God Dam Hydroelectric Plant, and other businesses had to start up to support their new home life. The newly accessible beach presented desirable resort possibilities, and so sprang up the new town of Alta Caca, California, founded 1921, straddling the Verdes Creek, under the afternoon shadow of the great God Dam. Lovely, affluent houses were built on the slopes lining the valley, while more affordable housing was built on the valley floor. And so, slowly, a small faux-artist's colonywasforgedoutofequalpartsimitation-LagunaBeachandsham-Santa Barbara.

By the 1970s, Alta Caca, had become an eclectic mix. The Alta Caca Arts & Crafts Festival attracted the arty liberal types, the expensive hillside and beachfront properties brought in wealthy conservatives, and the beach itself attracted tourists and surfers. In 1961, the Alta Caca Arts Council, a group composed solely of snooty rich Republican wives who wouldn't allow any of the actual, liberal, local artists to join the arts council, established the annual Alta Caca Summer Musical Theater, which each year staged a Broadway or would-be Broadway-esque musical theater production, featuring one, or at the most two, genuine name stars in their career decline, fleshing out the remaining roles with local talent. Generally, the stars also taught a youth acting seminar, to share their wisdom and experience with the stage-struck youth of the town. Over the years, The Alta Caca Summer Musical Theater had become an established steppingstone to memorable theatrical careers in Oregon, Florida, and the Catskills.

The Alta Caca Summer Musical Theater was the reason, one hot June afternoon in the early nineteen-seventies, that a sleek, gaudy Rolls Royce was to be seen slinking down the Gorge of Death Highway towards Beaver Valley and Alta Caca. It was being driven by a handsome Filipino man in his forties named Rudy. Riding in the back were two women. Onewasaprettybrunetteinhermid-thirtiesnamedIrisCole,personal assistant to the car's other occupant, the ageless (Though she was seventy-six on this particular afternoon, but Torquemada couldn't have made her admit that.) motion picture legend, now retired from film work, Miss Tallulah Morehead.

Miss Cole was reading a script aloud to Tallulah, who was ignoring her while knocking back vodka martinis, and daydreaming of tanned beach boys with tight Speedos and raging libidos. Glancing out the window she barked, "What the hell is all this nature crap? I haven't seen a decent liquor store in miles. Someone should do something about all this natural blight, and get some buildings up here, or at least a few scenic billboards! And dial back that sun! Doesn't God know soft light is vastly more flattering to ladies of a certain age, like you and I, Iris? Well, you anyway."

"I'm only thirty-six," Iris automatically replied, knowing full well it would make no dent on her employer.

"I know that, Iris dear," replied Miss Tallulah, "But fear not. I don't regard you as an old fogey simply because you're a year or two my senior. Gracious me! That lake, that gorge: good God, look at the size of them! Where are all the men?"

"Good question," piped in Rudy from the front seat, "I better see plenty of finely tanned man-meat in this two-bit burg."

"Keep your eyes on the road, Rudy darling," snapped Tallulah, "I'm too old, I mean *Iris* is too old, to go Rolls-surfing in this God Dam lake. I'll keep a watch out for penises."

Alta Caca would literally never be the same. Tallulah was coming to town.

Part One

Something Sottish This Way Staggers

(June)

Chapter 1
Tallulah Blows Into Town

(From the personal journal of Tallulah Morehead.)

"**L**ook Rudy," I said to my chauffeur/houseboy/ex-husband, a handsome Filipino man of a certain age, as we crested The Gorge of Death, and I saw the town of Alta Caca revealed through the prism of my slosh-proof travel martini glass, "there's Beaver Valley spread out below you. That's something you've never seen before. Look at all that wild, untrimmed bush descending the legs."

"Tallulah doll," said Rudy, in his lovely Polynesian accent, colored by the slightly superior attitude he never forsook, "I've seen beaver before." He shuddered with restraint. "I never trust a rodent that likes to gnaw on logs rather than merely lick. Where should we go first? The hotel or the theater?"

"Rudy darling," I trilled, "I never tire of your sense of humor. First stop is a bar of course. Then you and Iris can go to the hotel and get unloaded, while I relax at the bar and get loaded. What's the name of the hotel by the way, in case I wake up in a different city?" This last question may strike the new reader as odd, but numerous instances of my going out on the town of an evening, and then waking up the next day or month or decade in a strange city, state, or continent, and generally incontinent as well, has taught me the wisdom of taking simple precautions, or at least adult diapers. I have never, as yet, woken up on a different planet, but now that man has landed on my moon, I suppose I should also begin checking on which astronomical orbs I find myself as well.

"We're staying at The God Dam Hotel," replied Iris, my rapidly aging personal assistant, who has, it must be admitted, a rather common sort of prettiness that pales next to my legendary beauty, much as the planet Venus vanishes when the sun rises. Poor Iris, who has been with me now for six or ten years (I can hardly be expected to keep track of every single passing year. I never know when I have inadvertently slept through one, do I?), was divorced about six months ago, and is still a tad testy. The cause of her divorce remains a bit of a sore point between Rudy and myself. Iris's husband leaving her for another woman instead of for another man had resulted in Rudy having to pay me ten dollars, and to forfeit to me his next turn with Eduardo, my gardener's son.

"Really Iris, there's no need for such rude fucking language darling. You mustn't be bitter."

"I'm not bitter, Tallulah; that's the name of the hotel. The God Dam Hotel is named for The God Dam, of which, the brochure says, it has a magnificent view."

"Well first, let's find the God damn bar," I said, as usual, the only voice of reason.

"Speak of the devil," said Rudy, as he pulled my modest, down-market Rolls Royce into a parking spot directly in front of a watering hole which a neon sign, not as yet turned on as it was only mid-afternoon, clearly proclaimed as being *The God Dam Bar.*

"Well," said Rudy, "I see where I'll be spending my spare time." He nodded in the direction of what was clearly another saloon a few doors down. The name on that sign was *The Salty Seaman.* "I suggest you stay out of there, Tallulah, if you don't want to take home another husband at the end of summer, along with the usual View Master slides and suntan." Rudy never lets me forget that he has not been my only gay husband, although he was the only one who had told me he was gay up front. He may even have told me before we were married; I don't remember. As far as my memory goes, I met Rudy for the first time the morning I woke up next to him, already wed. We stayed married for ten years, and though we've been divorced now for sixteen years, I still keep him on as an employee, because he's damn good at his job, and never interferes with my fun.

"Should I send a note of polite greeting to Monica Montana, now that we're in town?" asked Iris.

"Who?" I asked.

Iris took her deep, I'm-being-patient sigh, and said, "Monica Montana? Your co-star?"

"Oh, that bitch," I said, annoyed at this irrelevant question delaying my drink order. I'd finished my last transit martini just as Rudy engaged the parking brake, and I wouldn't be able to get another until I got inside The God Dam Bar. Monica Montana is a fifty-ish former movie star I have never met, now in a well-deserved career downslide who was to play my sister opposite me in the original stage musical I was in town to star in for the summer. I didn't really feel that I needed a co-star hogging my limelight, but as the role was already written, the Alta Caca City Fathers hadn't responded well to my suggestion that we engage a talented drag queen to play the role, and as apparently I could not simply do the play with Rudy reading the sister's lines from offstage, though he read them awfully well, as I was going to be stuck carrying this elderly has-been for the summer.

"I really don't give a rat's ass, Iris," I graciously replied, "Do as you choose. I need a drink." I opened my car door and slid out onto the blacktop, which I quickly found did not taste nearly as good as some of the other black tops I've tasted over the years. I pulled myself to my feet with all the dignity I could simulate, and wobbled off into *The God Dam Bar.* It was as dark as midnight inside which meant that, once I'd had a drink or twelve, a compliant man might be doable as well.

I don't know how many hours passed before I saw Sir Ludwig walk in, but when I heard him say something to Gage The Hot Bartender about how "Johnny's guest line-up tonight sucks." I felt safe in assuming that midnight must have rolled around. California still having antiquated blue laws, I knew this meant I had only two hours left to drink in public, so I began ordering doubles.

I didn't know his name yet of course, but as he was quite a striking-looking man, with his distinguished graying beard and his sexy English accent, every bit as authentic as Ingrid Bergman's Cockney dialect was back in MGM's bewildering version of *Doctor Jekyll and Mr. Hyde.*

I asked Gage who "The Limey" was.

"Ah Miss Morehead," said Gage, a stunning blond man with huge bulging biceps, nicely displayed by the tank top he wore behind The God Dam Bar's bar, "That is one of our local luminaries, the celebrated

Sir Ludwig Von Isherwood."

"And just what is Sir Ludwig celebrated for?"

"He's an internationally renowned poet, knighted by the Queen for his services to poetry. He said so himself."

"An English poet?" I asked, always wary of artistic men when I had orgasms on my agenda, "Shouldn't he be drinking at *The Salty Seaman?*"

"Oh no. Don't let the accent fool you. He's a total pussy-hound."

"What an unusual combination of housepets, darling. Well, set me up another vodka double, and send him one of whatever he's having, on me. What does he drink, anyway?"

"Sir Ludwig's usual poison is a gin and French."

"Well, send him some gin, and I'll handle Frenching him myself."

"I should tell you," said Gage, "as he won't, that he is married."

"That's all right darling, for all I know, I may be married myself."

Shortly thereafter, Sir Ludwig and I were lolling in a dark booth, which at this point in the evening was considerably less of a challenge than trying to stay perched on a bar stool. Luddy had been regaling me with an adorable poem of his, a love ode to a lady from Nantucket who got around, to put it mildly. For a late-20th century poet, his work is groundbreaking and *outré*; by which I mean it rhymes, and you can understand what it is about.

Suddenly his recitation was interrupted by an onslaught of lightning. This was odd, since we were indoors, and there hadn't been a cloud in the sky all day. A glance about revealed that a man was taking flash pictures of a rail-thin, elderly woman with bright orange hair, who was seated at a booth across the bar from us. I was annoyed by the rudeness of someone taking flash pictures of a woman who wasn't me.

"What the hell does anyone see in that flaming-haired old bat when I'm around?" I asked Sir Luddy.

"Oh, there's no accounting for taste, luv," Sir Luddy slurred, "But I always say, 'If I'm not fondlin' the bird I fancy, I fancy the bird I'm fondlin'. Now if you'll excuse me, Tallulah me dear, I've got to go drain the Thames."

"I'll bear your bird fancying advice in mind the next time I'm applying glitter to a peacock's tail," I said, having no idea what he or I were talking about.

"Speaking of a peacock's tail, me luv," said Luddy, "you just keep your lovely tail planted right where it is, while I drain the pee out of my cock."

His last word getting my semi-divided attention (fresh drinks had just arrived), I began to grasp that he was excusing himself for an excursion to the little boy's room. He got up and sauntered with a slanted strut that would have made John Wayne proud, through a curtained doorway at the back of The God Dam Bar. Realizing that I was only two sips away from needing an adult diaper myself, I got up and wobbled my way through the same doorway Sir Luddy had just gone through.

There were several options available to me behind the curtain: a cigarette machine, a table full of flyers, and at least four different doors, each labeled. Sadly, I had left my reading eyes in my other head, and had no idea which of the doors was the one I needed. I decided to just take potluck, and choosing at random, opened the door at the end of the short hallway and stepped through.

Judging from the handful of men I saw, clearly this was not the ladies room. But I've always considered men's rooms more fun anyway, though it has taken me years of practice to learn how to use a urinal.

But if this was a men's room, it was the largest and most lushly planted one I had ever seen. It was spread over several acres, many times the size of the bar it served (no wonder men's rooms never have lines), had trees, grass, and bushes planted everywhere, and, in an architectural style you'd only find in a California beach town, it was open air with no ceiling at all. I was almost beginning to suspect that I had actually found the rear exit, when my original diagnosis of it as the men's room was confirmed by the sight of Sir Ludwig Von Isherwood unzipping by a shrub, and hauling out His Lordship to water the bush. I noted with admiration that he was spraying out of a hose that would make any fire man proud. I waited until his gush became a trickle, and then staggered up to him.

"Ishyerwood, Isherwood?" I slurred to him.

"Tallulah dear," said Sir Luddy, turning towards me while making no attempt to zip or cover up his noble tool, which was well worth displaying with pride, "So nice to see you here, luv."

"So nice to see you there. Was the sword the queen knighted you with anywhere near as impressive as your Excalibur?"

"It was sharper and more bejeweled, but this one knows tricks that queen will never learn."

"Really darling? Well let me kneel down and pay it homage, and you can dub me with any title you like." I knelt down and allowed Sir Ludwig to knight me, although rather than try to hit each of my fur-shrouded shoulders, he split the difference, and aimed his pork sword directly between them. *Bullseye!*

I was just getting into the meat of the ceremony, which judging by his moaning, Sir Ludwig found as moving as I did, when one of those lightning flashes went off so close to my face that I felt the heat hit my cheek. Looking up, I saw the man with the camera who had been photographing the orange-haired woman inside, standing two feet away, grinning ear to ear.

"Thank you, Miss Morehead. I'll have to blur out the center of the picture when I publish it tomorrow, but enough will still be in focus for everyone in Alta Caca to recognize the fabulous film legend Miss Tallulah Morehead still living down to her name, and with our own Sir Ludwig Von Isherwood as well. I must say, I am impressed that a woman over seventy can still find someone to commit acts of public lewdness with in Beaver Green Park."

"How dare you, sir?" I bellowed with rage once I'd swallowed, "I'll have you know, I am not a day over thirty-five, and haven't been for longer than you've been alive. You publish any malicious lies about me being in my seventies, and I'll sue your balls off!"

"I say, Billy old bean," stuttered Sir Ludwig, "You can't print that picture. My wife will go on the warpath. Have a heart."

"You know this libel merchant?" I asked Sir Luddy, while noticing that I was, as per my involuntary lifelong habit, drawing an audience, albeit of gawkers. Easily ten or twenty people were gathering from every direction.

"Sadly yes, Tallulah. This is William Randolph Hack, the editor, photographer, and nearly sole staff of our little local newspaper, *The God Dam Gazette*. I'm afraid, since he owns and operates the paper nearly single-handed, with the instincts of a gutter tabloid sleaze-peddler, he can print anything he wants, even near-pornographic pictures like the shot he's just gotten of us."

"But that was a private moment of devout religious worship. I'm a non-practicing Christian Scientist, so I worship The Little God, although in your case darling, it was a pretty *large* little god. You can't use that as an excuse to publish lies about my age."

"There's nothing private about blowing old drunks in a public park," the vile reporter smirked, "You're just lucky Sheriff Hermosa isn't here to arrest you for public lewdness."

"Is public lewdness a crime now, too?" I asked, incredulous, "Is this Topsy-Turvy World? Is this the Bizarro Planet? Did that serpentine mountain road deposit me in Russia today? What kind of degenerates make public lewdness a crime? I'll have you know, I live in Hollywood, California, where public lewdness is our primary export. Anyway, we're getting way off point here, which is, if you publish that picture, you can't give my age as anything over forty!"

Just then, a blinding light switched on behind a bush a few yards away, while a bullhorned voice was heard bellowing out, "Put it back in your pants, Snake. And you kid, stand up."

Outlined in the glare I could see that behind a bush not far from ours, a rough-looking, tattooed man of maybe thirty, dressed entirely in black leather biker regalia, with a most impressive manhood jutting up from his open fly, had been interrupted while being serviced in a similar manner by a teen age boy who stood and faced into the light, looking terrified, and in immediate need of a handkerchief.

As the boy's tender face hit the full light, Mr. Hack yelled, "It's Merle! Hot damn!" and went dashing towards the boy with his camera. Simultaneously, the voice behind the bullhorn said, "Oh shit. Kill those lights! Kill those lights *now!*"

The lights went out, and a man in a police uniform stepped out from behind the light and blocked Hack's run towards the boy. "Stop right there, Bill," the policeman said, "You can't take a picture of Merle."

"I certainly can. This is news, Henry. It's textbook First Amendment. Get out of my way."

"Bill, we both know Merle is sixteen. If you take a picture of him like that, I'll arrest you as a child pornographer. You want a sex offender tag hung on you for the rest of your life? Besides, we both also know Harry would have you run out of town in tar and feathers if you publish a word about this. You got your lewd movie star shot. Be happy with that and back off the boy."

Hack seemed to take that in, and said, "All right this time. But if you arrest him, then it's news even old Harry Mirkin can't hush up."

"I'm not arresting anybody. They're all going home with warnings to keep it out of the park. That's it. Now take off, Bill, or you'll be my one arrest this evening."

Hack started to head off. "Remember," I said to him as he passed, "I'm only thirty-five. And could you let me have a couple unblurred prints for my private collection?"

Then I noticed that the crowd was still staring at me with a hostility I usually tried to discourage in my audiences, however unsuccessfully. I decided to act.

"Folks, listen!" I hollered out, "May I have your attention please, attention please. I can deal with this trouble, friends, with a wave of my gland, this very gland. Please incline to me your foreheads, I'm the great Tallulah Morehead, and I'm here to teach your Alta Caca boys drama." I went over to the troubled young man they were calling Merle, and the rough-looking tattooed, leather-clad biker, took them by the hands, and led them forward.

"Now these young men may seem to you to have chosen the wrong path, or at least, the wrong bush, but think my friends, how can any rough sex ever hope to compete with a Neal Simon script? Hm? With training in acting from Tallulah Morehead they'll go from *being* an odd couple, to **starring in** *The Odd Couple,* the greatest play ever written in the English language."

"Hey lady," said the biker, "I ain't no faggot, and I ain't no actor. I was just gettin' a little blow job from a park pansy. It don't make me an actor."

"No, it doesn't," I agreed, "I'm glad you recognize that it takes more than anonymous public gay sex to make one an actor. It takes Miss Tallulah Morehead's Academy of Acting to accomplish. Yes, Tallulah Morehead's AA, where you'll get drunk on acting - for starters."

"I told you, I ain't no faggot."

"What's your name, young man?"

"Snake Bendix. Everybody knows who I am. I'm the leader of Heck's Seraphim, the baddest biker gang in Alta Caca. And we ain't faggots. We may gang-bang fags, and let 'em blow us if they pay us enough, but we don't enjoy it."

"Well Snake, here's a couple of things you need to know. First: 'fags' and 'faggots' are very rude terms. In the presence of a lady like myself, please refer to them as gay men, or homos, or trouser divers, or butt slammers, or Hershey highwaymen. Secondly, believe it or not, you don't have to be a homosexual to be an actor. Humphrey Bogart wasn't gay. Neither was Clark Gable. There's probably a third example; he just doesn't spring to mind at the moment."

Something like comprehension dawned on Snake's roughly handsome face. "Yeah, I guess you're right. I mean Marlon Brando, man, his movie *The Wild One,* it inspired my whole life. He sure ain't no fruitcake."

"Certainly he's not," I lied, deciding that perhaps this wasn't the time to open Snake's eyes to Marlon's - ah - sexual versatility, instead limiting myself to, "And if once in a while he is, well I'm sure he's an exclusive top."

"Huh?" Snake eloquently replied.

"Now young man, you're name is Merle?" I said to the still-scared teenage boy.

"Yes, ma'am. I'm Merle Mirkin."

"You want to be an actor, Merle?"

"I'm not sure, Ma'am. I'd enjoy to give it a try, though, ma'am."

"Good for you. Well Merle, here's a couple of things you should know. First, if you call me 'Ma'am' once more, I'm going to punch you in the balls. Call me Miss Morehead, or better yet, Tallulah, okay?"

"Yes, Miss Morehead."

"Good. Secondly, no matter what you've heard, you do not have to blow rough trade in the park to be an actor. Mind you, it may be of help later on, when you need to get an agent, but it isn't required. So from now on, Merle, when you feel the need for a little sword swallowing or snake charming, I want you to do it on the beach like civilized people. Okay, Merle?"

"Okay, Miss Morehead."

"Okay, Snake?"

"Okay, Miss Morehead. Come on, faggo - ah - I mean, *Merle.*"

"You can call me 'bitch,' if you like, Snake."

"Okay. Thanks. And you can call me 'sir.'"

"Yes, sir."

"So hop on my hog, and we'll head down to Beaver Beach, bitch."

"Oh yes, sir! Thank you, sir!"

And the boy and the man, hand-in-hand, ran off in the direction of the parking lot by the park. I turned to the remaining spectators and said, "There, you see? Just through the power of acting and my own special coaching those two young men have gone from being antagonistic scofflaws, one brutalizing and degrading the other, to new-found friends with a new-found respect for each other. Those are just some of the benefits of the acting workshop I'll be teaching while I'm here in Alta Caca this summer. Sign your boys up now for Tallulah Morehead's AA. No girls allowed."

I took a bow, and for lack of any other conceivable response the small handful of remaining gawkers applauded weakly, before petering out and wandering away. The policeman walked up to me and said, "Very impressive, Miss Morehead. I'm Sheriff Henry Hermosa by the way."

"Nice to meet you, Sheriff. I always love a man out of uniform."

"Thank you. As I said, a very impressive wriggle free from an embarrassing situation. You only made a couple of mistakes though."

"Oh? What were my mistakes?"

"First off, there's that Sir Ludwig Von Isherwood you're going to be seen blowing in the bushes on the front page of tomorrow's *God Dam Gazette*. He's married to Monica Montana, whom I gather will be your co-star in that big musical you'll be doing together, which I would say constitutes getting off on the wrong foot with her."

"I see. And...?"

"That teenage boy you just sent off to get sodomized by that lowlife biker?"

"I don't know that they will go that far on their first date. One can only hope. At least he won't get beaten up by the bikers anymore."

"Might be better for you if he was. You see, Merle Mirkin is the only son of Harry Mirkin, **Mayor** Harry Mirkin, and Harry is determined to straighten his son out and turn him into a girl-loving heterosexual."

"Sheriff Hermosa..."

"Call me Henry, Miss Morehead."

"Thanks, Henry. Call me Tallulah. You and I both know it's highly unlikely that boy will ever turn straight."

"Yes, I suppose we do, but that's not going to make the mayor any less of your enemy."

"You may have a point. Any other mistakes you can see that I've made tonight?"

"Just one."

"Yes?"

"You see that thin lady over there with the orange hair, staring at you like you're from Mars?"

"I can hardly miss her."

"That's the Broadway legend, Miss Carol Channing."

"What on earth is Carol Channing doing here in Alta Caca?"

"She's here to star in our summer musical theater production of *Hello Dolly.* The show you're booked to star in with Monica Montana is **next** summer. You're a year early, Tallulah, and you're off to a flying start."

"Oops."

Chapter 2
The Slut Who Came to Supper

Minge Mirkin, the wife of Mayor Harry Mirkin, even though she was officially the First Lady of Alta Caca, nonetheless felt cheated. She *should* have been the unquestioned leader of Alta Caca's social circle, the people who *mattered,* but she knew she wasn't. That damned Odette Snype, Chairwoman of the Alta Caca Arts Council, was richer, more admired, more influential, and worst of all, more *feared,* than little Minge Mirkin. Minge just wasn't a dominant personality. That was why she made a good wife to Harry. He was always in charge, and he wanted a wife who took orders without questioning them.

But while asserting herself had always been a problem for Minge, that didn't mean she didn't have a will of her own. She just couldn't bring herself to put it forth. She'd been a shy child, and while she had grown accustomed to being a public figure as an adult, she was still easily cowed by stronger personalities, (which was most everyone,) but especially Odette. She dreamed of outshining Odette, at *anything,* and Odette knew it.

But on this afternoon in late June, 1974, she was certain she had pulled off a coup that Odette wouldn't be able to top. The movie legend Tallulah Morehead, once one of the most famous and beautiful actresses in the world, was coming to the Mirkin House for supper, and Odette would be sitting there at the table herself, as far away from Tallulah as she could be placed without actually being served at the card table in the den with the children. Odette would be steaming with jealousy, something Minge had pined to see on her rival's face for years.

Tallulah had come to town to play the title role in the annual Alta Caca Summer Musical Theater production. The previous year's presentation of *Hello Dolly,* with the original Broadway star, Carol Channing, had been a rousing success, but Miss Channing had never accepted an invitation to dinner. Since she knew the show backwards, she had arrived only a week before opening, doing only the dress rehearsals with the local cast, who had rehearsed for five weeks before she arrived. Then she stayed each day in her hotel, dining in her room before the show. On her one day each week with no performance, she still wouldn't accept social invitations - **except** for closing night, when she'd attended the closing night cast party, delighting everyone with songs and comic monologues, around the piano in **Odette Snype's** living room. And Minge hadn't even been invited. She got to hear all about it, mostly from Odette, but only second hand. Minge had burned with envy.

But this time out, by contacting Miss Morehead herself, months in advance, Minge had scored the social coup of the summer. Tallulah had accepted an invitation to a Mirkin family dinner, graciously posing no objection to Minge inviting "A few select friends," which meant she could have Odette there, and rub her nose in Minge's triumph. Minge and Tallulah would bond and become allies. Minge would have a triumph over Odette that would last all summer.

Unlike Carol Channing, Tallulah was starring in an original musical, having its world premiere right there in Alta Caca, written by two locals, Ignatius Wambaugh, who'd written the adaptation of Mr. Farrell's book, and Phil Rains, who had written the lyrics and composed the score. Wambaugh taught English and creative writing at Alta Caca High school, while Rains conducted the Alta Caca High Concert Choir and the senior Choraleers. Alta Caca High was deeply involved with the show. It was being directed by Cyril Savoy, Alta Caca High's drama teacher, the music was being performed by the Alta Caca Philharmonic Marching Orchestra conducted by Butch Miller, the school's band director, and the show was being performed in the school's auditorium.

Since it was an original, Tallulah certainly hadn't played it on Broadway, and would be rehearsing it for six weeks with the rest of the cast, before it opened on August 7th. Odette would be thwarted for months. Minge almost purred at the thought.

The show they would be staging was a musical adaptation of the popular novel and film *Whatever Happened to Baby Jane;* its musical title shortened to the punchier *BJ!* Tallulah would be playing the title role, while Jane's crippled sister, Blanche Hudson, would be played by Monica Montana, another retired film star who happened to reside in Alta Caca, and who was a somewhat too-chummy friend of Odette's for Minge's liking. Fortunately, since Monica lived in town, her celebrity cachet was long since used up. She was now a mere local. Tallulah still lived in glamorous Hollywood, and was The Visiting Star.

Further, Minge had gotten her own youngest child, nine-year-old Fanny, cast to play Baby Jane as a child. Since her own daughter would be playing Young Tallulah as it were, this would further strengthen the bond she felt sure would spring up between them. Little Fanny had begged not to be cast. She was a painfully shy child, altogether too much like her mother had been at her age, and Minge was determined to force it out of her.

There had been some sort of strange mix-up the summer before, when Tallulah had come to town a year early, probably to see her old friend Miss Channing in *Dolly.* There had been a tasteless picture, obviously crudely doctored, in *The God Dam Gazette,* that local tabloid rag which only seemed to exist to embarrass good people. A number of persons had tried to tell Minge that Tallulah had been caught in some sort of public indiscretion, but Minge refused to believe a word of it. Tallulah Morehead was a survivor of the grand days of classic Hollywood, when class and taste had ruled supreme, not like these decadent days. The idea that she would have done - well - the unmentionable thing people had whispered to Minge was absurd. And this dinner would show the town just how ridiculous this rumor that so many people claimed to have been eyewitnesses to was. The Mayor and his wife would certainly never invite a scarlet woman to dine in their home.

And it was with such dreams of social success spinning in her mind, that Minge Mirkin prepared the dinner her servant would soon serve to her illustrious guest and the selected witnesses to her ascendency to her rightful place on the throne of Alta Cacan Society. Meanwhile, less than a mile away Tallulah Morehead was enjoying a cocktail in her rooms at The God Dam Hotel, while contemplating its panoramic view of The God Dam.

***

(From the personal journal of Tallulah Morehead.)

My first clue that I was not going to be happy at The God Dam Hotel was seeing the mini-bar in The Presidential Suite. I had very explicitly stated that I must have a maxi-bar, and they had laughed and ignored me. Where on earth had they gotten the idea that I made jokes?

"From that very funny faked photo you allowed them to print in the newspaper last year," The God Dam Hotel manager replied. "The joke was, perhaps, a bit vulgar, but I've always enjoyed a bit of ribaldry myself. Now come and feast your eyes on the breathtaking view of the Great God Dam." With that he yanked open the curtains, and my dissatisfaction was total.

The window might as well have been a wall. It was like looking into a dense fog, something with which I have a lot of experience. There was nothing visible through the glass but an unbroken expanse of gray.

The Presidential Suite does indeed have a view of The God Dam. The problem with the view is that the dam is only 50 yards away. It is almost 4000 feet wide and easily 100 feet high. All you can see is flat grayness. If you press your face against the glass you can catch a glimpse of a sliver of the hills on either side of the dam. "Does this window get any sunlight?" I asked the manager.

"Plenty," he replied, "The sun crests the dam around 11:40 a.m. and strikes the lowest third of this window."

"I don't get up that early anymore. That's why I retired from making movies."

"Then you're in the right place. This is the perfect east-facing room for late sleepers. Direct sunlight only enters the room this far." He indicated with his toe a point on the carpet five inches from the window. "By noon, the sun is over the hotel, and off this window again. Twenty minutes of sunlight is all it gets, but then it illuminates the dam, so you can see the full brilliance of the concrete, and watch the shadow of the hotel creeping up."

Good grief. A whole summer spent staring out that window at that blank, gray wall would send me over the edge. That mini-bar needed to get maximized pronto.

"Tallulah," said Iris, "we have about two hours to get you dressed and sobered up for that dinner at the Mayor's house."

"I'm sure you meant dressed and drunk enough to attend the

Mayorette's little show-off-the-movie-star meal."

"Yes. That's what I meant."

"Must I go? This woman is bound to be dreary. Small-town society. I've been to parties at San Simeon, soirées with Gable and Lombard, and orgies with the Rat Pack; now I've got to listen while some woman who thinks she's interesting prattles on about church socials and bake sales? Their vodka had better be good. *Rudy!*"

"Yes, Missy Tallulah?"

"Make me an *Invigorator*. This promises to be an ordeal by boredom."

"All ready mixed, doll. Here you go."

"Rudy, you're invaluable."

"I know."

Ninety minutes later, I was staggering up the front walk of a huge, neo-Victorian monstrosity of a mansion that made the Winchester House look tasteful and restrained. A fat, mustachioed fiftyish man with "gasbag" written all over him was standing on the veranda, which ran the whole width of the house fortunately, scowling at me with a distaste that brought back fond memories of my loathed old rival, the late-but-not-late-enough Delores Delgado.

Next to Gasbag stood a mousy, overdressed brown-haired woman pretending to be fortyish, who was just erupting with joy.

Beside her in this grim family line-up was a girl of twenty, pretty in a common sort of way, looking understandably awestruck.

Standing next to her was the only bright spot in the whole line-up. He was six foot three at least, had wavy brown hair, piercing blue eyes, a jutting, cleft chin, and a smile that made me weak in the knees, or perhaps I should say weaker, as Rudy's three *Invigorators* had left my gait a trifle unsteady.

The Adonis was standing with his arm around the young woman in a most un-brotherly manner, which combined with his clear lack of the deficient Mirkin family genes, led me to believe that he was a boyfriend.

On the other side of him stood a teenage boy who looked vaguely familiar. He was having difficulty tearing his eyes away from Mr. Hunk, as was I, but when he occasionally managed, he grinned at me in a way that seemed vastly more genuine than the rest of the motley welcoming committee.

Last of all was a little girl of nine or ten with large solemn eyes and freshly dyed fake blonde hair, and I speak as an expert on fake-dyed blonde hair, having been born a natural platinum blonde myself. The child was regarding me with a look that seemed to hold only dread.

I turned to Iris and said, "All right, I've seen the Mirkins. Can I leave now?"

"No," she stated, "You have to go inside and eat with them."

The mayor's wife stepped forward and dithered so hard, it was like hiccupping. "Miss Morehead, we are so *honored* to have you enter our humble abode."

"Humble darling?" I asked, "Please! If this Victorian eyesore is humble, then San Simeon is Mother Theresa."

The hunk suppressed a smirk. The Mayoress was stopped cold by this remark, which she was clearly completely unable to process. She blinked a few times, looking rather as if hit by a brick, then I could clearly see her dismiss my comment from existence. I could not have said it, therefore I had not said it. I saw at once that this was a woman who could rewrite reality at top speed if need be. She'd have made a good studio publicist.

"May I introduce my family to you before we go in and meet the others?"

"Others?" I said, "How many shirts have you stuffed in there."

"Oh, only family, and those who are like family."

"So no one fun then. Well I'll sway here and meet your tribe only if someone gets me a drink. I haven't had a cocktail since I got out of the car."

"But that was only fifteen seconds ago."

"Good *God!* Tempus is fugiting its brains out! **Rudy!**"

"Right here, doll," said Rudy, slipping a vodka martini into my hand, "Sorry. I had to park the Rolls before I could get your front lawn bracer to you."

"Bless you Rudy. You're worth all of them. All right, Mrs. Mayor..."

"Call me Minge."

"*Minge?* Really? Well it's clear what your parents were thinking about while they named you."

"What? Oh never mind. This is my husband, Mayor Harry Mirkin."

The Mayor stepped forward to shake my hand. His scowl never cleared, and his touch re-chilled my drink. "Miss Morehead," he said through gritted teeth, "I can't tell you how happy your being here is making my wife. At least it keeps you out of our park."

"Well, it's early yet. Harry darling, you look like you could use a drink yourself. I've met warmer ice sculptures. Rudy, give old Harry here one of your Invigorators."

"No really, I'm not..."

"Coming up," said Rudy. "Fortunately, I made a thermos full of them."

"I don't generally drink this early in the evening."

"Then it's high time you started. It's high time for a High Time," I said as Rudy thrust a drink into his hand, "Come on, Harry, bottom's up!"

As Rudy forced the mayor's arm up, so that he could either drink the cocktail or pour it on his suit, a light dawned in my memory. "*Bottom's up!* Now I know where I've seen you before, young man," I said to the teenage boy standing next to the hunk, "In the park last summer. You're Merle, aren't you?"

"You remember me?" The boy blurted, clearly delighted, "I'm so flattered. You don't know what you did for me last summer."

"Perhaps not, but I know what you did for Snake," Hearing the name "Snake," Harry did a spit take with his Invigorator that would have done Danny Thomas proud.

"Gracious Harry. Can't hold your liquor I see, in the most literal sense possible. Yes Merle, I remember you now. It's not often I meet a boy your age with oral skills to match mine. What is your age anyway?"

"I'm seventeen, Miss Tallulah. I just graduated from Alta Caca High last week."

"Nearly legal. I thought I smelt ripe fruit. Are you appearing in my show, darling?"

"No, Miss Tallulah, I'm no actor."

"Nonsense, I'll make you an actor, or at least make you, if it kills you. You must take my acting workshop."

"I'd be pleased to. But as far as your show goes; it's all cast, and I'm working on making the costumes."

"*A couturier!* A fine and noble profession. Well Munge, who are the rest of these waxworks?"

Minge, who looked like we'd all been speaking Chinese for three minutes, recovered herself and brought out the drab young woman, one side of whose face was now peppered with spray from her father's

Invigorator. "This is my older daughter, Susan."

The mousy twenty-year-old girl actually curtsied and said, "Pleased to meet you, Miss Morehead. I love all your quaint old movies on the late, late show. After Vivien Leigh, you're my favorite old actress."

"Aren't you sweet? I hope my not being dead isn't too jarring for you. Vivien was a lovely woman, and a role-stealing whore. But we mustn't speak ill of the dead, and Viv's being dead is the best thing about her. I wanted to play Scarlett O'Hara in the worst way, but Viv lived my dream, and *did!* If I had starred in *Gone with the Wind,* people would still remember it today."

"But people do still remember it. It played in our theater here in Alta Caca again just last month."

"Did it, dear? You must pine for some films made during your lifetime. Do you know they have wide screen now? Are you in the cast of my play?"

"No, Miss Morehead, I.."

"Good. And who is this Adonis?"

Minge, who seemed to shut off when not being addressed directly, clicked back on and said, "This is Susan's fiancé, Dick Rockwood."

Dick stepped forward, stretched out a massive, muscular hand, and spoke in a bass voice so deep it made my shoes oscillate. "Pleased to meet you, Miss More..." but I cut him off mid-sentence by drawing his hand around my waist, grabbing him in a bear hug, planting my largest open-mouth kiss right on his magnificent lips, and sending my tongue in search of his uvula. I heard a good deal of blustering around me, but my eyes were closed, and my womanly parts were producing enough moisture to power one of The God Dam Hydroelectric Plant's generators while just as much electricity flowed between us. For his part, Dick wasn't fighting me off either. Rather, his tongue was examining each of my fillings in turn. Suddenly a summer in Alta Caca didn't seem so horrible after all. Then, against my stomach, I could feel Dick's namesake miming how glad it was to meet me, too.

When I broke for breath, I gasped out, "I hope you're in my play, Dick."

"As a matter of fact I am, Miss Morehead."

"Call me Tallulah, day or night."

"I'll be playing your father in the prologue."

"Oh *Daddy!* Have you ever acted before, darling?"

"Yes Tallulah. In fact, I'm kind of interested in maybe having a real career as an actor. So I'd be pleased to hear any advice you might have for me."

"Well you're a tad too old to take my workshop, but I'll gladly give you private tutoring. I can feel your enormous talent right now, and I want to feel your huge talent resonating deep inside me."

"Miss Tallulah," said Susan, thrusting herself between us in a rude and pushy manner, "Dick doesn't mean that. He's going to go to work for my father, helping run his rental properties, and we're going to be married, and live right here in Alta Caca."

"That's 'Miss Morehead' to you, dear. And I can tell you already that Dick has a talent that is too big for this two-bit burg. You can't be so selfish as to keep his talent from the world."

"Oh yes I can be."

"Trust me," said Dick, "Susan has no problem with selfishness."

"*Ro-od!*" whined Susan, whom I now realized wasn't even pretty in a common way. No wonder her father spit his drinks on her, although Rudy's Invigorators were much too good for her, as was Dick.

Minge leapt forward, shoving the poor fake-blonde little girl ahead of her. The child looked like she'd rather be doing homework than meeting me. "Tallulah..." Minge said.

"Miss Morehead."

"Miss Morehead, this is my youngest child, Fanny."

"This is your youngest child's fanny? What a strange thing to exhibit to guests. Well twirl her around and I'll take a gander, though God knows why."

"No. This is my daughter, Fanny. She's going to be playing you as a child in the prologue. Say hello to Miss Morehead, Fanny."

"Hello, Miss Morehead," Fanny said, forcing out each syllable as though they were physically painful to her.

"Hello, Fanny darling. So you're going to be Baby Baby Jane are you?"

"That's what Mother says."

"Have you ever acted before?"

"No."

"Do you want to be an actress?"

"No."

"Oh Fanny," said Minge, "that's not true. Little Fanny has done nothing but talk about how much she wants to be an actress, just like you."

"What a noble ambition. Is that true, Fanny?"

"No."

"Fanny! It is so. You mustn't mind what she says, Miss Morehead. She's a bit shy with strangers."

"Don't worry about a thing, Munge dear."

"It's Minge."

"I know that, Mange darling. I was shy at Fanny's age also, but I hid it so well, no one ever knew. Fanny, since you'll be playing me, the role of a lifetime, we'll have to spend *lots* of time together, *without* your parents, so you can study me. And I know just how to loosen up your shyness. Rudy! Fanny here needs a cocktail."

"Miss Morehead," gasped Minge, "Fanny is only nine years old. We don't allow her to drink alcohol."

"No wonder the child looks so morose. What kind of monsters are you? Rudy, make Butt-girl's drink a double."

"Already done, doll," said Rudy, handing Fanny a glass.

"What is that you've given my daughter?" asked Harry, looking ready to explode.

"Relax, tubs," said Rudy tactfully, "it's just a Shirley Temple. Hollywood kids drink them all the time."

"Sh-shall we go inside now and meet the others?" stuttered Minge, trying to herd everyone in the extra-wide front door.

As we walked into the house, I asked Rudy in a whisper, "What is in that 'Shirley Temple' you gave her?"

Rudy whispered back, "Well, that *Shirley* was more of a *saloon* than a *temple*, because it was one of your Invigorators."

I glanced back at the child. She had winced at her first sip, but she was now downing the whole thing. "Make sure she gets another when she's finished. That child needs more loosening up than Doris Day at a kitten drowning."

"I'll keep her company," said Rudy, flashing the three thermoses he kept with him under his jacket at all times in case of emergencies, or in case prohibition ever came back.

I glanced about at the murky Mirkin home interior and said graciously, "What a dump. What's that from? Who said that?"

"Liz Taylor in *Who's Afraid of Virgina Woolfe,*" said Merle.

"Bette Davis in *Beyond the Forest*," said Rudy.

"You're both wrong," I said, "It was my mother back when I was being toilet trained."

"An ongoing process," Rudy added unnecessarily.

There were eight more gruesome stiffs waiting in the living room. Apparently this "Informal Family Supper" had more guests than a White House State Dinner, especially these days, as Richard Millhouse Toxin wallows ever deeper into his self-made Watergate morass, the investigation into which has now supplanted all the soap operas on daytime TV.

A man of forty who was what I would call professionally handsome, which is to say photogenic but not sexy, and who appeared to have borrowed the fine, wavy brown hair of Vincent Price, stepped up. On closer inspection I could see he was wearing pancake makeup.

Minge almost purred as she said, "This is our local version of Paul Newman, only better. He stars in all our Alta Caca Players Community Theater Productions."

"My condolences to your audiences," I said. They all laughed, as though I had made a joke.

"No," Minge insisted, "he's wonderful. You should have seen his Charlie Brown."

"Charlie Brown? In What? *You're a Good Middle-Aged Man, Charlie Brown?*"

"Anyway," said Minge, who was a master at ignoring any comments she couldn't process, "he's Nelson Baker Eddy. He'll be playing Edwin Flagg, your leading man in the play."

"*You're* playing Edwin Flagg?" I asked, astounded. "You're not half the man that Victor Buono is. In fact, by volume, you're barely a third."

"I take that as a great compliment," Nelson Baker Eddy smoothly purred. This man was smarmy enough to host game shows.

"You would."

"In *BJ!*, the role of Edwin has been built up into more of a love interest for Jane Hudson. How I look forward to our duet."

"Well, the play is supposed to be scary. That should do it."

"May I present my wife, Miss Tallulah?" he said, bringing up a woman as patently phony-gracious as he was, "This is Jeanette Baker Eddy."

"So pleased to meet you, Miss Morehead," she said, laying it on with a trowel, "I was raised on you. You were my mother's favorite actress, and her mother's favorite as well."

"So I wasn't good enough for your great-grandmother then?"

"I don't know," she said, missing my point entirely, "She died before I was born, but I'm told she enjoyed you."

"Are you in our play, Mrs. Eddy?"

"Why yes. I'm playing Mrs. Bates, your nosy next door neighbor."

"Well, perhaps you could get the feel of your character by having dinner next door."

"But..."

"Perhaps I should introduce the rest of our creative team," Nelson gallantly interrupted, "These are the authors, Ignatius Wambaugh, book."

A small, ratty man with an attempt at a mustache stepped forward, kissed my hand, and said, "I'm charmed to be putting words in your mouth."

"Well," I said, "As long as you confine yourself to words. Did you ever Meet Kaiser Wilhelm? You know, it's thanks to me we're not all speaking German. I personally licked the Kaiser. Of course, it's hard to do it impersonally."

"And this," Nelson continued as though introducing contestants on *Concentration,* "is Phil Rains, the composer and lyricist. He'll be the musical director also."

As Rains shook my hand and said "So pleased," with a listless, defeated air, while not even sparing my eyes a glance, I noted that, for a high school choir director, he was a surprisingly handsome man: a little bit of Sean Connery, a tiny hint of Farley Granger, quite tall, and with the smell of a heterosexual. He would bear watching. I noticed with approval that, though he was wearing a wedding ring, his wife was not with him. I did notice that he continued to mutter to himself after I moved on.

"This," Nelson relentlessly continued, "is our director, the maestro himself, Cyril Savoy."

Cyril was a short, thin man, who was desperately trying to be dapper and English, and not genuinely succeeding at either.

"Frightfully delighted to be working with you," Cyril said, "To be directing someone who was directed by Hitchcock, well, I can't express it."

"An inarticulate director. How refreshing," I said.

Nelson was not to be stopped, "This is the gentleman who will be conducting the Alta Caca Philharmonic Marching Orchestra in the pit, Butch Miller."

Butch Miller, who looked as awestruck as Minge, stepped forth and said, "So excited to meet you." He may have been descended from millers, but he was about as butch as I am.

"And here," the unstoppable Nelson continued, "is the last member of our creative team, our choreographer, Floradora Windwillow."

Floradora was forty-five if she was a day. She was dressed in gossamer layers of chiffon, which floated about her in a multi-colored cloud. She wore a black leotard under the drifting wisps, and was draped in love beads and peace symbols. She had the watery eyes and the blissed-out smile of a stoner. She had flowers in her brown hair, which came down to her waist. Some of the blooms appeared to have been tangled in there for weeks.

"Oh Tallulah," she said in a high, fluting voice, "I know you and I will be courting our muses together in joyful union."

"Floradora darling," I said, "I never swing that way, unless there are no available straight men in the room." I glanced at Dick, and at the bulge in his trousers that could say, "Howdy Ma'am" from across the room. He was staring directly at me, and seemed oblivious to his drab fiancé beside him. Phil Rains wasn't looking so bad either, though he wasn't looking back at me. Whatever tiresomeness this summer held, I could see that there were pleasures awaiting as well, although this dinner didn't look to be one of them.

"I simply mean," said Floradora, who seemed incapable of being insulted, "that we are two sisters in the arts. I anticipate we will share moments together that none of these others will ever comprehend."

"I'm not even comprehending you now. I see one more guest lurking by the dining room archway. Who have we here?"

Minge pounced forward, dragging towards me a severe, grim-looking woman. She was taller than Minge, in fact taller than me, dressed in rigid good taste with an armored face that no smile had ever cracked. "This, Tallulah, is my great friend," at these words the woman spared a glance of withering contempt for Minge, "the chairwoman of our Alta Caca Arts Council, Mrs. Odette Snype."

Snype gripped my fingers with all the warmth of a steel vise and said, "So pleased to meet you at last," managing to convey with her tone the exact opposite of her words. "Such a shame I missed you last summer, as your Suck-Spears-in-the-Park performance sounded, on its numerous retellings, to be far more *outré* than anything we can expect from your Baby Jane Hudson, I hope."

"Oh let's not bring that old nonsense up," twittered Minge.

"And where is Mr. Snype this evening?" I asked the odious dragon.

Something like a smile, but equally like a sneer, spread across her face as she said, "Oh, my husband died."

"I'm sorry," I lied.

"So was he," she said, "But it was too late."

"Dinner is served," announced Minge, "Tallulah, I'm sure your - ah - servants will be fine at the card table in the den with Fanny and little Shirley Knott."

"Why not?"

"No. That's her name, Shirley Knott."

"Oh, Surely not."

"Yes that's right. She's the little girl who will be playing your sister Blanche as a child in the prologue. You can meet her after supper."

"At last," I said, "Something to live for."

"May I escort you into dinner?" asked Dick, who had materialized at my side, more handsome, rugged, and masculine even than Odette, if not as tall.

"Dick darling, you can escort me anywhere. I can't wait to call you 'Daddy.' You must demonstrate your siring technique for me."

Susan, Minge, and Harry all had simultaneous coughing fits, as we went in to the wretched meal.

Chapter 3
Din-Din

"**W**here the hell's the vodka around this catacomb?" I asked with my usual charm.

"We don't serve vodka with dinner," Minge replied insanely, "Just a nice table wine."

"Well here's a nice table whine," I answered, "I waaaaannnnnnnt some vooooooooodkaaaaaaa. How do you expect me to choke down this - what is this?"

"Caramelized caramel."

"Why did I ask? An *un*-appetizer. As I was whining, how do you expect me to choke down this garbage without a vodka tonic, **heavy** on the vodka; just the merest *whisper* of tonic?" I turned to Dick, "How do you choke it down without vodka?"

"I don't," he said, slipping a hip flask out of his jacket pocket, and pouring some of its contents into my water glass, which I had quickly emptied into Minge's lap, a locale which probably hadn't experienced any moisture in over a decade, and I'm taking into account that her daughter Fanny was under ten years old. Minge, unable to accept that a celebrity guest had just used her for a sink, simply erased it from her awareness.

"A man after my own heart. What brand of vodka is that?"

"Actually, it's generic. It comes in a bottle with a white label that has a blue stripe, with just the word Vodka written on it."

"Darling, that's my preferred house brand!"

"***Concepcion!***" shouted Minge, while also tinkling a tiny little bell that sat beside her to summon her servant, although it could not possibly be heard from over two feet away, even in a silent room with acoustics superior to the Senate Chamber, let alone a room in which Minge was bellowing "***Concepcion!***"

A tired-looking, middle-aged, frumpy Hispanic woman whom a paramecium could see was Minge's vast intellectual superior, stepped up to the table from where she'd been standing, a foot and a half away from Minge. Apparently, to Minge, Concepcion became a piece of furniture when not needed.

"Concepcion," said Minge as though addressing an unusually slow three year old, "Mrs., ah, I'm sorry, Tallulah.."

"You will be if you keep calling me Tallulah."

"I don't know your married name."

"Am I married at the moment?"

"***NO!***" Iris's lilting voice came echoing in from the den, where she was seated with Rudy, Fanny, and the Shirley child I had yet to meet, bellowed out louder than Minge summoning a servant from a foot away.

"Well then, my married name, in so far as I can recall, is Countess Knight Thalberg Tepes Karloff Towers Whatever-the-hell-Rudy's-last-name-is - you can ask him yourself - Borgnine Bronze. I may have overlooked a few. And it grows regularly. Ask me again tomorrow. Rudy can issue you updates, if necessary."

"Concepcion," said Minge, looking as though I'd maced her, "Miss Morehead would enjoy a vodka tonic with her main course. Would you bring her one please?"

"*Heavy* on the vodka, Contracepcion darling, just the merest *whisper* of tonic. And better make it a triple. Just to save yourself steps, make that three triples. Now then, Dick, have you nailed Susan yet, or are you two waiting for the wedding?"

Susan, Minge, and Harry managed simultaneous spit takes this time, while Merle smirked. Perhaps I was wrong about Minge's lap not experiencing any recent moisture. In this household, you needed an umbrella just to sit through din-din.

Once she could speak again, Susan said, "Miss Tallulah, you're *teeeerrible!*"

"In what? It was a bad script! The director was a *hack*! The cinematographer went blind and never told anyone! I was never a member of the Communist Party! *Why are you tormenting me this way?*

I'm all about the craft."

"Nooo," said Susan, who was quite a table whine herself, "I meant that of *coooouuurse* we're waiting for the wedding."

"That's right," said Dick, winking at me, "*she's* waiting for the wedding."

"And what are we waiting for?" I asked him.

"Dessert." he said with a charming leer. I began wolfing down the caramelized caramel, which sadly, shortly thereafter caused me to wolf up the caramelized caramel. Thank heavens for Minge's nearby lap. We were then served caramelized beefsteaks with caramelized asparagus shoots. When the caramelized applesauce was ladled out, I realized that Minge was just using the word *caramelized* to cover over that all the food was burned. I lived in terror of receiving caramelized vodka.

Throughout the grizzly, carbonized meal, Odette Snype stared at me with condescending loathing from the far end of the table. On the rare occasions when, by accident, I said something to Minge that wasn't insulting, Minge would turn and flash a smug grin at Odette. Conversely, when I did insult her, Odette would come as close to a smile as her frozen face could manage.

Once in a while we would hear the roar of a passing motorcycle, and young Merle would perk up and glance at the window, only to find his father glaring at him.

Phil Rains received a telephone call from his wife at one point. He could be heard in the next room, arguing into the receiver. When he returned to the table, Minge said, "We're so sorry Claudia couldn't be here this evening, Phil. Isn't she feeling well?"

"Your wife is sick? What a shame," I lied, "Is she hovering on the brink of death? Do you need bucking up?" Minge choked on her ash-coated applesauce, so I clarified my question, "I said *b*ucking. Although feel free to mishear me, Phil."

"Claudia ill?" Phil asked, "Hardly. The woman is as strong as a horse."

"A racehorse or a Clydesdale?" I asked.

"A drayhorse," Phil said, rolling his eyes. For a songwriter, he didn't smile much.

"Well," said Minge, "if she's not ill, why didn't she come to dinner?"

"Maybe she wants to remain healthy," said Odette, "She has eaten your cooking before, Minge dear."

"*Odette*," Minge said, duplicating her daughter's whine, "Miss

Morehead won't know you're joking."

"One more vodka," said Odette wisely, "and she won't even know her name."

"Good idea!" I chimed in, "Contracepcion darling, another vodka please, hold the tonic."

Phil decided to answer Minge's question, "Claudia doesn't like to go out in public with me anymore. She's lost the knack of maintaining the illusion of graciousness while ordering me about."

"What was her call about?" Minge asked.

"She likes to check up on me whenever I'm out of her sight for more than three minutes."

I winked at him and said, "Can't trust you with the ladies, eh? I don't blame her a bit."

"No. She just likes to grind any life out of my soul that may have popped up while I was away from her baleful presence for a few meager seconds. And she didn't come tonight because this evening is about *my* project, and has nothing to do with *her*."

"Well," I said, "you can tell her that you're safe with me. What she doesn't know won't hurt her."

"What she doesn't know can at least try."

"So she's jealous of you?"

"Not at all. She's certain no woman on earth would be interested in me."

"Blind is she? I'd love to prove to her just how wrong she is. I think I should send you home with some lipstick smears on your pe-"

"Miss Morehead!" Harry rudely interrupted just as I was getting to the good part, "There are ladies and young people at this table. Please try to at least *pretend* to have some decency. We are a Christian household."

"I knew that, Harry dear, as soon as I inhaled the strong aromas of mendacity and hypocrisy that you give off like background radiation at Hiroshima. Now then, Phil darling, as long as your wife treats you like a cheating dog, why not give her some justification? Once I've thrown up dessert, I'll be free."

"Not that I'm not tempted by a woman older than my mother," Phil answered flirtatiously, "but believe me, you do not want to get on my wife's bad side."

"Which side is that?"

"Frankly, both."

"So Phil dear, what drew you to *Whatever Happened to Baby Jane*? for a project? You don't look like a typical Bette Davis fan to me. For one thing, you married a woman. Your wife is a woman, isn't she?"

"Well, she has female genitalia. I'm not sure what drew me to *BJ!* I read Henry Farrell's novel, and its portrayal of two members of one family, shackled together in a vicious cycle of hatred and soured love, inflicting psychological damage on each other behind closed doors just somehow connected with me. Oh, and its two main characters are women who are monsters. I related to that. I didn't want to write the usual boy-meets-girl-and-gets-married type of musical, because I don't care for horror stories."

"Isn't *BJ!* a horror story?"

"I think of it as a normal, every day, slice-of-life type of tale, with a soupçon of Hollywood glamour, to make it look removed from the audience's lives so no one commits suicide in the lobby."

"Well then, I won't have din-din at your house. I'm trying to cut down on sautéed rats. Oh, I'm sorry Minge. Did I just give away your dessert?"

"No," said Minge, looking puzzled, "We're having lemon meringue pie."

"Caramelized?"

"If you like."

"Contracepcion darling, more vodka. In fact, maybe you should just set me up an intravenous vodka drip."

Once din-din had ground to its longed-for conclusion, I unhooked the vodka drip and staggered with the rest out into the Existing Room. The Mirkins call it their "Living Room," but theirs is not my idea of living. There's not even a bar.

"So, Miss Morehead," said the Snype woman, who was within earshot of me for the first time since we'd sat down, "is it true that you've had every disease known to man?"

I laughed, took her hand, patted and stroked it, and kissed her on the cheek as I replied, "Absolutely true, Odiferous my darling. In fact, I was just diagnosed with leprosy today. Highly infectious I'm afraid." Odette leapt away.

Minge saw and heard this exchange, and burst out with a scream of laughter. She doubled over with hilarity, laughing so hard I was worried she'd hemorrhage. Well, perhaps *worried* isn't the right word. *Hoped* she'd hemorrhage would be closer to the truth.

"Oh Miss Morehead, you are so funny," Minge gasped out. "It's too bad you ever have to leave. How I wish you were staying here with us, instead of at our hotel."

Remembering that picture window and the mini-bar at The God Dam Hotel, I instantly said, "I accept! *Rudy!*"

"Yes, Missy Tallulah?"

"You and Iris pop over to The God Dam Hotel, pack me up, check me out, and bring my luggage here. And stock up on liquor while you're at it. We're moving in with the Mirkins."

"**WHAT?**" hollered Harry.

"I've just accepted Mange's lovely invitation to stay here in your home, rather than in that dreary old hotel."

"Dreary?" sputtered Harry, who was a world-class sputterer, "I'll have you know that I own that hotel. Minge! Did you invite this - this - *woman* to stay here, in *our* house, around *our* children, for the entire summer?"

"I - I - I - I," Minge had clearly studied sputtering under her husband.

"She certainly did," said Odette, with a look of vulpine triumph that would have given Hitler a case of the heebie-jeebies, "I heard her. Surely you weren't just making an empty, insincere offer, were you, dear?" Minge looked terrified. "You having this glamorous slut, I mean star, in your house all summer, why I'll just be dripping with envy." Odette was dripping with something, but I don't think it was envy. Does envy burn holes in carpeting?

Minge looked supremely unhappy, which suited her face, but Odette's ironic claim of envy was too tempting for her to resist. She turned to Harry and said, "Yes, dear. I have invited Tallulah..."

"Miss Morehead. Just because I'm sponging off of you for the rest of the summer doesn't give you license to get all familiar."

"I have invited Miss Morehead to stay with us. It will be a - ah - a *broadening* experience for the children."

Merle cheered. "Oh, Miss Morehead..."

"Tallulah, darling."

"Oh, Tallulah, having you here will be *heaven!*"

"Thank you darling."

"Tallulah," said Iris, "would you mind if I kept the hotel suite for myself? I can come over here days for work. Rudy can stay here with you."

"Why not? The city's paying for it anyway." I said.

"Lovely," said Odette who, it turned out, could laugh without smiling.

"In that case," I said, "would you all clear out of **my** living room now? I need to unbuckle, and get down to some serious evening imbibing. Merle, you can stay."

"Do you think I will refrain from entering my own living room for the whole summer?" asked Harry.

"Well, I just meant for the evening, but since you've offered, that would be very nice. Thank you, darling. You can come and go by the back entrance."

"But, that's the servants' entrance," said Minge.

"Mange, don't put yourself down. You have me for that now. Besides, servants are paid. You're not getting a cent from me. And my friends and my staff will be using your front door anyway, so the back will be clear for you. And I must insist that you stay silent as the grave until at least noon each day. I am *not* an early riser. Now, who is up for a couple rounds of strip poker?"

"I am," said Dick.

"Me, too," said Merle.

"Count me in," said Floradora.

"Great," I said, "We'll play my own version of *Texas Hold 'Em*. You show me your big panhandles, and I'll hold 'em. We'll use *my* deck. Or we could just strip, and then, Dick, you poker."

There was a loud thump as Minge passed out cold on her own luxurious shag carpet. "Hmmm," I said, "Can't handle her liquor. I'm not in the least surprised. I'll deal."

Chapter 4
Morning Becomes Tallulah

At 4 a.m. the next morning, a ground floor window opened on the side of the Mirkin house, and a large male figure slipped through it. He tiptoed to the back gate and let himself into the alley. He took the motorcycle parked there and silently rolled it to the end of the alley, where he mounted it, fired it up, and roared off.

Inside the house, a face watching from behind the window heard the distant sounds of the bike starting up. The person listening then closed the window again, as quietly as possible. A moment later, a pair of bare feet tip-toed up the stairs and went into a bedroom, shutting the door silently. No one noticed another face, watching from another window.

At 4:30 a.m., Rudy slipped out the kitchen door into the Mirkin backyard, carrying a small garden spade and a burlap bag. Picking a spot behind Minge's geranium bed, as close to the house as possible, he dug a shallow hole, and then placed into the hole a human thighbone he had removed from the bag. He covered it up with dirt, patting the earth down flat, so no one but he would know where the bone lay, secure in the knowledge that the Mirkins had no dog to sniff it out and dig it up again. Rudy then let himself back into the house.

Moments later, the spectral figure of a headless Indian brave, clad only in a ragged loin cloth, appeared in the dimness of the master bedroom. A deep, whisky-soaked female voice murmured, "Is that you darling? So glad you could come along. Don't wake whoever this is. I'm going to snooze some more now."

The Headless Indian Brave then watched over the woman and the man sleeping in the bed, at least so far as a headless man can be said to *watch* anything, until the dawn forced him to vanish again.

In the guest room, Harry and Minge Mirkin tossed and turned, devoid of rest, as they tried to achieve some small measure of comfort on the lumpy bed they usually employed to encourage house guests to cut short their stays.

September seemed a long way away.

***

(From the personal journal of Tallulah Morehead.)

Noon dawned early in Alta Caca. As my eyes slowly cleared, I glanced about the Mirkin master bedroom. I was going to have to ask Rudy to take down all the horrific Mirkin Family pictures then disfiguring the room every bit as badly as the ugly flowered wall paper. Rudy could put up something attractive for me to look at for the three months I would be stuck in this hellhole. Maybe some posters from my movies, and perhaps a few foldouts of well-built naked men. I was going to need decor that would encourage me to open my eyes, or I'd be likely to spend the whole summer in bed.

Speaking of well-built naked men, there seemed to be one sleeping beside me. I had no idea who he was or where I'd acquired him, but judging from his broadly muscular, hairy pectorals I must have picked him out myself, as he certainly suited my taste, what with his being alive and all. (Not that I have anything against dead men, as the Headless Indian Brave could tell you if he had a head, but if someone is just going to lie there motionless in bed like a dead lump emitting a foul odor, I'd rather it was me.)

My memory of the end of the evening before was a bit hazy. I recalled how the strip poker party had terminated in a shambles when Floradora had deliberately thrown the game, exposing the sort of female body that could turn a bulldyke straight and make a homo out of Warren Beatty. There was a stampede for the lifeboats.

I remembered taking a gander at the minuscule guest room where I discovered that its bed had a ghastly excuse for a mattress. It had felt a bit like a rock quarry covered in sandpaper, only not so luxurious, the sort of bed that would entice one into borrowing Gandhi's bed of nails. I'd had no choice but to roust the Mirkins out of their own roomy but repellant room, which featured a very comfy king-sized bed, and commandeer that room for myself.

Then I trundled off to The God Dam Bar while Rudy broke out his tool kit, and began fitting together and stocking my pre-fab, on-the-road, bedroom wet bar. I recall nothing else until awakening next to the snoring stud. A pair of muddy prints of a man's bare feet told me that Rudy had also handled his other assigned task, making it possible for my longtime spectral companion, the Headless Indian Brave, to accompany me for the summer.

Whoever-He-Was and I stumbled downstairs half an hour later for breakfast. Mayor Harry, who was apparently home from city hall for lunch (God alone knows why), spat his cigar across the room at the sight of me in my shorty negligee and my unknown companion, who was wearing only pair of white briefs and a bathrobe we'd found in Harry's closet.

"When's breakfast in this dump?" I enquired sweetly.

"Who the hell is that man in *my* dressing gown?" Harry replied non-responsively.

"How the hell should I *know*?" I sensibly answered, "Do you think I could ask him his name when my mouth was full? I can't keep track of every man I do. Who can? Do you, Harry?"

"You know me, Mr. Mayor," the near-naked stud said, "I'm Bill Eastman. I fill your gas tank whenever you pull into the Union station at Main and Morella."

"You've brought a gas jockey into *my* house, done God-knows-what with him in *our* bed, and then brought him down here naked for lunch?"

"That reminds me," I said, "you better tell Minge that what's left of your sheets need changing. And sadly, he's not naked, although that can be remedied quite quickly if you'd like. A gas jockey, eh? No wonder I brought you home. I like a man who knows how to stick in his hose and pump. But now we need some breakfast. I'll have Eggs Benedict and a screwdriver."

"This is not an hotel," said Harry unnecessarily, "and my wife is not accustomed to preparing breakfast at all hours. It happens to be lunchtime."

"Your wife?" I said, "Don't be macabre. I've had enough of her cooking to last me a lifetime. Rudy cooks my..."

"Breakfast is served," trilled Rudy, entering the dining room from the kitchen carrying a tray with Eggs Benedict and a screwdriver for me, and a plate full of scrambled eggs, hash browns, pork sausage, an English muffin, and a virgin screwdriver for Bill. Appraising Bill by eye as he set down the tray, Rudy said, "Not bad. Nice biceps. Is he any good?"

"I don't remember. Bill darling, were you any good?"

"You thought so last night."

"That's good enough for me," said Rudy. "Can I have him while you're at rehearsal?"

"You'll have to ask him."

"Hey, handsome," said Rudy, plopping himself down in the chair next to Bill and reaching into his lap, "want some nice man-butt after breakfast?"

"I'm not gay, fella," Bill babbled senselessly as he removed Rudy's hand. Honestly, he'd had sex with me; how gay is that?

"Well then, close your eyes and pretend I'm Jane Fonda. You'll never know the difference."

"Unless you've had Jane," I put in, "Rudy smells exactly the same, but he gives much better head."

"I don't care how he smells. I'm no homo," said Bill.

"How narrow-minded," I said.

"Okay, muscle boy. Your loss," said Rudy.

"But I wouldn't mind some afternoon delight with you again, Miss Morehead. I can still close my eyes and pretend, can't I?"

"You certainly can. That looks like a much nicer breakfast even than Rudy's eggs," I said, bending over to stick my face in his crotch, which was rising to the occasion nicely.

"My eggs are still fresher than yours," Rudy snapped, as he left for the kitchen.

"What in the name of hell is going on in here?" shrieked Harry as he glanced over his newspaper at my harmless breakfast snacking, "This is my dining room, not some brothel!"

"Mgggggggmmmmmffgglllh," I tried to reply, which is hard to do when you're eating. I came up for air and said, "Of course it's not a brothel. If it was, he'd be charging me, and this room would be decorated *far* more tastefully."

"Cease this indecency at once!" Harry screamed, turning a shade of

purple which clashed dreadfully with the wallpaper. The man had no taste at all.

"And you, Eastman, get out of my robe..."

"He's trying," I said from below the level of the table.

"Eastman, get dressed and get out of my house at once, or I'll have you arrested!"

Bill broke free of me, stumbled to his feet and ran for the stairs, nearly colliding with little Fanny, who turned out to be standing in the door archway. I returned my attention to my eggs. "Harry," I said, "could you hold it down. I'm trying to eat. Hello, Fanny darling. Come sit here by me, and tell me what tickles your fancy."

Fanny came and sat down beside me and began eating Bill's abandoned breakfast. Harry was still fuming. "Miss Morehead, I will *not* have you filling my house with your sordid conquests and indecent behavior. I would appreciate it if you would pack up your motley collection of perverts and leave my house at once!"

"Well I would appreciate being allowed to drink my breakfast in peace. You know, breakfast is the most important cocktail of the day. Maybe you should lunch at your office for the remainder of my stay. But ten–out-of-ten for vocabulary. We haven't been called 'motley' in decades."

"Your stay is over right now! I want you out of my house by the time I get home this evening!"

"Harold!" it was Minge in the archway, "Please don't talk to our celebrated guest that way."

"I will *celebrate* our guest when I see the back of her."

"Thank you, darling," I said, "My backside has been beloved by millions for decades. Bill certainly enjoyed it. I suspect you named your little Fanny here in its honor." Fanny laughed into her hash browns. It was the first time I'd seen the saturnine child crack a smile.

"Harold," said Minge, "we can't evict Tallulah."

"That's Miss Morehead to you, toots. Just because you're defending me, that's no excuse for being fresh." Little Fanny snorted another laugh.

"Harold," Minge went on, "if she left, Odette would never let me live it down."

"I don't give a Democrat's behind what that Snype woman thinks about anything. I'm not having this whore in my home one minute longer."

"Darling," I said, "I am *not* a whore. I've never charged for it in my life. I am a slut. Please try and understand the distinction." I turned my attention to little Fanny, who was wolfing down stud-puppy's uneaten breakfast.

"Did you get a nice night's sleep, Fanny dear?"

"Sort of," she replied with a mouth full of scrambled eggs, "I'm in the bedroom next to yours, and a lot of very odd noises were coming through the wall."

"Odd noises? Such as?"

"Well, moans, cries, gasps, shouted phrases like: 'Oh yeah,' 'Just like that,' 'Harder,' and 'That's it baby, send Grandma to Disneyland!' and of course, the creaking, and the half hour of thumping against the wall."

"Don't you hear the same sort of thing every night when your parents are in there?"

"No. The only noise I ever hear from them in there is Daddy's tremendously loud snoring."

I glanced at Harry and Minge. Although Harry's rage was still evident, both were blushing crimson, and neither could meet my eyes.

"Well, I've got to get to the first rehearsal. I'll see you folks later. By the way, Rudy will need the exclusive use of the kitchen to prepare my dinner this evening, so perhaps you should eat out tonight, and every night. Fanny and Merle can stay and eat with me. Coming Fanny? We can chat in my limo."

"Yes, Miss Morehead. Can I finish this pork sausage while you get dressed? Then we can ride over."

"What a wise child. I'm so relieved to hear you can speak. And I don't blame you a bit. When I'm getting porked by a nice, plump sausage, you can't tear me away either." As I went upstairs to change for work, I could still hear Harry and Minge arguing while little Fanny suppressed giggles.

Chapter 5
When Stars Collide

The first rehearsal for *BJ!*, which would consist of a read-through of the entire script, was scheduled to begin at 2 p.m. in the Alta Caca High School auditorium. At 1:55, the cast, production crew, and Tallulah's assistant Iris, were all assembled around a large table on the auditorium's stage, waiting for the two stars to arrive.

There are important traditional protocols for stars. One is that stars keep people waiting. If you can keep people waiting for you, you are a star. If you are kept waiting for someone else, they are the star.

At 2:10, a black Mercedes cruised slowly down Goldenwest Street, past Alta Caca High. The driver noticed that the two spaces in the parking lot closest to the auditorium doors were empty, but had signs reserving one for Tallulah Morehead and the other for Monica Montana. The Mercedes continued a block past the school, made a U-turn at the next intersection, pulled over to the curb, and waited.

At 2:20, a Rolls Royce drove up Perry Drive, which crossed Goldenwest Street at a right angle at the entrance to the parking lot. This car's driver also observed the two empty parking spaces, and a sharp pair of eyes in the back seat noted the Mercedes biding its time up the block to the left. The Rolls made a U-turn, and went a block back up Perry Drive. There it made another U-turn, and pulled over to the curb to wait out the Mercedes, which it could no longer see, nor be seen by. A Mexican Park-Off was now fully engaged.

At 2:45, the Rolls blinked first. It pulled out from the curb and drove down into the school parking lot, coming to a halt in the spot for Tallulah Morehead. In the Mercedes a block away, a pair of eyes strained to see what would happen next.

Those eyes saw a man get out of the driver's door and open the passenger door. The woman who emerged was wearing high heels, a "summer fur," and a bejeweled turban. Supported on the arm of the man, the woman wobbled her way into the auditorium.

At 2:50, the Mercedes pulled away from the curb, drove down to the school, and parked in Monica Montana's reserved spot. A man emerged from this car's driver's door and opened the passenger door. A tall woman with hair that had recently been restored to an approximation of its former blackness, and wearing the face that Joan Crawford had discarded during her last facial procedure, walked arm-in-arm with the man into the school theater, crossed the lobby, and entered the auditorium proper.

As the woman stepped through the doors, Cyril Savoy rose from a chair at the table and said, "Welcome, Miss Montana."

"Please," said Miss Montana, in a tone even Olivia de Havilland would have found mannered, "call me Monica."

Cyril said, "Come take a seat. As soon as Miss Morehead arrives, we'll begin."

"*What?*" snapped Monica, all pretense of mannered graciousness suddenly a distant memory, "She's not here yet? But I saw her! I saw her come in - Wait! There she is right there!" Monica pointed at the turbaned woman sitting at the table with her back to Monica. The female in the turban turned to face her.

"That's hardly Tallulah Morehead," said Cyril, "That's our esteemed mayor's daughter Fanny Mirkin."

It was indeed little Fanny, dressed up in wobbly high heels too big for her small feet, draped in the stole Tallulah had been wearing when they had left the Mirkin house and one of Tallulah's hundreds of turbans.

"Why is she dressed like that?" Monica sputtered.

Rudy, seated beside Fanny, explained, "Fanny here will be playing Baby Baby Jane in the prologue. Since she is, in essence, playing Tallulah when slightly younger, Tallulah is mentoring her. She felt Fanny would get more of a feeling for being her by wearing some of Tallulah's clothes. And drinking some of Tallulah's vodka."

"But I saw her get out of Tallulah's Rolls Royce."

"Yes," Rudy continued, "Tallulah is staying in the Mirkin's home while she's in Alta Caca, so she naturally gave the child a lift here with her."

"*Then where is Tallulah?*" Monica almost screamed.

"Well, it was such a nice day," said Rudy, "that Tallulah decided to get out of the car a few blocks back, and stroll down here on her own. She'll be here shortly, I'm sure, unless she meets a really hot and compliant surfer. Just cool your heels, babe."

Monica looked ready to explode. "*She **what**? That's - that's ---- that is just incredibly **rude!** How **dare** she make **me** wait like this? Who the hell does she think she ---*"

At that moment, the double doors to the lobby at the head of the center aisle both opened and there, silhouetted in the doorway, stood Tallulah Morehead, swaying slightly. It was precisely 3 p.m.

"Darlings," she said as she perambulated down the aisle to the stage with her world-famous unsteady wobble, "please forgive me for keeping all of you waiting like this. I know it's *inexcusable*. But your town looked so lovely in the brilliant summer sun that I couldn't resist a relaxed stagger down your beachfront, drinking in the beauty, and also enjoying the beauty of a drink. I don't think I saw a single male under thirty-five who wasn't shirtless. It's *paradise* in this town."

"Miss Morehead," said Cyril, who knew this game, "we're honored to have you."

"If you have me, you'll be honored all right. Well," said Tallulah, now standing directly beside Monica, "where's this elderly co-star of mine? Hasn't she gotten here yet? Keeping us all waiting around just to pretend she's still a star, is she? How typical."

"*I* am Monica Montana, you drunken twit!" Monica yelled into Tallulah's face.

"Darling!" cried Tallulah, air-kissing Monica's head's immediate vicinity, "I didn't recognize you without any makeup." A blind man in the next county could have seen that Monica was wearing makeup almost two inches thick in a vain attempt to erase two decades from her face. "How wise of you to come *incognito*, and dressed down as well, to pretend to be common. I too just threw on any old rags I happened to find lying around the discard bin." The clothes and jewels Tallulah was wearing probably cost more than building the school had.

Spotting the man beside Monica, Tallulah squealed, "Luddy darling! I didn't recognize you from this angle," as she grabbed Sir Ludwig in a bearish embrace. No air kiss for him. She planted a deep one on his lips, with her tongue seeking his tonsils. For his part, Sir Ludwig's tongue found time to convey "Nice to see you, too," to her tongue in the privacy of his mouth.

As they broke the kiss, Monica said, "Keep the memory of that kiss fast, Tallulah, because it's the last one you'll be getting from *my* husband, that is, if he still wants to be capable of experiencing a woman."

"Well aren't we just a teensy bit insecure? Relax, toots; I was only testing his bridgework. Can't we get down to business now? We've already wasted an hour waiting for *you*." Tallulah turned from the speechlessly enraged Monica and spotted Dick Rockwood sitting at the table, wearing a tank top that exposed a lot of chest hair and an impressive set of shoulders and biceps. "I'll just have a seat. Dick's face looks free."

"Over *here*, Tallulah," said Iris, indicating the vacant chair beside her.

"Well aren't you the little spoil sport?" pouted Tallulah, as she wobbled over and plopped into the chair. "Where's my -?"

"Right here," said Rudy, handing her a martini.

"Uh, Miss Morehead," said Cyril timidly, "I'm afraid drinking isn't allowed on school grounds."

"Fine," said Tallulah, rising to her feet again. "It was nice meeting most of you. You'll find me at Morehead Heights, my legendary mansion. Goodbye."

"No! Miss Morehead, please," said Cyril, "I'm sure we can make an exception in your case. This isn't the school year or even a school function after all. And it's not like you're a student."

"I'm certainly not," said Tallulah, sinking back into her seat and resuming her drink, "In fact, this summer I'm a teacher, and my first acting workshop will be held as soon as we're done, so can we get moving please?"

Monica took a seat, and the rehearsal began.

***

(From the personal journal of Tallulah Morehead.)

Once I'd finished pulling the stick out of Monica Montana's uptight ass we were able to start work on the silly script.

When I sat, I felt an odd sensation near my behind. Reaching around demurely, I found a small envelope had been slipped up my dress, apparently by Sir Ludwig during our brief, chaste, tongue-wrestling match.

Phil Rains, looking handsome yet hangdog, sat down to a piano and began banging out the *BJ!* overture as he glared at his sheet music and grimaced. As he played, I slipped open the envelope. Inside were two pieces of paper. On the first page was written:

> "Dear Tallulah,
>
> As a private gift, just between us two, I've written you a little verse. I hope you enjoy it.
>
> Sir Ludwig Von Isherwood
> Poet Laureate Presumptive of England."

The second page read:

> ## "*Ode To Tallulah*
> by Sir Ludwig Von Isherwood.
>
> *A glamorous lady named Morehead,*
> *Made all of the menfolk adore bed.*
> *As she opened her thighs,*
> *She admired my size,*
> *But said, 'That's a mighty large sore, Fred.'*"

I glanced over at Luddy as I suppressed my giggle. He was watching me read it. I smiled. He winked. Monica, sensing something passing between us but not knowing what, sent me a puzzled scowl. Rains's gloomy music thundered louder.

The read-through went fairly well. We all read our dialogue while Phil sang the songs we were going to perform in a clear, rich baritone voice I can only hope to approximate, being a bass myself. There was, however, one exception from Phil solo-performing his entire score. They hadn't been able to clear the rights to the song from the movie, *I've Written a Letter to Daddy,* so Phil had written Baby Baby Jane a new show song, *I'm Sending Mother to Heaven, Where Daddy Wants Her Bad,* a ditty a bit more disturbing than the film song, combining the same wretched sentimental bathos of the original, but with an undercurrent of impending matricide that foreshadowed the show's themes of familial homicide.

It turned out that Little Fanny was more of a pro than expected, as she had already learned the number and sang it for us. Phil had worked with her on it, and Minge had made her rehearse it at home. I admit to grinning at the thought of Minge drilling into her daughter a song in which Fanny sang of her intentions to send Mommy to Heaven. Remembering my problematic relationship with my own mother, I have to confess, I looked forward to singing it as well, although Heaven isn't where I suspect my mother ended up. And if it was Heaven when Mother arrived, it wasn't Heaven for long.

Nelson Baker Eddy, as Edwin Flagg, has a bitter second act song to perform about how all the women in his life: his mother, all the girls he'd known in school, me, have conspired to make his life a misery. Phil sang the song, titled *All the God Damn Bitches in My Life*, with a ferocity I doubt Nelson will ever achieve. I don't understand why, since the play is set in Hollywood, the song references the local hometown landmark. Why, even as he bewails that all women are harpies devouring his guts for fun, should he nonetheless encourage local Alta Caca tourism?

During a break, I asked Phil Rains when I was going to get to meet his much-talked-of-and-dreaded wife.

"If you're truly lucky, never," he replied, "Claudia's only interest in this project is whether it might ever earn me enough extra money for her to visit Paris, by herself."

"Ah, Paris," I said, "How I love being plastered in Paris. I narrowly escaped a gruesome death there years ago at the fiendish hands of my arch-nemesis, Delores Delgado, only to see her meet a watery fate in the Seine. You can't buy memories that lovely. I should write a book about it sometime."

Phil flashed a grin that would have chilled the blood of Peter Lorre, all teeth, with the eyes not participating. "That *is* a romantic notion. It would almost be worth the trip. But really, does one have to go all the way to France just to arrange a gruesome death? I wonder."

"Have you been married long?"

"A thousand years, squeezed into seventeen."

"Does she encourage your composing?"

"In a way, since it's only when I'm deep in my muse that I can escape, however briefly, the torture of her voice, the misery of her company, and her unrelenting demands. Maybe that's why she seems to treat my muse as though she were a rival, another woman." He laughed a particularly nasty laugh, and added, "As though, after her, I'd ever want to risk having another woman."

"So she's spoiled you for other women?"

"Oh yes. Spoiled. Spoiled like rotting meat. Rotting, stinking carrion. That's what my Claudia has done for me."

"How romantic. Well, if you ever feel like cheating on her, you know where to find me." Phil was clearly a hopeless romantic, with the emphasis on *hopeless.*

The highlight of the play for me was certainly the finale of Act One, when I find Blanche trying to phone for help, and I attack her, kicking the living crap out of her, which has been re-imagined as a dance number with plenty of kicks.

"One, two, kick, turn, kick, turn, kick.

One, two, kick, turn, kick, turn, kick.

Punt, kick, step, kick, turn, kick,

Step, step, step, Turn, turn, turn, kick, kick, kick," Floradora chanted to the high-spirited dance music.

I almost began to like her again as I envisioned the many kicks I would have to give darling Monica when we rehearsed this sure-fire showstopper. It would be a lot of hard work, but work like kicking Monica was more fun than play. That's entertainment. Fortunately, a lifetime of lifting my legs heavenward has left me with thigh muscles of iron.

The most unusual piece of casting was a lady named Henrietta Shemp, who was playing Elvira, the maid I murder in Act Two. Nothing against little Henrietta, who seemed a very nice lady, if a tad odd, and was apparently a member of Odette Snype's Alta Caca Arts Council, which is sponsoring the play.

It is just that she is about as white as Governatrix Nancy Reagan (whom she claims as a pal and personal heroine. *Gad!*), while the character of Elvira is black. When I mentioned this discrepancy, she explained that it was all right as she'd be playing it in black face.

"What?" I asked, actually flummoxed, "I thought black-faced impersonations by white people had died out with minstrel shows, with the occasional *weird* exception, like Larry Olivier's black-faced *Othello*, and that certainly hadn't fooled anyone. Well, it fooled Rex Reed, but nobody else."

"We don't have much choice, do we?" Henrietta said, "We don't have any black people here in Alta Caca."

"You don't?" I asked, even more amazed.

"Of course not. Only Darien the librarian, and he's much too all-man to play a maid. Besides, he's not *very* black. And he's one of the good ones. Did you know there are good ones? There are. Honest. I've read about them."

"I know, dear. I've acted, among other things, with Paul Robeson, and he is a *great* one!"

"Isn't he a commie? I heard that he... wait a minute. When you say 'Other things,' do you mean you, ah, *made* love to him?"

"Well, if by 'made *love*,' you mean hot, sweaty, hard-pounding, raw animal sex, then yes. We did make the beast with two colors."

"Oh my gracious! You've had *sex* with a *Negro*?"

"That's right, sister. Actually, I've had sex with a rather large number of rather large black men over the years, going back to a lovely man I knew named Antoine, back when I was in high school."

"Oh! Oh, deary me!" Henrietta's eyes were growing so wide, they were in danger of meeting at the back of her head, though whether in shock or envy I could not be sure. "What are they...? I mean, well, is it true what they say? I mean about their..." She looked around to see if we were being overheard, then whispered, "Is it true what they say about their *endowment*?"

"If you're asking me if it's true that all black men on earth, without exception, are hung like engorged bull elephants, or horny sperm whales, I'd have to say that that is a racist stereotype, and absolutely true."

Henrietta's face drained of color, an ironic turn of events given the subject of our chat, and she looked like she might faint. To keep her from passing out, I tried steering the conversation back to our original topic. "So you're okay with playing a role in racial makeup? This doesn't bother you, or your audiences?"

"Oh, no," she said in a poo-poohing tone once she'd regained her composure. "Good Heavens, we did an all-white production of *Porgy and Bess*, with the entire cast in black-face makeup, seven years ago, and everyone just *loved* it! For once, Gershwin's music really sounded authentic! And we fixed all that bad grammar as well. You should have heard Nelson sing *Bess, You Are My Woman Now.* And I loved when Sportin' Wood sang *It's Not Necessarily So."*

"The character's name is Sportin' Life, not Sportin' Wood."

Henrietta, who was maybe fifty-five, going gray, and unmarried, giggled and said, "You're right! 'Sportin' *Wood*'? What was I thinking of?"

"I have a working theory on that."

"Anyway, our all-white *Porgy and Bess* was terrific. It was like seeing Negro Music Night on *The Lawrence Welk Show* in person. We're hoping to get the rights to do an all-white production of *The Wiz* as soon as we can."

"And wearing that black-face makeup doesn't offend you?"

"Well, why would it? It washes off. It's not like anyone will think I'm really a Negro trying to pass as a normal person."

And people think *I* live in my own private world.

When rehearsal was over, Fanny said she had some kind of summer job to go to, so I asked Rudy to give her a lift to her little jobette and then come back. I had about twenty minutes to kill before my students would arrive for the first of my acting workshops, so I retired to my dressing room for a rejuvenating drink or three. I hadn't been in there thirty seconds, barely time enough to pour one of Rudy's premixed martinis from the thermos to the glass, when there came a quiet tap on the door. I opened it and there stood Dick Rockwood, who quickly slipped in, closed the door, and then quickly slipped in.

"Gracious darling," I said as I experienced how well he deserved his name, "Aren't you - *Oh my God!* - and that mousy little Susan - *Oh yes! Right there!* - person engaged to be married?"

"That what she thinks," he panted into my ear. "It's very convenient for me just now. *Oh yes!* Could you turn slightly to the left? - *Oh yes!"*

"You aren't bothered by - *Oh sweet Christ on toast!* - cheating on her?"

"No. Why would I be? After all, we aren't - *Oh, Momma!* Where'd you learn to do **that?"**

"From Errol Flynn. What were you - *Hello! You can do that some more!* - What were you saying?"

"I was saying Susan and I aren't married yet, so it isn't - *O Holy Mother of God, do that again!* - so technically it isn't - *Oh God!* - cheating just yet."

"Wgggggghhhlgphhmmmmrgh."

"What?"

"Sorry. I shouldn't try to talk with my mouth full. I was just asking if Susan would - *Yeah baby! That's Mamma's hand of glory!* - if Susan would feel the same way about it."

"Who cares? Besides, I think our engagement's days are - *Uuuuuuuuuhhhhh!* - our engagement's days are numbered. Who wants a girl when they can have a woman? *Oh! Oh! Oh! Yes! Yes!* **Yes!"**

Then suddenly there came a rapping, as of someone gently tapping, tapping on my dressing room door. At first we thought it was just my heels rattling against the wall, but when we heard the voice of Sir Ludwig whispering, "Tallulah old bean, are you indecent?" we realized it was the door.

"He probably shouldn't know I'm here," Dick whispered in my ear.

"In the closet," I suggested. Dick got off of me and slipped into my closet. I clambered back to my feet, took a swig of martini, and opened the door. Sir Ludwig slipped in, closed the door, and slipped in.

"Won't your wife be angry if she catches you with me, getting sloppy one-and-a-halfs?" I asked, while noticing that it was easier to concentrate and speak while Sir Ludwig was making love to me than while Dick was dishing out his somewhat more energetic moves.

"Oh, who gives a Corgi's behind? If she isn't angry about that she'll be angry about something else. Anger is what she does. *Oh blimey! That's positively spiffy!"*

"Language dear. There's a slutty woman present."

At that moment there came a loud pounding at the door. There was no mistaking that for any noise my feet were making, as Sir Ludwig wasn't nearly so athletic, and besides, we were doing it standing up. Then we heard Monica's voice asking, "May I come in Tallulah?"

"She mustn't find me," hissed Ludwig.

"Tallulah," asked Monica through the door, "may I come in?"

"I'm full at the moment, dear," I said.

"What?" she asked, as Ludwig made a dive towards the closet.

"Ah, *occupaddo*," I said, as I grabbed Ludwig. "Not in there," I whispered to him, "it's the first place she'll look. Get under the daybed."

Ludwig wriggled his plump, aging body under my day bed as I opened the door. Monica strode in like an officer with a no-knocker warrant. "By any chance is my husband in here, you ancient trollop?"

she asked politely.

"What would Luddy be doing in here?" I asked with sweetness, as I plopped down on the daybed, which groaned in response with a British accent.

"You, of course. He's been lusting for you since 1940."

"Well, who can blame him? You have to expect a man to dream of steak, when all he gets at home is gruel."

"Who are you calling gruel?"

"Who is the only grueling woman in the room?" An English snort came from under the bed.

"What was that?"

"What was what?" A sudden thump came from the closet.

"*Ah ha!*" said Monica, like Nancy Drew discovering a treasure map in The Old Mill, "So he's in *here!*"

Monica yanked open the closet door. Needless to say, we didn't see Sir Ludwig. What we did see was Dick with his jeans and white cotton briefs pooled at his ankles, and the woman who was stage managing the play clinging to him, with her legs wrapped around his waist, her arms around his neck, and her panties dangling from her left ankle. I noticed with admiration that she was a natural redhead.

"Do you mind?" asked Dick, giving a better performance than he had reading his lines, "We'd like a little privacy. Two's company and four's a crowd."

Seeing Ludwig's foot sticking out from under the end of the daybed I said, "Let's test that theory," and shoved Monica into the closet, sliding the door closed.

"Get out now. I can't keep her in there long," I said to Sir Ludwig, my words ironically obscured from Monica by all the noise she herself was making as she squawked in the closet, pounding on the door and yelling unimaginative clichés like, "*Let me out of here!*"

Ludwig wriggled out and fled the room. I opened the closet and Monica fell out in a fury. "What did you do that for?" she yelped.

"You just have no sense of humor at all, do you?" I replied with all the innocence of a week-old baby born able to speak.

"This summer can't be over soon enough for *me*," she snarled, before storming out the door.

"Don't be shy. Drop in again anytime!" I called after her graciously, "Now then," I said to the closeted couple hurriedly extracting themselves from each other, "what were you two doing?"

"I was just keeping him warmed up for you," the woman said, all wide-eyed innocent guilt.

"A little too well," I observed, noting the evidence of things having gone just a tad too far trickling down her leg.

"Sorry Tallulah," said Dick, pulling up his pants, "things got a bit out of hand. Rain check?" And he bounded out of the room.

"Ah, Miss Morehead," said the woman, who was attractive in a sluttish, been-around-the-block-twice sort of way, "you probably want some sort of explanation."

"About what? You hiding in my dressing room closet, and getting nailed by Dick while he hid in there with you?"

"Yes. About that."

"No explanation needed, darling. The only odd thing about this to me is that usually when this sort of thing occurs, *I'm* the slut in the closet. This time, it happens that I'm out of the closet. If only all of my husbands had been. What's your name, darling?"

"Rita Morecombe. I'm stage managing this show, and I run a little beachfront bar; *The Wet Spot.*"

"You're a bartendress?" I asked.

"No. I'm a bar owner."

"A bar ownerette, and a woman who'll just hop on any random pantsless man with whom she suddenly finds herself crammed in a closet? I think I might be beginning to like you."

"You're not mad at me for doing Rockwood?"

"Am I mad at you because Dick was screwing you behind my back when he was interrupted screwing me behind his fiancé's back so I could screw Sir Ludwig behind Dick's and Monica's backs? Dear, I may be a drunken slut, but I'm not a hypocrite. I am just a tad curious as to why you were in my closet in the first place. Not mad. Just curious."

"Oh that. Well, while Cyril allows you to drink on the campus, he doesn't exempt me from that rule, so I slipped in here for a snort, and hid in the closet when I heard you unlocking the door."

"A snort?"

"Oh, yeah," she said, pulling a hip flask from her purse, "Want some?"

"Darling, if it weren't for your age, I'd think you were my little sister."

"Us? Sisters? I'm only forty."

"Okay, my *older* sister," I took a swig from the flask. It was throat-burning rotgut. "Rita my dear, I think this may be the beginning of a beautiful friendship."

Chapter 6
Higher Education

The day I arrived in Alta Caca, now some two eternal days in the past, I had discovered to my horror that The Alta Caca Arts Council, in promoting my acting workshop, *Tallulah Morehead's Acting Academy*, better known as *Tallulah Morehead's AA*, while they had remembered my insistence that the class be all-male (under the excuse that I didn't need to create competition for myself), had nonetheless forgotten my other condition: that all my pupils be post-pubescent. Just what the hell was I supposed to do with a bunch of little boys? Rudy and I had put our heads together, though not close enough to touch, and come up with a plan.

At the first class meeting I would instruct all and sundry in the basics of my special, revolutionary acting system, and then all the little kiddies would be sent off with Rudy with whom I had prepared a forty-five-minute condensation of a fairly recent, popular, all-male Broadway play, which he would spend the summer directing them in for a single performance for their parents and friends, if any, the same week *BJ!* opened. Meanwhile, I would devote the summer to coaching the more mature boys on how to reach my inner potential, taking them in hand, and working my fingers to their bones if need be, or even if not.

So now I found myself facing a room with seven teenage boys of varying degrees of promise, that is to say looks, and nine prepubescent boys, whose ages ranged (if their applications are to be believed; eight-year-old boys are notoriously vain about their age) from seven to twelve. The only pupil there I knew was Merle.

Since Rudy would be taking the wee ones to the auditorium later for the first read-through of the play I'd chosen for them, we were in a classroom, and the boys were all sitting at school desks, onto which Rudy was setting the paper cups into which the boys' drinks would soon be poured. I sat down on the top of the teacher's desk facing the boys, legs a bit spread, so the lads' educations began instantly. I hadn't been a star for decades, without learning how to command an audience's attention effortlessly.

"All right, boys," I began, "First off, I need to know who here has gone through puberty, and who hasn't, as there are separate curricula for each group. So please raise your hand if you've gone through puberty. After all, if you've really finished puberty, you probably only have one hand free."

"Ma'am?" asked a boy who was clearly not over eight.

"Don't call me ma'am, darling. It makes me sound like an old lady. Call me Miss Morehead, and you older boys can call me Tallulah."

"Uh, Miss Morehead, what is 'puberty'?"

"If you don't know what it is, you haven't gone through it."

Another question came from a spotty-faced boy, whose voice cracked and leapt about from octave to octave, "I think I'm going through puberty now, Tallulah."

"It's 'Miss Morehead' to you, and you can go with the smaller boys. Rudy, he's your stage manager. Now then, about acting, or as you've been calling it all your life, lying. Tell me, have any of you ever seen any movies starring Joan Crawford?"

Several hands shot up from the teenage boys.

"And did you ever believe a single word out of her mouth?"

All the hands went down again.

"I wouldn't think so. We have a technical term for Joan's style of acting. It's called 'fakey.' Joan couldn't communicate an honest emotion if her life depended on it. You see, an actress like Joan, and I use the term quite loosely, has no access to her emotions. She's put so much dedication into hiding her true self, and creating a completely synthetic persona, that her emotions are all damned up deep inside. Admittedly, given what her true self is like, it was probably a wise decision on her part, but that's not important right now. The trick to honest acting is finding a way to break through the barriers we all erect to hide our true selves.

And for that I have perfected a system which I have used to achieve my acclaimed performances in ninety motion pictures, all of which I am sure you're intimately familiar with. I call it The Drink System. Rudy, pour."

Rudy began pouring beer into each student's glass. I thought that I'd start them on beer until I determined who had enough talent for wine, whisky, or vodka.

One boy, seven years old according to his application, stuck his hand up. "Miss Morehead, is that true? Because my mom says drinking is bad."

"Dear, it's time you faced this fact: your mother is lying to you. *All* mothers lie to their kids on a daily basis. I was a mother myself for a while, and I can assure you, I never said a true word to my daughter in her whole life. Mothers do this to prevent their children from enjoying the same things they do. This is because all mothers are hypocrites, especially mine."

"But..."

"Do your parents drag you to church?"

"Yes."

"Do your parents tell you church is good?"

"Yes."

"Do they give you wine in church?"

"Yes."

"So how does your mother justify that?"

"What does *jussify* mean?"

"I mean, how does your mother explain why she says drinking is bad, church is good, and then makes you drink in church?"

"Uh, she says it's the blood of Christ."

"*Is* it blood?"

"I don't think so."

"Is drinking human blood a *good* thing? Would you worship Dracula?"

"No! He's scary!"

"Perhaps, but he was a damn fine lay. However, this is no time for me to wax nostalgic. Does your mother drink when she's not in church?"

"Sometimes."

"So your mom is a big, fat liar, isn't she?"

"I guess."

"Damn right she is. So, do you know the *real* reason people drink in church?"

"No."

"It's so they can act like they believe in God. And it also helps with the stultifying boredom. Now quit asking questions and chug that brew. Everyone else is on their second already."

"Yes, Miss Morehead."

Once everyone had had at least two cups of beer, I explained further, "Drinking relaxes your inhibitions, and allows your emotions to run free. A sober actor is a lousy actor, and a pretty rare actor, I might add. Of course, the irony is that Joan Crawford drank like a fish. But then, if you have no talent, all the booze in the world can't set it free.

"Now, you younger boys, Rudy here is going to take all of you to the auditorium to cast and begin rehearsing the play you're going to be putting on this summer. The rest of you young men will remain here for a fun acting exercise with me."

Once the little kids were gone, I explained to the teenage boys what we were going to do next.

"Now boys, first off, as you are all older, I think we can break out the harder stuff. Vodka anyone?" Not surprisingly, they were all up for it. In fact, two of them had brought their own. One had brought a better brand than mine.

Next, Step Two.

"Okay, boys, in order to break through your inhibitions in class this has to be a safe space where you can behave naturally without fear of consequences. So we have to have two hard and fast rules here. The first is, obviously, that whatever I say goes. In theater and movies someone has to be in charge, and in here, it's me."

"Now the second rule is this, whatever happens in here is just between us. It has to remain secret. You are never to tell anyone, not *anyone* at all, what goes on in here, *especially* not your parents. Everyone clear on that?"

"Yes, Tallulah," they all said in unison.

"Good. Now then darlings, another thing we use to hide our true selves from others are clothes. So everybody strip!"

To my surprise, it turned out that teenage boys are not always all that eager to get naked together, not even when half drunk. I can't imagine why not. They just sat there staring at me, some of them turning ashen, others turning beet red.

"I gave you a direction! I expect my directions to be taken at once, and without question. What's the problem, boys?"

There was some fumbling and indistinct mumbling. I was sharp.

"Boys! I can't make out a word any of you are saying. Silent movies are gone and, inexplicably, they're not coming back. Actors must speak clearly. Now just what is the problem with getting naked?"

One boy raised his hand. Of all the boys present, he was the one I most wanted stripped. "Yes? What is your name, young man?"

"Martin Lewis. Uh, I don't want to get naked with a bunch of guys. None of us do. Except maybe Miss Mirkin." Martin smirked at Merle.

"Get this, Martin, and get this now. I will not tolerate gay taunting or ridicule in this class. Some of my best husbands were gay. Besides, if you're going to act, you're going to be surrounded by gay people, so you better get used to it. Now, don't you boys take gym classes together?"

"Yes, Tallulah."

"Doesn't that involve all of you taking showers together every day?"

"Yes, Tallulah."

"I don't mind," said the oldest boy there, a long-haired blond boy whose application gave his age as 18.

"What is your name?"

"Moondog Hickcox. I surf, man. Clothes are a drag. Man is not meant to wear clothes, man. I got no problem stripping off in front of these uptight dudes, man."

"Me neither," said the long-haired brunette boy sitting next to Moondog. "If Moondoggie will, I will."

"And your name is?" I asked.

"Sandcrab, man."

"Thank you, boys, but I am not a man, as you'll see when I take off my clothes."

"You're getting nude too, man? Far out."

"Of course. I wouldn't ask anything of my pupils I wouldn't do myself, except for hard work. So what made you want to try acting, Mister Dog?"

"Ride the Wild Surf."

"Excuse me? I am not above riding a wild surfer, but..."

"No, man, I mean the movie *Ride the Wild Surf*, with Fabian and Tab Hunter. I saw it when I was like eight, and it was like I saw God. That was when I knew that no life could be better than surfing. But if I could be a great actor, like Fabian or Tab, well then, man, I could surf, and get paid for it."

"Well, as it happens, Moon, Tab Hunter, one of the greatest thespians of the Twentieth Century, is a dear friend of mine. We even co-starred together in *1,000,000 Years Ago*, one of the finest dinosaur movies ever made."

"I know, babe. I saw that flick. It was gnarly. That's how I know you're cool. So, are you gonna get naked or what?"

"I am." And with that I stood up, gave a practiced shrug, and was instantly standing naked before a room full of openmouthed teenaged boys. Moondog spoke for all when he said reverently, "Gnarly, man."
Within two minutes everyone in the room was nude.

"Now stand up, boys." They did. "Take hold of yourselves." They did. "Only our own, Merle."

"Sorry, Tallulah," said Merle.

"A natural mistake of the enthusiastic. Now boys, that is your instrument. Hold on to it. Cherish it. Don't let anybody else play around with it, not even me, not even you, until you *feel* you're ready."

"Mine feels ready," said Moondog.

"It certainly *looks* ready," I said, "Now then, I thought long and hard, much as Moondog seems to be doing now, about an opening exercise, one to show you how to open your mind to empathize with all manner of things, not just people, but animals, plants, objects, even tenors. And I found the answer in a great book by the master himself, Patrick Dennis. A book called *Auntie Mame.*"

There was hushed silence in the room.

"*Auntie Mame* is a quintessential acting text. It was first a novel, then a Broadway play, then a movie, then a Broadway musical, and finally, just a few months ago, a musical movie. Perhaps some of you saw *Mame* with Lucille Ball, back in March."

"Yeah, man," said Moondog, "I did. Lucy is gnarly, man. She just can't sing at all."

"No," I agreed, "she can't."

"And like, the whole movie was out of focus," added Sandcrab.

"Only her close ups. Anyway, my point is..."

"And what's with that Bea Arthur chick, man?" Moondog rolled on, "Is she a chick, or a dude?"

"I have no idea," I said, "Now to return to the topic, there's an acting game mentioned in every incarnation of *Auntie Mame*. It's called *Fish Families*. This is a game in which we will learn to feel what it's like to be fish. There is an expression you heard me use a few minutes ago, when I said Joan Crawford drinks like a fish. From this you can deduce two things. One: fish are heavy, nonstop drinkers, and two: Joan Crawford smells like a dead fish. So, to help you get more in touch with your drinking we're going to play this game, which will help you feel what it's like to be a fish. Once you've learned to feel like a fish, we can work up the food chain until you're ready to feel what it's like to be a person. Now first, I need you to clear all the desks to the side, so we have a big empty space in the room."

The boys hopped to it, and shortly the room had a big open space in the center.

"Excellent," I said, "Now, I'm going to pretend to lay my eggs. In order to become little fish, my eggs need to be fertilized. So I'm going to lie down over here, and I want each and every one of you to come over to me, one by one, and do what gentleman fish do. And remember, I'll be grading you."

And so, like good little fish, they did, and even managed to act like they enjoyed it. The Drink System was working.

Chapter 7
The Happiest Place on Earth

After class ended with a quick trip through the gymnasium showers (Well, maybe not all *that* quick), I had Rudy drop me off at Rita's little waterfront bar, *The Wet Spot*, telling him to take the rest of the night off; I'd catch a cab home. Rudy was off to *The Salty Seaman* faster than you can say *gay miscegenation*, or at least faster than I can say it.

The *Wet Spot* is directly across Seaview Drive from the beach, adjoining a small, lovably seedy motel. Through the bar's large picture window in front you can watch the surfers while you drink. Sadly, it was well after dark, so all one could see were the breakers in the moonlight.

As soon as Rita plopped herself down next to me on a bar stool we commenced gossiping about this circus of freaks we were working with while knocking back vodka stingers.

"What is the story with Phil Rains?" I asked her.

"You haven't met the fabled Claudia, have you?" asked Rita.

"No, I haven't had the pleasure."

"No pleasure to be had. A greater harridan I have never met. She is the castrating battleaxe to end all castrating battleaxes. I remember when Phil first arrived in Alta Caca fifteen years ago, he was darling. Handsome, sweet, smart, and he can sing like a dream. Well, you heard today; he can still sing, but that witch has sucked all the life out of him."

"I wonder if I could suck some life back into him."

"More power to you, but don't hold your breath."

"So Dick Rockwood; the people's fiancé. His pants aren't exactly padlocked."

"Well, that may be because Susan Mirkin keeps her woohoo locked in a vault that makes Fort Knox look like a paper bag. I think that girl plans to take her hymen with her, intact, to the grave. She'll either immaculately conceive, or she'll die barren. Dick on the other hand, believes in sharing what he has."

"A generous lad."

"Well, he does have plenty to go around. I think that young man wants out of this town and, Tallu doll, he may very well see you as his ticket to Hollywood."

"Darling, if he's half the man he looks to be, he's got a ticket to ride. So I have to ask, what is with this Henrietta Shemp woman and black face? It's 1974. Who is so idiotically insensitive that they're okay with corking up on stage anymore? Al Jolson is dead, thank God. And let me tell you, Jolie didn't confine the burnt cork to his face. You could always tell when Mammyman had paid me a visit, because I'd have a black tongue for days."

"Did she mention Darien?"

"She did mention someone by that name. Said he was the only black person in town, I think."

"That's right. He's the town librarian. He's kind of a sweet, shy widower. Must be sixty. But in Henrietta's eyes, he's Cassius Clay and Shaft all rolled into one, and she wants herself a king-sized Hershey bar with nuts."

"No."

"Yes. Visit the library most any afternoon. She's in there every day, pretending to read, except she never takes her eyes off of him."

"So, are they breaking the laws of Alabama or not?"

"Not yet. I think he's barely aware of her, at least as a romantic option. He likes, well, he likes books. I think that, where and when he was raised, the idea that touching a white woman was a quick ticket to being lynched was so deeply ingrained that it just doesn't occur to him that the dumpy, middle-aged, white biddy is sitting there undressing him in her mind, and mentally buffing him up.

"You know, Cyril told her that she could play Elvira white, only Henrietta *insisted* on playing her black. I'm not sure if she's doing it to get Darien to notice her, or if she gets off on imagining she's black. Possibly both. Another stinger, dear?"

"I'm still breathing, aren't I? Rita darling, how do you know all this? Where do you get all your info?"

"Can you keep this between us?"

"They'd have to torture me, or cut off my booze supply."

"You saw that motel next door?"

"That adorably sleazy dive? Of course."

"I own it, too. It's the only place in town that caters to locals instead of tourists. We charge hourly rates. Ten dollars gets you one hour. I have eight units, and do a land office business. It's completely anonymous. The primary entrance is off the back alley instead of the street, so people don't see you come and go. You go in the office and ring the buzzer. The clerk is behind a wall. You don't see him; he doesn't see you. You push ten dollars through the slot. A key comes out. There's no ID. No need to speak, unless you want to request a particular room. When you close the door to your room, a timer starts. At exactly one hour, the door pops open, so you know it's time to go. If you want a longer session you can purchase tokens for additional hours that you feed the lock from inside."

"How efficient. What do you call this place?"

"What else? Pay Ten Place. It's The Pay Ten Place Motel."

"Okay. But how does this get you the inside dope on folks?"

"Come with me. Bring your drink."

"Just you try and get it away from me. People have lost fingers."

She led me through a curtained doorway. On the other side was a padlocked door Rita unlocked with a ring of keys she pulled out. We stepped through and found ourselves in the motel's office.

"Now, this is my private retreat. No one comes in here except with me, not even my desk clerks. And over here is the real secret."

We went to another padlocked door. She unlocked it and we stepped through.

Now we were in a long, dark room. On one side was a series of large windows, through which came the only light. Opposite each window was a sofa. There was a stairway beside us up to a floor above.

"Can we get some light in here, darling? This place is darker than Jack Warner's soul."

"No. There are no lights in here. It would give the game away. Look through one of the windows."

I did. It looked into one of the motel's rooms. A man and a woman were on the bed, doing the horizontal mambo.

"It's a one-way mirror," said Rita. "As long as it stays dark in here, all they see is a big mirror. This place was built in 1920, as a brothel for the God Dam workers. This is a common feature in classic brothels."

"I know. Never mind how. How many of your rooms are equipped like this?"

"All of them. Four down here. Four above us. Believe me, in here, you can learn more about the real Alta Caca than anywhere else. Listen."

She flipped a switch beside the window. We could now hear from a wall speaker the woman saying, "Ow! Not so rough, Waldo."

Rita flipped the speaker back off and said, "Shall we stroll?"

We strolled. In the second room I recognized my new student, Martin Lewis. Apparently our round of Fish Families hadn't been enough for him, even though he'd fertilized my caviar twice, as he was in this room with two young women, apparently teaching them how to play Fish Philanderers.

Through the next window we saw a young man face down on the bed, and a man I recognized as Snake Bendix vigorously sodomizing him. When Snake grabbed his date by his hair and pulled his head up, the face of little Merle popped into view, looking strained and sweaty. I flipped on the speaker switch.

"You like that, don't you, you little bitch?" Snake snarled as he pounded away.

"Yes, sir. Thank you, sir. May I have some more please, sir?" Merle panted. He looked pained, yet somehow, I believed him. His "Yes, sir." just reeked of sincerity.

"Shut up bitch!" Snake barked, shoving Merle's face back down again. "I'll decide how much you get, you whore." I could see a brief glint of a grin flash across Merle's face as Snake called him a whore. I must admit, that kind of sweet talk gives me a tingle, too. I flipped the switch back off.

"Ah, young love," I said, "Is there anything as sweet?"

Rita laughed, and then said, "Check out room four. We call it The Dungeon."

Room four did look like a dungeon. The walls looked like dingy old stone. The bed had shackles at each corner, and had a roller with additional shackles at one end, to make an unusually comfy stretching rack. There were stocks and even a wooden pillory. "Are those walls really damp stone work?" I asked.

"It's just painted wallpaper, but it looks real enough for their purposes."

There was a man locked in the pillory. Its height was adjustable, and it had been lowered to where he had to stoop over at what must have been a most uncomfortable angle. The man was wearing a black leather corset, a black leather hood and mask. He had a ball-gag in his mouth, and he wasn't wearing pants, instead displaying quite an overlarge butt coated with thick curly hair. On a scale of one to ten, with ten being best, I'd rate it a three.

A tall woman was standing behind him. She was also wearing a black leather mask, a leather teddy, and was wielding a black-leather riding crop. As we watched, she let fly with a nasty swat to the man's butt, adding another bright red welt to the ones already there. Between his legs, the man's enjoyment of the abuse made itself evident.

"Rita darling," I said, "you should sue Disneyland, because this is clearly the actual 'Happiest Place on Earth.'"

"Two of the rooms upstairs are also occupied at the moment. Want to see?" Rita asked.

"I wouldn't miss it. This is what I call entertainment."

We climbed the steps to the second level. The first two rooms were empty. In the third, my two surfer dudes, Moondog and Sandcrab, were seated naked, cross-legged, on the bed. Between the two of them, also cross-legged, sat Floradora Windwillow, clothed only in her long, wavy hair. In some sort of cost-saving tactic, they were all sharing the same small cigarette, which they were passing around. Flipping on the sound only filled our room with sitar music. We couldn't flip it off again soon enough.

But the strangest scene was reserved for room eight. Through that mirror we could see Phil Rains, fully dressed, sitting in a chair, reading a book. The title, as far as I could make it out, was *The Boston Strangler*. There was no one else in the room. Switching on the speaker filled our room with Mozart. It took me a minute before I could put my finger on what looked odd about Phil. Then I realized what it was. He had a look of serene happiness on his face. I had never seen him smile before.

I turned to Rita and said, "No doubt about it; Pay Ten Place *is* The Happiest Place on Earth."

My taxi dropped me off back at Mirkin Manor around midnight. I was surprised to see the living room lights still on. When I let myself in, I found Harry and Minge waiting for me. Minge looked distressed, while Harry looked smug. "Miss Tallulah," he said with a nasty politeness, "we've been waiting for you."

"No need to wait up for me, darling. Rudy made me my own key."

"Be sure to leave it when you go."

"Go? The only place I'm going is to bed."

"I'm so sorry about this, Tallulah," said Minge, who was nearly in tears.

"It's Miss Morehead to you, Mange. Now what's all this about, Harry?"

"It's quite simple, Tallulah," said Harry, getting awfully familiar, "I'm tossing you out. You have fifteen minutes to pack up your belongings and get the hell out of here, or I'll have Sheriff Hermosa toss you out on the street bodily."

The doorbell rang. "Get that, Minge," snapped Harry. "Now then, I suggest you get packing, as I - what is it?"

Minge had returned from opening the door, and was now tugging at her husband's sleeve. "The man at the door. He has a delivery for you."

"Then sign for it."

"He says he has to deliver it to you in person."

"Honestly. Can't I ever get a minute to myself?" Harry grumbled as he crossed over to the door, "What is it?" he snapped at the delivery man.

"I'm sorry to disturb you so late, Mister Mayor," said the quite attractive young man on the porch, "but my instructions are to put this only into your hands, for your eyes only. It's marked 'Rush' and 'Most Urgent.'"

"All right. It must be city business, although I can't imagine what couldn't wait until morning."

Harry signed for the package, a flat, nine-by-eleven manila envelope, slammed the door in the young man's face, and turned back to me. "I'll finish throwing you out in just a moment."

Harry picked up a letter opener from a desk by the door and slit open the envelope. He slid out two pieces of paper, took one look at the first sheet, which appeared to be a glossy photograph from where I stood, turned ashen, and almost fell into a chair that was every bit as overstuffed as Harry.

Minge, alarmed, started towards him. "Harry, what is it?"

Harry slammed the papers against his chest and yelled, "None of your business woman! This is official city stuff, and *secret!* Now go back over there."

Minge stopped in her tracks, and then backed slowly over to me. Harry lowered the papers again, took another look at the top sheet, winced, and then took a look at the second page. It apparently was text, as Harry was obviously reading it. He read it over two or three times before sliding the papers back into the envelope.

He held the envelope with white knuckles as he walked back to me and said, "Miss Morehead, please accept my apologies." He looked as if the words made him nauseous, but he forced himself to continue, "Please consider our home to be your home for the remainder of the summer." He took a deep breath and continued through gritted teeth, "Your wishes will be our commands."

Minge kissed her husband's ample cheek, a task I was glad wasn't mine. "Thank you, dear. I felt sure you'd come around. You know, she is really a very..." But she was interrupted by the front door opening. Rudy entered, dragging along by the hand a young man I recognized as one of the butcher dancers from *BJ!*

"Excuse us, everyone. Just ignore us. Mrs. Mirkin, what is that you're wearing? I *love* it. Excuse us." Rudy and his temporary friend pushed past us, heading to his room off the kitchen in the ground floor servant's quarters.

"Wait a minute!" blustered Harry, "Who is that person you're bringing into my home?"

"How should I know?" asked Rudy. "His name wasn't what interested me."

"I didn't expect you to get in this early, Rudy," I said.

"Oh I'm not getting in. He is," said Rudy as he and the dancer disappeared into the back of the house.

"Is this the sort of thing I can expect all summer?" roared Harry.

"With any luck," I said, "Rudy knows how to pick 'em."

"*I can't have this sort of thing in my house!*" Harry started shouting, raising his hand, only to notice the envelope he was still holding.

He froze, staring at it for a moment, then he took a deep breath, and resumed speaking through gritted teeth. "I'm sorry, Miss Morehead. I have to remember that that - *person's* - customs aren't those of civilized - aren't like mine. I can't very well expect your servant to forgo a personal life all summer. Come, Minge. It's past time we were in bed."

He took Minge by the arm, and the two of them mounted the steps, he with his eyes staring straight ahead, she looking bewildered. She tried to reach for the envelope, but he smartly slapped her hand away.

Realizing that my liquor was by my bed, I went up also. Opening the door to my room, I saw a not-unwelcome surprise. Dick Rockwood was lying in my bed, and from what I could see of him above the blankets, he was as naked as a Nixon lie. Shutting the door I said, "Dick darling, however did you get in here?"

"Well, I had a date with Susan earlier, for an evening of *Scrabble* with her and her parents." We both shuddered, and Dick went on, "While she was in the little girl's room, I went into the kitchen and unlocked the back door. Then, after I 'left,' so to speak, I went around, let myself in the back way, crept up the servant stairs, and have been waiting for you in here ever since. I thought maybe we could pick up where we were interrupted this afternoon."

"Dick, doll," I said, placing my bedtime libation on the night stand and dropping my clothes with my usual practiced skill before slipping under the covers beside him, "you're just the tonic this vodka needs."

As Dick rolled over and took me in his powerful arms, all I could think of were Ira Gershwin's immortal lyrics from Alta Caca's all-white production of *Porgy and Bess*: "Summertime, and this actress is easy."

This looked to be a long, lovely summer indeed.

Part Two

Suddenly, This Summer

(July)

Chapter 8
Scrambled Legs

The first of July in 1974 was a Monday. The cast of *BJ!* had enjoyed the weekend off, as did Tallulah's pupils, though many of the more enthusiastic ones had spent much of the weekend studying The Drink System on their own, one supposes for extra credit.

At the Eddy house, Nelson and Jeanette had spent the weekend rehearsing their lines and songs together, to little noticeable effect.

At the Rains Residence, Phil had listened to his wife's incessant criticisms, complaints, and harangues in stoic silence, envying those who had the luxury of living lives of *quiet* desperation.

Floradora Windwillow had scored some primo Maui Wowie from Moondoggie on Friday evening, and had conceived some brilliant new dance moves, which she was now struggling mightily to remember. She *had* to start jotting her inspirations down. Her mood took a decidedly nasty downward turn when she received a manila envelope from a delivery man. The contents of that envelope could prove hazardous to her freedom, and would certainly prove expensive. There was only one way to face such a challenge. Fortunately, she still had some of the Maui Wowie. She reached for her rolling papers.

Moondog Hickcox woke up when a similar envelope was pushed under the door of the apartment he lived in over his parent's garage, which they had allowed him to move into when he hit his 18th birthday. His brain wasn't so fogged yet that he didn't immediately realize that, if his parents saw the contents of the envelope, he'd be back in the house, and grounded as well. And if Sheriff Hermosa were to see this, his freedom would be even more severely restricted, for about ten years. This required serious attention, when he could get to it. Right now, surf would be up, and he wanted to ride some waves before acting class this afternoon.

Snake Bendix and his Heck's Seraphim had spent the weekend roaring up and down the coast like the badass bikers they thought themselves to be, even if no one who actually knew them shared that opinion. Snake had picked an argument with his companions Saturday evening, roaring off in a huff alone. He had a hot date waiting, and he preferred it if his gang didn't know with whom.

When he went out to his bike Monday morning, he found an envelope taped to his saddle. When he saw the contents, he turned as green as his tattoos. Who the hell had taken these? And how? Maybe it was time for him to stop *pretending* he was a badass butt-kicker, and *actually* kick some butt. But whose? Who the hell had left this for him?

The Alta Caca Public Library was open on Saturdays, closed on Sundays and Mondays, so Darien Littlewood, the town librarian, had spent Saturday sitting behind the library counter. Ten minutes after opening, Henrietta Shemp had come in. She'd picked a copy of *Black Like Me* from the non-fiction shelves, and sat down at a reading table facing the counter, opened the book, and proceeded to spend the day gazing at Darien over the top of the book. When the library closed at six, she was still on page one.

Darien had thought nothing at first, some months back, of Henrietta's library days. She always came in early, stayed all day, always in the same seat, and she was certainly a slow reader for someone who read so much. But as time passed, he came to realize that she wasn't reading at all. She was just staring at him. Maybe she'd been assigned by some paranoid batch of old white people to keep an eye on him, in case this sixty-year-old librarian, who perhaps weighed 150 pounds soaking wet, might be a secret Black Panther, plotting a one-man race riot.

When he finally began noting the dreamy-eyed expression on her face, he began to develop another hypothesis. Once, after she'd spent an entire day reading the first page of *Soul on Ice*, he'd tried asking her a couple of casual questions about the book. She'd confessed she "hadn't been able to follow the plot," and he realized she thought it was a novel. Oh dear.

But today was Monday, and Darien had the day off. He intended to spend the day off his feet, watching TV. He never read in his time off. That was work.

He was enjoying *Edge of Night* when his doorbell rang. Who the hell could that be? He wasn't expecting anyone. In fact, as the lone black resident of Alta Caca, *no one* ever visited him. He was officially tolerated, but not socially.

It was Henrietta Shemp standing on his veranda, holding a dish covered with a cloth. She was looking around nervously, and said, "Hello Darien," (He had long before noticed how no one in Alta Caca over the age of 17 ever called him "Mr. Littlewood." He supposed he should be glad they didn't call him "Boy") "may I come in?" She charged in without waiting for a reply, and he allowed it, as he knew damn well she was hoping no one saw her on his porch. He wondered to himself how many blocks away she was parked, and whether she'd walked here from her car on the sidewalk, or skulked down an alley. When he saw the grit on his doormat before closing the door, he knew it had been the alley.

"I hope you'll forgive my boldness in dropping in uninvited, but I did bring you a pie." She pulled off the checkered cloth. It had covered a still-steaming-hot, fresh, home-baked apple pie.

"Please sit, Miss Shemp," he said, "I'll get us some plates, forks, and a pie slicer. I don't get many visitors."

"Oh please," she said, "you can call me Henrietta, at least when we're *private* like this. I baked this myself. In fact, I even grew the apples in my backyard."

"Well then, let us enjoy the fruit of your - ah - fruit." Darien winced inside. He shouldn't attempt banter. He was simply no good at it. But it had been many years since he'd entertained a female caller, even a dotty middle-aged biddy like Miss Shemp, and he'd never before entertained a *white* female caller at all. The times, they *were* a changin'.

"So Miss Shemp," he said, once the pie had been dished out, "what did you want to pick my brain about? Oh my. This pie is *delicious!"*

"Thank you. Well, Darien," she said, apparently deciding not to insist on the familiarity of "Henrietta," "as you may have heard, I've been cast in our new musical *BJ!* with Tallulah Morehead."

"No, I hadn't heard. Congratulations. Who are you playing?"

"I'm playing the maid, Elvira. That's what I wanted to ask you about. I wanted you to help me make my character more *authentic*."

"Well, I don't know how I can help you. I've never been employed as a domestic."

"Oh I realize that. But, Elvira *is* a Negro."

"But surely you'll be playing her as white?"

"And change the author's intentions? Certainly not. I will be playing it in Negro make-up." Darien resisted the impulse to spit his mouthful of pie across the room. "I wanted you to help me to understand The Black Experience, in order to give my performance greater verisimilitude."

Darien was appalled. *Oh brother,* he thought, *this woman is loonier than I realized.* But then, the pie was awfully good, and it was pleasant to have company, particularly female company, and it wasn't as if she was *deliberately* patronizing him. He didn't have any pressing engagements. In fact, he had no engagements at all. There were worse ways to spend an afternoon. "All right, Miss Shemp."

"Henrietta."

"Henrietta. What would you like to know?"

"It's simple really. Just tell me exactly what it's like to be a Negro. Omit nothing."

Darien quickly stuffed a large chunk of pie in his mouth, to keep from responding honestly. Maybe he'd been wrong about there being worse ways to spend an afternoon.

The Mirkin household had also had a pleasant weekend. There had been no sign of Tallulah. She'd gone out with her chauffeur Friday at 1 p.m. for her rehearsal, and hadn't been seen since, although the Mirkins had heard her letting herself back into the house around 3 a.m. Monday morning. All Mirkin hopes that she'd staggered into the Gorge of Death and drowned in Swan Song Lake were dashed.

Up in Tallulah's bedroom, when noon rolled around, she woke up to find Dick Rockwood still snoozing beside her, naked as a naked jaybird. "Dick darling," she said, "shouldn't you have snuck out before sunrise?"

Dick opened his eyes and said, "Why?"

"Well, that shrill little fiancé of yours may be in the house."

Dick took her in his arms and said, "Susan stopped being my fiancé Saturday afternoon, when you became Mrs. Rockwood."

"When I did what?"

"Don't you remember?"

"Things slip my mind once in a while."

"You did have a lot to drink."

"That would be me all right. What did we do?"

"Dear, we just got back from Las Vegas a few hours ago. We're married now."

"I *married* you?"

"Yes, dear."

"Well, old habits *are* the hardest to break."

***

(From the personal journal of Tallulah Morehead.)

Good Lord, I am married again! And to a man a year or two my junior. Would I never learn the value of casual sex? Oh well, I'd had less-attractive husbands. And there's nothing like a summer marriage.

"However, my love," Dick said, "it might not be a bad idea to withhold our wedding announcement until the play closes, and we're free to leave for Hollywood."

"Perhaps that's wise," I said, "although wisdom isn't my specialty."

"What is?"

"Well, *this* for one."

"Oh my darling!"

An hour later I tiptoed down the stairs as best I could, in a silent-yet-graceful forward somersault, only to discover that Dick and I were alone in the house, except for Contracepcion and Rudy. "You can come down now, Dick," I hollered discreetly up the stairs.

Dick, now dressed, came downstairs. "Tallulah, I do really think we should just go ahead and let Susan and the others believe I'm still engaged to her for the time being."

"So you want me to help you lead that poor girl on all summer?"

"Essentially."

"Sounds good to me. And I think that, to help maintain the illusion that we're both still single, I should go on shagging as many men in this berg as I can manage, *strictly* to throw the suspicious off our scent, of course."

"Fine with me."

"It is? Where were you in 1925?"

"My parents were still children then. Anyway, as long as it's a two-way street, I'm on board with it."

"You want to shag all the men you can also? Don't tell me I've married yet *another* homo!"

"*No!* No. God, no. I meant I should go on nailing a few of my regular

Alta Caca hosebags, I mean girl friends, to also maintain the illusion of being single."

"Does Susan know about these other women?"

"Of course not."

"So you want to have sex with other women Susan knows nothing of, making sure she still doesn't find out about them, in order to fool her into thinking that you're faithful to her?"

"That's it."

"You're afraid that if she finds out that you've stopped the fooling around she knows nothing about, she'll wonder why you're not still doing what she doesn't know you're doing in the first place?"

"You get it."

"You know the worst thing about that darling? It somehow makes sense to me. But how will you be able to perform with these other, lesser women now that you've had *me*?"

"I'll keep my eyes closed, and pretend they are you. That should help me delay orgasm as well."

"Is that why you keep your eyes tightly closed when you're making love to me?"

"That's right. I'm pretending you're youn - ah – someone else, to keep my excitement in check. You don't mind, do you?"

"Of course not. I do the same thing."

"I wondered why you kept calling me *Kong*."

"Ah King Kong, talk about **hung!** His penis was larger than whole, entire husbands I've had. Well, I don't have time to reminisce all day. I've got rehearsal. I need breakfast. Where's...?"

"One screwdriver, freshly swilled," said Rudy, always one step ahead of me.

"Rudy," began Dick.

"I know. You want to keep our Vegas trip and your wedding secret."

"You're certainly right on top of things," said Dick.

"If that's what you like, big boy," said Rudy, "but I prefer to be underneath."

"Rudy! You know the rules. Glands off my husbands."

"Yes, Tallulah," Rudy answered, though giving me as sullen a look as he dared. "Now drink your breakfast. We have to get you to work."

"What about me?" asked Dick, "Wedding weekends take a lot out of you."

"Suffering from depleted fluids are we?" said Rudy with a smirk, "Well, keep your shirt off, Hairy Tits. I've whipped up a plateful of my own special-recipe version of *Huevos Rancheros* for you. Dig in."

Rudy slapped a plate full of scrambled *Huevos Rancheros* in front of Dick. Sadly, it failed to occur to me that perhaps I should warn him. A few measly decades of moderate, full-time, heavy-drinking had toughened my taste buds to the point that I needed fairly vivid flavors to even notice solid food in my mouth anymore, and so Rudy, who had been preparing my meals for twenty-seven years by this point, was accustomed to making my food, well, let's say strongly flavored.

Consequently, his *Huevos Rancheros* tended to be fairly spicy. In fact, they usually required rather rapid consumption, before they ate through the plate and began burning their way through the table. Once, when introducing the President of France to Rudy's Filipino-Mexican cooking, the garrulous old Frenchman made the mistake of letting them sit on his plate while he chugged a bottle of particularly fine wine, and Rudy's Mexican-style eggs accidentally destroyed a two hundred year old, Louis XIV gold table, and ate a four-foot hole in a marble floor.

Therefore, it occurred to me just a moment too late that perhaps I should have mentioned to Dick before the food hit his ever-so-talented tongue to expect them to be a tad spicier than he was accustomed to. I was just recalling that the Mexican ambassador, on sampling them, had suggested renaming the dish *Huevos Godzillus*, when we heard the front door open. The ever-shrill voice of Susan Mirkin assaulted our ears from the living room, hollering for Contracepcion, just as the first forkful of spicy eggs hovered at his lips.

"*Concepcion!*" Susan bellowed. The harried maid rolled her eyes and scurried into the living room. "Where have you been, you lazy woman?" Susan politely inquired, apparently miffed that Contracepcion's psychic abilities had not informed her of her junior mistress's arrival in advance, "I've been looking all over town for Dick. He's been missing all weekend. What if he's been waylaid by some horrible fiend?"

Dick's eyes bugged forward until he looked like Bette Davis imitating Peter Lorre. (Always a showstopper at Bette's parties.) He glanced about, seeking escape.

"You must be new at this," I said, "The traditional hiding place in these circumstances is under the table."

As we heard Contracepcion saying, "I don't think she's damaged him," Dick nodded quickly, dropped the forkful of eggs into his mouth, swallowed almost without chewing, and dove beneath the table, pulling the tablecloth down again behind him.

Susan strode into the room, still with a full head of steam. "Miss Morehead," she stated, "I haven't been able to find Dick all weekend."

"I've had weekends like that myself. Don't let it get you down. That's what lesbians are for."

"Do you have any idea where he is?"

A roar that would have frightened a tyrannosaur came from under the table.

"None whatsoever," I said.

"*What* the hell was that?" Susan asked in her most ladylike manner.

"Mice?" I suggested.

"*Mice?* That sounded like King Kong."

"Now, Susan dear," I said, as I saw Dick's face emerge in my lap, just where I liked it, his eyes flooding tears, his mouth twisted in a grimace of pain. "That sounded nothing like King Kong. I should know. We were quite the scandalous couple back in 1933. Did you know that human/giant-mythical-ape sexual relations are still illegal, even here in California? It's like living in the Dark Ages. Excuse me, my lap's on fire, as usual." And I took the water pitcher, (which I assumed had been put on the table merely as a centerpiece. I'm not a flower. I never drink the vile swill) and passed it down to Dick. Instantly we heard a gulping, glugging sound.

"Then what is making *that* sound?" Susan continued nosily.

"Don't get personal, dear. You drink your way, and I'll drink mine. At my age, my Magic Tunnel sometimes requires external sources of moisture. Not all of us are fortunate enough to have fathers who habitually target us with spit takes."

"What is under there?" asked Susan, bending down and reaching for the tablecloth.

However, her investigation was delayed by the front door opening and the voice of Harry Mirkin calling for his daughter.

"In here, daddy," Susan called out, and then asked me, "Who is that plateful of eggs for?"

"The dog?" I ventured.

"We don't have a dog."

"Sorry. I meant your mother Mange. It's a natural mistake."

"Susan," said Harry from the next room, "I've brought Sheriff Hermosa. Come out here. We'll find Dick's kidnappers."

Susan went into the living room, saying, "Daddy, there's something very strange about the dining room table."

As I heard Harry say, "This is no time to discuss your mother's peculiar tastes in furniture," I lifted the tablecloth and gestured to Dick to scoot. He sprinted out from under faster than I'd seen a man move on all fours since my third husband (Vlad could scurry down a wall, headfirst, fast enough to shame spiders), and slipped through the door into the kitchen.

"No, daddy," said Susan, "I mean there's something *under* the table. You should have heard it roar."

Harry, Susan, and Henry Hermosa strode into the room. Only Sheriff Hermosa had the manners to say "Good morning, Miss Morehead."

"Daddy," whined Susan, who had a fine summer whine, "look under the table. She's hiding something under there!"

"Sheriff, would you investigate that please?" said Harry, who was apparently accustomed to allowing others to check under his furniture for him.

Hermosa bent down, looked, and stood up again, holding the now-empty pitcher. "Am I supposed to arrest this pitcher, or just protect you from it?" he asked Susan and Harry.

"Miss Morehead," asked Harry, "what is the meaning of this?"

"I don't think that pitcher has a meaning. It just is. It's zen."

"But what was it doing under the table?"

"Plotting the overthrow of all that's good and decent?"

"She put it there," said Susan. "I saw her."

"Well, Miss Morehead?"

"Some idiot filled it with water. Naturally, I was offended, and wanted it out of my sight. Imagine impugning my reputation by implying that I would drink *water*! Did I commit some crime? Sheriff, perhaps you should arrest me for first-degree pitcher-stowing."

Hermosa laughed. As the only sane man in the room, he stood out. "That's all right, Miss Morehead. Susan's fiancé has gone missing, and she's a little worried. That's all."

"Well where is Dick then?" Susan demanded.

"Right here,' said Dick, strolling in from the living room. "Susan, my mother says you've been looking for me."

"*Where have you been?*" said Susan, rushing into my husband's arms.

"I took a drive up to Carmel for the weekend, to relax from the stress of rehearsals, and to study my lines."

"Well, why didn't you tell me?" She cuddled up to him and said more suggestively, "Why didn't you take me along?"

While my stomach lurched at that thought, Dick said, "Well I wouldn't have gotten much studying done that way."

"My daughter is a virgin, sir," said Harry with enough pompousness for three Victorian Prime Ministers combined.

Dick rolled his eyes and said, "I know. Believe me, I know."

"Well, clearly no crime has been committed," said the Sheriff, "So if you can handle your family squabbles yourself, Harry, I'll get back to real police work. Mr. Rockwood, Miss Mirkin, Miss Morehead, good day all." And he left.

"But wait," said Susan, "what are those eggs for?"

"Self defense?" I suggested.

"Self defense?" blustered Harry, "How can a plateful of eggs be for self defense?"

"Try 'em."

Tentatively, Susan and Harry both picked up forks and each took a small bite of Rudy's deluxe *Huevos Rancheros*. There was a momentary pause, before both of them shrieked and bolted for the kitchen. My husband and I shared a glance and a laugh. Sometimes breakfast *is* the most important meal of the day.

Chapter 9
Singing in the Rains'

J ust what the hell is the appeal of Live Theater anyway? You have to learn the *entire show all at once*, which means endless memorization and rehearsal. In the movies I never had to learn more than about three pages at any one time. Great Thalberg, I haven't even memorized my full married name. I believe I'm Tallulah Clytemnestra Morehead Knight Thalberg Tepes Karloff (Actually Pratt, but who the hell wants to be known as Mrs. Pratt?) Towers (Actually Suderstrombork, but who the hell can even spell it?) Whatever-The-Hell-Rudy's-Last-Name-Is *[Note from Iris: "It's Herkert."]* Borgnine Bronze Rockwood, but I may well have forgotten a few altogether. Now they expect me to memorize an entire play, and the largest role in that play as well, plus songs.

And then there are the dances. Songs at least are fairly easy to learn. The rhythms, melodies, and rhyme schemes make them easier to remember. All I generally forget are the pitches. But the dances?

In movie musicals, my dance double did all my dancing. All I had to manage were my close ups. But here I had to do *all* my own dancing! Haven't they noticed that it's pretty much all I can do to walk across a room steadily? So when Phil announced he'd written another new song for me, *Buzz Off, Mrs. Bates*, which I was to sing to that snoopy neighbor character, I was a tad annoyed. The nice thing about it was I got to sing a nasty song to the odious Jeanette Baker Eddy. The bad thing about it was, I would have to learn it.

And then Phil mentioned that he'd neglected to bring it with him to rehearsal. This is July 3rd. We have July 4th off, and in fact, are having a cast pot luck picnic on the beach in the late afternoon.

This meant a whole day I could use to learn this new song would be utterly wasted. As it was, memorization was seriously cutting into my drinking time, and the time I had to sneak over to the Pay Ten Place Motel to hump the living brains out of Dick, who, probably wisely, still wanted to keep us a secret from my husband's fiancé. ("My husband's fiancé" I believe that's the first time I've ever encountered that phrase.)

So, just as I was settling onto my favorite stool at The *God Dam Bar* for an after-rehearsal aperitif, it occurred to me, why not just drop by The Rains' house and pick up a copy of the song tonight?

And I could meet the fabled Mrs. Rains while I was at it. I'd yet to set eyes on the notorious woman. So far, Claudia Rains had been The Invisible Woman, which must have frosted Virginia Bruce. Was she even a real woman, or was she just a fiction, used as a beard to aid Phil in maintaining the illusion of heterosexuality, and keep women at bay? It wouldn't be the first time I'd fallen for such a ploy. I don't want to end up accidentally marrying another gay man, even if I am already accidentally married at the moment. After all, my husband is engaged to another woman, so who knows how long this marriage will last?

So I slipped off my stool, got back up on my feet, and wobbled off to *The Salty Seaman*, two doors down, to retrieve Rudy to drive me over to Phil's domicile.

It took Phil forever to answer the door, and when he did he was just in an undershirt and jockeys, all disheveled and covered in sweat, with even a few drops of what tasted like blood.

"Tallulah," said Phil, a bit out of breath, "what are you doing here?"

"I dropped by to pick up a copy of *Buzz Off, Mrs. Bates* so I could start learning it over the holiday. Did we come at a bad time?"

"Well yes, actually."

"Did we catch you and Mrs. Rains *in flagrante delicto*? You certainly look *delicto*. I love a hot, sweaty man."

"What? You mean did you interrupt sex? Oh, you're several years too late to catch us at that."

"Is you wife blind?"

"Not yet. It's still early."

"Then I cannot believe you have a chaste relationship. Perhaps I could meet your wife now?" I asked, charging past him into the house.

"This isn't really the best time," said Phil, chasing after me, "Claudia's indisposed."

But as many a studio head had found out before, when I get my steam up, I am not to be stopped.

Phil turned to Rudy, "Rudy, this is really not a good time. How do we stop her?"

"You don't. But she can be distracted. Watch this." Then Rudy hollered out, "What a charming wet bar."

"Wet bar?" I said, "Where?" The next thing I knew, Rudy was serving me some of Phil's *Jack Daniels*, which happened to be sitting out. Apparently Phil had been trying to drink his miseries away. I *knew* I loved this man!

Then Phil retrieved a couple copies of *Buzz Off, Mrs. Bates*. We sat around his piano as he sang the song for me, so I could learn the melody, making it easier to absorb the lyrics. During my second attempt at the number, Rudy wandered off down the hall to use the little boy's room. As I opened my mouth to hit my big, showy high note, a high-pitched scream shattered the air.

"No," said Phil, "that was extremely sharp. This is the note."

"That may have been sharp, but you're not. That wasn't me. It sounded like a woman being tortured."

"That's why I thought it was your singing," said Phil.

"Point taken," I said, "But who was it? Was that Claudia?"

"I extremely doubt it."

"It was me, you idiots," said Rudy, stumbling back into the room, his normally tan skin pale and ashen, "He's torturing her. Come see."

"A tortured woman? Oh goody," I said, bounding down the hall in the direction indicated by Rudy.

"*Please!*" called out Phil, "***Don't!***"

But there was no stopping me at this point, short of a hammer to the back of the skull. I ran down the hall and into the doorway left open by Rudy. A terrifying sight met my eyes.

Claudia Rains is a big woman, tall, muscular, broad-shouldered, like the huge actress Hope Emerson (One of the nicest lesbians I've ever met), only not as dainty. Above her on the bed was a traction rig. Her hands were duct-taped together and chained to the traction rig, leaving her upper torso hanging, while her ample butt and thick, powerful legs lay on the bed, which was stained with substances I'd not care to know the composition of. A large swath of duct tape was also slapped across her mouth. She looked shrunken and starved, and her eyes stared out at me from deep, black sockets. If eyes can be said to scream, hers were shaming Fay Wray.

"Phil!" I said in a severe tone, "You *lied* to me!"

"Tallulah," pleaded Phil, "you don't understand."

"The hell I don't," I said, insulted, "Any fool with two eyes and the ability to focus images into distinct blurs can see what is going on in here."

"Tallulah," said Phil in the sort of pleading tone I've always found appealing coming from men, "you can't imagine what I've been going through..."

"Oh yes I can. You've been going through the prop room. These are the rigs I use to truss up Blanche in Act Two."

"I was going to return them."

"You said I hadn't interrupted you."

"Well I could hardly say you'd interrupted me when I was..."

"...having extremely kinky S-and-M sex with your wife," I finished for him, "After all the complaining I've heard you do about her, I must say I am surprised to find you two love birds livening up your love life with a little bondage inspired by Act Two. This really takes me back. Remember, I was once married for a night to Vlad the Impaler. When I think of all the blissful hours I've spent trussed up like that..." I couldn't help it. I began singing, "*Memories, light the corners of my mind...*"

"Kinky sex..." said Phil, "Ah - ah - yeah! You caught us all right. We both love a little bondage, don't we, Claudia dear?"

Claudia's eyes seemed to be trying to leap out of their sunken sockets as she frantically shook her head from side to side. A muffled, indistinct sound, like the Bride of Frankenstein shrieking under twenty pillows, emanated from behind the duct tape gagging her mouth. Tears poured from her eyes.

"My Gracious," I said, "you weren't kidding. Look at the intense passion just mentioning it triggers in your wife. She wants you in the worst way, and judging from this set-up, that's just what she's been getting."

"Yeah," said Phil, "you've caught us at our little love game. I borrowed the props for us to reenact Blanche's torment for our little fun.

It's such an intimate thing. I'd really appreciate it if you'd never mention it to anyone, ever, not even under oath. I mean, you know, if Claudia ever, oh say, disappeared without a trace, or was found dismembered, as though hacked to pieces in a rage, or you know, something like that, and Sheriff Hermosa leapt to a silly, *erroneous* conclusion, you'd never tell them about this. Claudia, you want it kept secret too, don't you?"

Claudia was now violently thrashing her whole body about, as though trying to tear herself loose from her rigging. Fortunately, Phil had done a great job of binding her, and she had no chance in hell of ever getting loose without help.

I leaned in to whisper to her. "Don't worry, Claudia dear. I'll never tell a soul what Phil is doing to you here. No one will ever know, or interrupt you again. I'll leave you forever, safe in his loving hands."

Claudia's frantic gratitude was shown in the tears which glistened in her eyes as I withdrew. "Come Rudy," I told my Filipino companion, "let's leave these lovebirds to finish the ancient intimate ritual we so rudely interrupted."

"Thank you, Tallulah," said Phil, as he ushered us to the door, past the little entryway table on which rested the day's mail and a hacksaw he must have put down hurriedly when answering the door earlier.
"And remember, never speak of this, ever. Claudia would be mortified if anyone ever knew how much she craves being bound up and abused."

"Mum's the word," I assured him. "I'll be as silent as the grave."

"Just exactly what I had in mind," said Phil, adding, "I'll see you at the pot luck tomorrow."

As we walked back to the car at the curb, Rudy said to me, "I'm sorry about screaming. When I first saw her trussed up like that, I thought she was being killed."

"A common mistake, Rudy. You must remember that you are in a civilized country now, not like the primitive island village of your youth."

"I'm from Manila. It's a modern city. Anyway, being caught in such a kinky act, how embarrassing."

"Exactly. That's why we must *never* tell anyone about it. If anyone knew about their private games, well, it would just be murder. Now let's get home. I want to dictate this all out on tape for Iris to type up before it fades away. This is way too juicy to lose."

As Rudy opened the car door, the piercing scream of a woman in pain and terror ripped through the evening air, only to be suddenly, permanently, silenced. I took Rudy's arm, smiled and said, "Ah *l'mour, l'mour.* Let's be off."

Chapter 10
Pot Luck

A round 2 p.m. Rudy pulled my tasteful economy Rolls Royce into a parking lot for Beaver Valley Beach. The Alta Caca Arts Council was throwing a 4th of July pot luck beach party for the cast and crew of *BJ!*, their families and "friends," by which they meant "insignificant others."

I was bringing my famous rum cake; *heavy* on the rum, almost no cake. In fact, it was more "caked on" than cake. It's the only cake that is served in a glass, neat or on the rocks. It's a two-layer cake, because "if you give her two, you'll lay 'er".

I had also brought a new seafood dish I had invented for the occasion. It's boiled lobster served in a uniquely flavorful sauce that I found in a cookbook titled The *120 Days of Sodom*, where it had not been used on lobster. In honor of my host city, I have named it *Lobster ala Caca*. I had actually snagged the lobsters myself while down at the *The Pay Ten Place Motel*, catching crabs.

Rudy had also prepared a huge amount of his notorious *Huevos Rancheros*, which he had garnished with a small notice reading, "Eat at Your Own Risk."

The Mirkins were already there. Earlier there had been quite a kitchen *contretemps*, as Minge had mistakenly thought she could use her own kitchen to force Contracepcion to prepare Minge's special Cottage Cheese, powdered Barbecue Potato Chips, ground Bologna, Campbell's Cream of Mushroom Soup, and Miracle Whip Vindaloo Surprise casserole, a dish recommended by gastroenterologists in need of new yachts everywhere, while Rudy was busy preparing his and my offerings. I thought Rudy and Minge might come to blows, which was alarming, as Rudy would be seriously overmatched, but Harry, attracted by the noise, came into the kitchen and told Minge she could use The God Dam Hotel's kitchen to prepare her inedible dish. As they left, Contracepcion said to Rudy, "I owe you one."

At the beach party site, Harry was lounging on a beach chair, his vast bulk draped in the ugliest purple-and-yellow Hawaiian shirt ever made by color-blind wahinis, and a pair of Bermuda shorts that should have been left in the Bermuda Triangle. He was reading a newly published book called *All The President's Men*, which sadly, wasn't a gay porn novel despite one of the main characters being named "Deep Throat."

"Honestly," he exploded, using a term I felt was rather inappropriate at best when used in reference to Richard Nixon, "how can something be illegal if the president does it? Get a clue, Woodstein! I'm *certain* the Constitution says that the president can do whatever the hell he feels he must. It's in the article on Executive Privilege."

Minge was setting out her horrific unappetizer on the buffet table. Even the other foods looked revolted.

Merle was lazing on a beach towel, clad only in swim trunks so tight you could tell he wasn't circumcised, admiring the equally mostly-naked stage hands who were leaping about, playing volleyball in front of him, as though for his own private entertainment.

When Carl, a thirty-year-old set-builder with muscles rippling across his form and a two-day growth of beard stubble on his darkly handsome face, asked Merle if he'd like to join in their "ball handling," Merle's swim suit suddenly grew several inches larger. But then the sound of a motorcycle roaring by on Seaview Drive made him turn his head. Whoever he hoped it was, it wasn't, but when he turned his head back, Carl was serving again.

Little Fanny was running about with her stage sister, Shirley Knott, snapping pictures of the festivities with a little Brownie camera.

That homely little bitch, Susan, was sharing a large beach towel with my husband. Susan was wearing a one-piece bathing suit that even Queen Victoria would have considered excessively modest, while Dick was wearing only loose hanging shorts that came down to his knees, which meant they exceeded the length of his best feature by fully an inch and a half. Well, an inch. All right, half an inch. It depends on how interested he is in his companion, or how cold the water is.

Susan, seeing me, made a smug face, grabbed Dick by his abundant chest fur, and pulled him to her for a deep, lingering, gratuitous kiss. Dick winked at me over his whore's shoulder as she brushed his teeth with her tongue.

"*Susan!*" snapped Harry from behind his book, "Don't behave like a scarlet woman in public. We have an image to maintain."

"Are you saying I can behave like a scarlet woman in private?" asked Susan, showing more wit than I thought she possessed.

"Don't you sass me, young lady," Harry said, "There will be plenty of time for...for...for *that* sort of filthy behavior *after* you're married."

"At least for the first month, anyway," piped in Minge in a rueful tone.

Dick began coughing convulsively. I decided to leap into the breach, since leaping into his breeches just then would have involved wrestling Susan out of the way. "I always say, *any* time is the time for filthy behavior. As for scarlet women; you know, I almost played Scarlett O'Hara, so I know a thing or two about scarlet women, and Susan falls even shorter of that beloved goal than that untalented twat Vivian Leigh did, rest her soul. Maybe if Susan slept around more, she'd get the idea. Isn't there a biker gang around here she could gang-bang for practice? Merle darling, do you know any bikers that could give your sister a crash course in serial copulation?"

"*Miss Morehead!*" said Susan, "*I'm a virgin!*"

"I know, darling, I'm trying to arrange for you to be cured of that Tragic Condition, without involving my hus - co-star. Virginity isn't the incurable scourge it used to be. Many former virgins have gone on to lead comparatively normal lives. Look at your mother. Ew. Bad example. Well look at me. Believe it or not, I was a virgin once, for several months. It nearly killed me. However, a young man named Kevin gave me the cure, but good. Still, to achieve that, young lady, you need to get poked, and not by young Rockwood here. He saved it for marriage."

"Miss Tallulah," roared Harry in full pompous mode, "I will not have you corrupting my child with your filth!"

"Mister Mirkin," said Dick, standing in a rage, "don't you dare to speak to my - *friend* like that! Tallulah has wisdom far beyond your years and mine combined."

I was touched to see my current hubby leap to my defense with such passion, although I could have done without that "far beyond your years and mine combined" crap.

Harry also attempted to leap to his feet, although at his age, bulk, and condition, it was more of a haul to his feet. "Who do you think you are to speak to me like..." then Harry trailed off, and looked at Dick oddly, his fat head askew, a suspicious look in his eyes. Then he turned to me and said, "I apologize, Miss Morehead. I realize you're only trying to help my daughter. Perhaps we take a slightly different view of intimate matters here than you are used to in Hollywood. Here we have morals."

"Is that what you call them, Harry?" I replied, "You should try sharing them with your buddy Nixon."

Dick said, "Harry, I'm sorry, too. Let me make it up to you. Here, let me get you and Susan some food."

"Thank you, Dick. That sounds delicious. I didn't mean to fly off the handle. Sometimes I can be a bit hot-headed."

"You won't know what *hot-headed* means until you've tasted this."

I saw Dick winking at me as he heaped Rudy's *Huevos Rancheros* onto doomed plastic plates, and covering it with Minge's ghastly offering, to hide from them the same dish that had blistered their mouths only three days earlier. I decided this might be a good time for a stroll.

"If you'll all excuse me, I think I'll go for a wobble about. Whoever put all this sand on this beach was most inconsiderate. It's nearly impossible to walk on this grit in high heels, even sober, not that I've tried it that way. And even my flats are *high* heels. In fact, the higher my heels are, the more fun I'm having."

I sauntered about as best I could on this quicksand, seeking for more agreeable company. Sir Ludwig was looking suitably pickled and welcoming, but Monica Montana was lounging beside him, giving me a look so icy that it was refreshing in the summer heat. It's bad enough I have to carry the untalented cow in the play, without making nice with her at a party.

The Baker-Eddys were ensconced in their own beach tent, Jeanette wisely draped in a caftan, and Nelson in a swimsuit tighter than Merle's (cut) displaying a body that was probably mildly attractive, in an unattractive sort of way, back during the Truman Administration. They smiled and waved me over. I pretended to have the sun in my eyes, which wasn't easy given I had my back to the sun, and wandered on.

"Looking for fun?" asked a voice in my ear. I turned, and there was Floradora Windwillow, in a light, billowing, tie-dyed summer dress and sandals.

"That depends on what you mean by 'fun,' darling. I'm not really a disciple of Lesbos unless there are no men about, or the woman is a lot hotter than you are, no offense."

"You misunderstand me, Tallulah dear," Floradora replied, "When I say fun, I mean..." she whipped out a hand-rolled cigarette as she said, "...reefer!"

"Where do you suggest we light up your Mary Jane, in front of the Mayor, or over there with Sheriff Hermosa?"

"Follow me," said Floradora, heading off down the sand towards a little beach shack which made a teepee look like Windsor Castle. Just as we stepped onto the porch, I heard Harry let out a shriek in the far distance that reminded me of the roar of Maleficent's dragon in Disney's *Sleeping Beauty*, only with a greater amount of fire shooting from his mouth.

Inside the shack, Moondog, Sandcrab, and Rita Morecombe were lounging about on mismatched, threadbare furniture. The room was decorated with macramé and surfboards, and Simon and Garfunkle's *Bridge Over Troubled Waters* album was playing on a portable stereo.

"Miss Morehead," said Moondog, "welcome to Mellow Manor, our beach hangout. We are most honored to have such a major movie babe in our shack. Here, toke up."

Although not my usual stimulant, I have always found marijuana a pleasant social lubricant, especially if you're out of real lube, and it mixes well with vodka. But then, vodka mixes well with most anything except Cottage Cheese, powdered Barbecue Potato Chips, ground bologna, Campbell's Cream of Mushroom Soup, and Miracle Whip Vindaloo Surprise Casserole. I transferred my martini to my other hand and accepted the joint from Moondog as I asked him, "Do you live here?"

Moondog and Sandcrab laughed hard enough to hemorrhage, literally rolling around on the frayed sofa they were splayed on. When he could manage speech again Moondog said, "No way man, this is like our clubhouse, where we hang between riding the big waves. Come on. Toke up. That roach is burning."

"What style is your furniture? Early dumpster?"

"You got it, Miss Morehead."

"Please, call me Tallulah, as long as we're flaunting drug laws together."

"Tallulah, would you like to use our carburetor to toke up deep?" asked Sandcrab, holding up the cardboard center of a toilet paper roll with a small hole in the side. "You stick the joint in the hole here, cover the end with your hand. Suck the carb full of smoke, and then drop your hand from the end and inhale fast. It shoots a gnarly load of dope straight into you."

"Sandcrab darling, I was toking the wacky tobaccy with John Barrymore before your parents were born. Oh, the pot-scented nights I spent with Bobby Mitchum. Mmmm. He is a man and a half. Let me show you just what real sucking is all about." And then I put the joint to my lips, and applied my patented full-Morehead mouth-vacuum to it, actually consuming the entire reefer in one long, deep suck.

"Whoa!" said Moondog and Sandcrab reverently. Sandcrab added, "That was the most bodacious suck I've ever seen."

"Thank you, darling," I said in a high-pitched, strangled tone, as I tried to speak while retaining the smoke in my beleaguered lungs. "You know, alcohol isn't the only intoxicant on earth. If I'm not mistaken that was three parts Maui Wowie to one part Acapulco Gold, from the southern slopes, vintage 1974. Perky, full bodied, and just a little insolent."

"Whoa," said Moondog, who had a limited vocabulary, "You are absolutely right. You know your grass, lady. I am most utterly impressed."

"Open your mouth, Moondog," I said, still retaining most of the happy smoke in my lungs.

"Okay," he said, dropping his jaw low.

I leaned in, planted my lips on his, and then exhaled the load of reefer fumes directly into him. Moondog's eyes bulged as he drew in all the smoke I transferred to him. His lips broke free, and he fell back on the tatty couch in bliss.

"Bitchin'!" said Sandcrab, "That was incretastic! I got major wood just watching."

"How major? You want to try it?" I asked Sandcrab, as Moondog suddenly broke into a coughing jag that would do credit to a tubercular patient in his final hours.

"Please, ma'am," said Sandcrab, dropping his jaw in preparation.

"Florawhora," I asked, "where's that reefer you had?"

"Right here, honey," said Floradora, handing me the burning one she had just been passed by Rita, who was watching all that went on silently with glassy eyes and a happy grin.

I inhaled that entire joint in one suck as well, held it in as Rita finally broke her silence by saying, "Tallulah, you have talents the movies haven't even touched."

I leaned in and exhaled the dreamy dope into Sandcrab's waiting orifice. He held it as best he could, and then he went into a coughing jag so violent it suggested that his lungs were trying to jump ship.

"Wow, Miss Tallulah," said Moondog, who somehow now appeared twice as stoned as he had when I arrived, "you are like a human carburetor."

"Darlings," I said, the pot and the vodka putting me in a very mellow, friendly, sociable mood, "I have oral skills you've never dreamed of. Allow me to demonstrate."

And I dropped to my knees in front of Moondog, fumbled open his blue jeans, and showed him just what sucking was really all about. After a moment Rita said, "Why should she have all the fun?" and knelt beside me to demonstrate her skills on Sandcrab, thus initiating a competitive Suck-Off, an event I have never lost. Floradora sang along with the record, as she danced happily about the room, waiting for her turn at bat.

***

A while later, I began to feel a bit peckish, despite the creamy, protein-rich beverage the boys had served us several fresh loads of, and asked if anyone else was hungry.

"Man," said Moondog, the first sounds he'd uttered apart from moans for about half an hour, "I have like major munchies."

"Well, let's hit that buffet," suggested Rita. So we all staggered to our feet, the boys did themselves up again, and we tottered out of the shack and off back to the food tables a hundred yards away.

Much of the repast laid out when we had wandered off was now just empty foil pans, or in the case of Rudy's *Huevos Rancheros*, a charred hole in the table still slightly smoldering, with a pool of hardening new glass in the sand below it. However, Minge's Cottage Cheese, powdered Barbecue Potato Chips, ground bologna, Campbell's Cream of Mushroom Soup, and Miracle Whip Vindaloo Surprise Casserole was almost intact, having had but a single serving scooped out, and most of that serving was now in a balled-up napkin lying beside it.

However, several new dishes had arrived, and Phil Rains, clad only in tasteful loose swim trunks, sunglasses, and go-aheads, which showed off a marvelous mature body, about what Dick Rockwood should look like in 20 years if he keeps himself in shape, was laying out two new dishes on the table, and peeling the tin foil back off of them. One was a blood pudding, just starting to clot, while the other was a steaming hot meat loaf, the odor of which smelt like Heaven. And, wonder of wonders, Phil had a huge grin on his face, and seemed to be radiating joy.

"Phil darling," I purred, feeling in love with the world, and surprisingly hungry, "I had no idea you could cook."

"Me, Tallulah?" he replied in a cheery tone, "No. I'm helpless in a kitchen. I wouldn't let you in my kitchen at this moment without a search warrant. This meatloaf is pure, one hundred percent Claudia Rains."

"*Claudia* prepared food for this party?" said a horribly familiar voice, in a tone of incredulity. Turning, I saw Odette Snype standing behind me in a sun dress that seemed to repel light. "Claudia has always seemed so anti-social as far as our little civic *soirées* went in the past."

"Claudia?" said Phil, "Nonsense. She loves all of you. She was literally beside herself making this meal."

"Then why isn't she here?" asked Odette.

"Oh, preparing this meal ground her to pieces in the kitchen, but she threw herself into this food. I can say with absolutely no fear of successful contradiction that her whole heart is in that meatloaf."

Moondog, who had already dished some meatloaf out for himself, and was chowing down greedily on it, added, "It tastes like some liver is in it as well."

"Right you are," said Phil, "quite a large chunk of liver, in fact. Very fresh. Also a *soupçon* of pancreas. And she sweat blood making that pudding, so that every one here could enjoy her offering. She may not be sitting here, drying out in the sun, but she wanted to be a part of every one of you. So dig in and enjoy."

Being inextricably stricken with a severe case of the munchies, even though my mouth had been stuffed full of hot meat for the better part of an hour now, I dished out a large, glistening serving for myself, and began wolfing it down like a savage with a platter full of fresh missionary. "Mmmmm," I said, "this is good. Unusual. Not just liver. Tastes of chicken, too."

"Is there any pork in this?" asked Floradora, inhaling the aroma arising from her plateful, "I might be Jewish. I keep meaning to find out."

"Sort of," said Phil, "a rare type called 'Long Pig.'"

"Haven't you been porked enough for one afternoon?" I asked with a friendly wink, while Moondog and Sandcrab choked on their mouthfuls and blushed.

"So, Phil, is it Claudia's own recipe?"

"No. She found it in *The Ellie Lovett Cookbook*."

"I'm not familiar with that one," said Minge through a mouthful of meatloaf, which was proving tremendously popular. Nearly the whole cast and crew were lined up at the table now for some, although neither Fanny nor Shirley were having any, being busy snapping pictures and running around. As if to make up for them, Harry was trying to slip a triple serving through his now-scabbed lips.

"It's very obscure," said Phil, "A 19th century English publication, never reprinted. Never really became popular."

"English cooking, I should think not," I said, "I'd rather eat Mange here than most traditional English dishes."

"*Oh Tallulah!*" said Minge, blushing.

"Don't get your hopes up, Mange; I didn't mean anything sexual, I think."

"Must everything in your mouth be revolting?" said Harry through a full mouth-load of meatloaf, "No one needs the image of you devouring my wife in their heads while we're eating Mrs. Rains's full-bodied dish."

Henrietta Shemp was handing a plateful of meatloaf to Darien the Librarian. Just what he was doing at the party I do not know, as he isn't affiliated with the play. Apparently, Henrietta had invited him. I guess that, as part of preparing to play a black maid, she needed to observe a black man devouring White Woman Meatloaf. They sat a bit apart from the others, giving each other surreptitious glances and furtive grins as they ate.

"I must get a shot of this buffet layout for the paper," said William

Randolph Hack, the boorish editor of *The God Damn Gazette*, who had materialized out of whatever hole the slimeball normally lived in.

"Everyone, say 'Cheese'!"

The folks around the table all turned to the camera, except for Phil, who must have heard some noise from the parking lot, as he turned his back to Hack just as it clicked off.

"Bill," said Harry to the loathsome editor, "I've been meaning to ask you about your extracurricular photography."

"What do you mean, Harry?" Hack asked.

"Have you been using your camera for purposes other than filling out the pages of your rag?"

Hack replied, "I don't know what you mean, Harry." Harry put an arm on Hack's shoulders and walked off with him, whispering together. Whatever Harry was hearing, it wasn't making him happy.

"Aren't you going to have any?" Minge asked Phil.

"No. I've had more than my fill of this dish at home over the years. To be frank, I'm sick of it. But you all have seconds."

The sheriff walked up and said, "Phil?"

Phil took a small leap when he heard his name, and said, "Yes, Sheriff?"

"I know I'm not involved in your play, but would you mind if I have some of your wife's leftovers here?"

Phil grinned from ear to ear. "Not at all, Henry, not at all. You just stuff yourself full of as much of it as you want. I can't think of anyone I would rather have chowing down on what my wife has left behind."

"What do you mean, 'left behind'?"

Phil blinked, glanced about, and then said, "Well, in this town nothing remains a secret long anyway, so I may as well spit it out now. Claudia has left me. She fixed this food for the picnic as her last gift to the town. That was why I was so late. I drove her inland to the Coast Highway, where she caught the bus for Los Angeles, and then I came here."

Minge put a hand on his arm, "Phil, I'm so sorry."

"We all knew you were having troubles," said Nelson Baker Eddy, "but we hoped you'd work it out."

"Well," said Phil, "we have worked it out, only this is what we worked out. It's better for both of us this way. Eat up, Nelson. Have some more. With her meatloaf on your tongue, it's like she never left."

"That's so odd. She seemed so happy when I saw how you had her all trussed up on the bed last night," I pitched in supportively.

Phil turned red, then green. He took me aside by the arm, and whispered to me, "Tallulah, you *promised* not to mention that to *anyone*! That was *very* personal and intimate. It was, ah, it was our last attempt to come together the way we used to, but it didn't work out. **Please**, don't mention it to anyone else ever again!"

"Mum's the word, Phil. Although I don't see what there is to be embarrassed about. I'm sure everyone here has tied up their spouse, hung them from the ceiling, and starved them once or twice. We all like a little spice in our marriages. Minge should really try it. Harry could use the weight loss. Claudia certainly looked enviably fit."

"Trust me; she's a total bone now," said Phil. "But let's keep it just between us, shall we? It will be fun to keep a secret."

"Anything you say, Phil baby. So, now that Claudia has disappeared, how would you like to jump *my* bones? I think we've waited a decent interval to be indecent."

"Tallulah, I'm honored, but I'd like to take a little break from women for a bit. I just got rid of one. I don't need to take on another."

"Well, I wasn't asking for a lifetime commitment, darling. I think I may be married myself at the moment anyway, although that needs to be kept a secret, too, even from me. I was just looking for some mutual recreational orgasms."

"Give me a few weeks, will you? Then we can talk. I have a few loose ends that still need to be buried somewhere before I can completely move on, you know what I mean?"

"I haven't a clue."

"Good."

***

As the afternoon wore on towards sunset, Nelson Baker Eddy brought around his motorboat and started taking partygoers on an activity called parasailing, which seemed to be a cross between waterskiing on air, and flying people like kites. As the sun approached the horizon, being a natural-born thrill-seeker, I decided to give it a try. After all, I've spent most of my life trying to get high as a kite without leaving the ground. Why not, I thought, try it for real?

Stripped down to my zebra-skin bikini, the top part of which, oddly enough, actually hangs lower than the bottom part, and equipped with a belt pouch containing thermoses full of emergency martinis and another joint Moondog had given me in a drug-induced fit of generosity, I was soon high aloft, gripping the tow-bar, speeding northward along the coast, enjoying the spectacular sunset on my left, and the California coastal mountains on my right. All that was needed to make the moment complete was a martini.

I let loose of the tow-bar with one hand to retrieve the thermos, and then let go with my other hand to unscrew the thermos. When I reached back for the tow-bar I saw that it had thoughtlessly fallen down to the ocean, a hundred or so yards below, and I was now flying, unfettered, straight towards the jagged mountain range.

I was headed for *Certain Death*, which would probably make telling you about it now very challenging! The only things preventing me from experiencing total panic was the mellow stone of the four or five joints I had shared with Moondog and crew all through the afternoon, the soothing effects of a full belly of Claudia Rains's meat, and the firm grip I had on the martini thermos.

Meanwhile, as the sun disappeared into the Pacific Ocean, the jagged cliffs, peaks, and chasms awaited me with their rocky horror!

Chapter 11
The Goddess Descends

The mountains on either side of Beaver Valley, California are unusually steep and sharp for the Pacific Coast Range, which for the most part is far milder than its more dramatic brother to the east, the Sierra Nevadas.

The intrusion into the range of the low, flat land which became Beaver Valley, shoved apart the mountains to each side, forcing them up, into loftier crags and steeper slopes. As a result, they have been far less explored by man than the remainder of the range.

But that is not to say no men have ever ventured into this final American frontier. Roughly a thousand years ago, a lost handful of Indians, separated from their tribe by a ferocious storm, found their way deep into the mountains north of Beaver Valley. While wandering there, a massive earthquake, unrecorded by history, opened a chasm beneath them, tossing the poor, lost people into the gulf below.

The fall wasn't far at first and some twenty or so of the men and women survived the fall. But then the patch of flat earth they had fallen onto sank further, carrying them down into a sheer-faced pit just over a hundred feet deep.

When their cataclysmic ordeal was over, the surviving band of Indians found themselves deep in a broad pit they could not climb out of. However, on the north side a wide high opening into the mountains led into a gentle cave. The cave spread for miles, with occasional openings in the roof, illuminating some patches with sunlight. The ground proved to be fertile.

A waterfall sent fresh water pouring into a subterranean lagoon full of fish. Animals and birds sometimes visited, not always by choice. But there was no exit. And so the band of Indians settled down to live, cut off from the world outside, eventually forgetting the land and the life beyond their isolated refuge.

By 1974, they were a colony of some fifty or so individuals, still undiscovered by the descendants of the Europeans invaders they had never encountered. They sometimes saw the metal birds soaring high above through the gaps in the cave's ceiling, and worshiped the gods who lived in the sky and traveled in these noisy, silver birds. They called themselves the Imawankahs. And on July 4, 1974, their tribal life was to be shaken and changed forever.

For as the sun set, a group of ten Imawankahs standing in their primary, southernmost pit looking up into the skies saw a white sky goddess descending from her celestial domain, borne on a giant, billowing wing. The younger Imawankahs ran off into the cave to summon the tribe elders, while the others prostrated themselves on the ground in worship of this goddess who had deigned to pay them a personal visit.

Tallulah's parasail carried her gently down into the pit which served as the entrance into the Imawankah village. She thudded to a halt, seated, in the midst of the Imawankah's patch of corn stalks. She rose to her feet, still clutching her martini thermos, and emerged wobbily from the cornrows. She saw before her four men and two women, clad in loincloths and beads, prostrate on the ground before her, chanting something in a language unknown to her, or indeed to anyone but Imawankahs, for it was the speech they had evolved through a millennia of isolation from all of mankind.

If there was anything she liked besides booze and sex, it was people on their knees worshiping her. Realizing immediately that these were primitive, simple people, not unlike Mormons or film censors, she spread her arms and said, "Darlings."

The Imawankahs looked up, and murmured in imitation, "Darlings."

Tallulah repeated her greeting, "Darlings, I come in peace. What have you got to drink in this hellhole?"

"Darlings," the Imawankahs replied, as more tribe members came running up from within the cave.

"Oh dear." said Tallulah, "This sounds like a conversation with Zazu Pitts. Look, darlings, I'm Tallulah Morehead, the Nearly Living Legend."

She patted her head, "You must have heard of me; I'm a screen *immortal!* Morehead. Tallulah Morehead. *Morehead.*"

"Morehead," the Imawankahs mimicked.

The Imawankah chief approached Tallulah. He had never seen the likes of her before, and was stunned, but determined to demonstrate his bravery and leadership.

Tallulah patted her head. "Morehead." she repeated. Then she patted the chief's head, and said, "Who are you, darling? The local president of my fan club?"

The chief grasped the general nature of the inquiry, and patted his own head, and said, "Imawankah."

"Don't put yourself down, darling." said Tallulah. "I think you're adorable. *Love* the beads!"

The chief patted her head and said, "Morehead." then he patted his own and said, "Imawankah." He then patted them each in turn, repeating the information, "Imawankah. Morehead. Imawankah. Morehead."

"Darling," said Tallulah, "This is beginning to sound like the cast party of a high school play. Have some martini, chiefy. It's just dry enough." She swigged some martini, and then passed the thermos to the chief. He took a swig, coughed, and then smiled.

"You like that, do you?" she asked, "You have excellent taste. Here darlings. All of you have some." She pulled the other two emergency thermoses from her belt pouch and handed them around. Each Imawankah there had a swig. "This should run both ways, darlings. Do you have any firewater in this burg?"

One of the Imawankahs evidently recognized the drink as alcohol and grasped the nature of her request. He produced an earthen jug of the corn liquor the Imawankahs made for themselves and handed it to Tallulah, after which he prostrated himself flat on the ground before her. Tallulah took a gulp, belched, and said to him, "I like the cut of your jib darling."

She turned to the chief and said, "You know, my longtime companion, the Headless Indian Brave, is one of your people, so I have great respect for your customs, especially when your customs are to welcome strangers with this delightful firewater. It's fierce, and just a touch impudent. I like it."

The chief, knowing only one word of English so far, repeated, "Morehead."

"Well darling, if you insist," Tallulah said, and then dropped to her knees and lifted the Chief's loincloth. "We call this 'giving head,'" she added, just before speaking became rude.

It's amazing what a people completely cut off from the rest of the world will and won't discover. With so much of the Imawankahs' village forever in darkness, their sense of smell had evolved over the millennium to a level that would shame a bloodhound. They had learned to brew their own corn liquor, to farm their small plots of land that received sunlight, to hunt the animals that came within range, to live in their closed environment, to mate and to maintain a stable tribe on limited resources, but they had never before discovered oral sex.

The Chief repeated, "giving head," before suddenly starting to moan.

And thus did the goddess who descended from the sky bearing the gift of "Martini" also teach them "The God's Pleasure," soon to be known as "The Sacrament of Tallulah."

As she went round, pleasuring each of the men in turn, and instructing them on how to similarly please their women as well, the Imawankahs took to it - and her - like cats to shredding sofas.

**

The orgy of oral sex Tallulah had unwittingly begun with the Imawankahs was going full blast when the sound of propellers and the blinding illumination of a spotlight flooded the pit, catching the parasail on the ground. A voice amplified by a bullhorn called out "Tallulah! Are you there, Tallulah?"

The Imawankahs, terrified by the noise, light, and the godlike voice calling out "Tallulah," scurried back into the cave and crouched there, watching.

Tallulah waved happily at the helicopter, as likely to invite the new arrivals down as to leave the party she'd begun. "*Did you bring vodka?*" she hollered upwards.

"She's there!" the voice called out. A moment later, a rope ladder unfurled down from the hovering helicopter to the bottom of the pit. A bottle of vodka was tethered to the ladder, like bait. Rudy was leaning out of the helicopter door, waving. Tallulah staggered over and clambered onto the rope ladder.

"Goodbye, my darling Imawankahs!" she cried, waving, and then began climbing the ladder.

The bravest of the Imawankahs crept out and saw their goddess ascend back into the skies. Just as she entered the helicopter, and word of her rescue was radioed back to Alta Caca, the celebratory Fourth of July fireworks began shooting off, startling Tallulah momentarily. Her startled foot accidentally detached the rope ladder from the 'copter and sent plummeting it down into the pit.

So the Imawankahs below, at the climax of the most amazing day in their entire history, lifted their booze-and-orgasm bedazzled eyes upwards to see their goddess fly away as the sky erupted in multi-colored explosions. They had seen these fireworks displays before, but had always believed they were the gods warring among themselves. Now they knew the truth. The gods were celebrating the return of their queen.

They heard her voice one last time, amplified by the bullhorn, "Goodbye, my darlings. Come up and see me sometime."

The meaning of those words would be debated with increasing vehemence, and even violence, amongst the tribe members for weeks to come as this divine visitation changed the Imawankahs forever.

***

(From the personal journal of Tallulah Morehead.)

Frankly darlings, I was exhausted when I got back to my room at the Mirkin House. Poor Harry Mirkin could barely conceal his disappointment at the proof of my rescue and utter lack of injury.

I felt, for the good of all concerned, that it would be best not to mention my encounter with the Imawankah Indians to anyone, since I felt that further contact with outsiders might corrupt their peaceful lifestyle just as they had learned the pleasures I had taught them. Also, there was a better than average chance no one would believe me, just thinking I was drunk, stoned, or mad, when I had only been two of the three, though I can't remember which two. And getting declared mad and committed to an asylum would seriously interfere with my rehearsal schedule.

But the day's adventures had left me more tired than an audience member at a Greer Garson triple feature (known in The Trade as a "Noble-athon"). All I wanted was some sleep. Frankly, I was glad my husband was off with his fiancé tonight as, after my cavorting with

Moondog and Sandcrab, and my servicing the entire male population of Imawankahs, including doing enough of the females for the men to get the idea, suppress their natural nausea and give it a try, I really had had enough sex to last me until morning, and I can't remember the last time I said *that!*

As I entered the bedroom, there was a silent whoosh of blurred movement. When I switched on the light, there was the Headless Indian Brave lying on my bed. He was naked, his transparent loincloth flung on the floor, and his transparent penis (also headless) was fully erect. Oh great, I thought; it wasn't enough to deal with thirty horny live Indian Braves in a cave, now I had a horny dead Indian Brave in my bed. Much as I loved him I frankly prefer a man I can actually feel when I'm having sex.

"Not tonight, darling," I said, "And how many times must I ask you, if you take your loincloth off, hang it in the closet?"

With that I slid open the closet door. Inside was a most unexpected sight: a tall naked woman was standing there, hiding I suppose after I had accidentally caught she and my ghostly companion *in flagrante necrofilo*. Along with being naked, she was also transparent. Even that was not the oddest thing about her. The real eye-catcher was that she too had no head!

"Oh," I said, "Hello. Don't be shy, my dear." I turned back to the Headless Indian Brave, "Sweetheart, you've made a friend? How lovely. I'd have knocked first if I'd suspected you two were - ah - necking." I turned back to the headless woman in the closet, "Come on out, my dear."

She tentatively stepped out of the closet, her ectoplasm quivering. The Headless Indian Brave walked over and took her hand in his.

"Is this love I'm seeing?" I asked the blushing shades. The Headless Indian Brave nodded his neck stump. After a moment, so did the woman.

"Well, that's just angelic," I said, "Tell you what. I am absolutely pooped, and must sack out in here. But why don't you two lovebirds go down the hall to the guest room where you can materialize, scare the living hell out of Harry and Mange, and send them fleeing off to their crappy hotel? Then you can consummate your brains out in there. Oh, I'm sorry. If you don't have heads, you're not likely to have brains. Well, you can consummate your butts off. How's that?"

The two charming, cranium-free phantasms nodded their stumps vigorously, and trotted off through the closed door.

"When you come back," I hollered after them, "I expect you to be buttless as well as headless."

A few moments later, as I settled snugly under the covers, I heard Minge scream her shrill little lungs out, followed quickly by Harry bellowing in terror. I drifted off to sleep listening to the sweet music of the Mirkins pounding along the hallway and down the stairs, shrieking all the way. There was more than one kind of fireworks shooting off in Alta Caca tonight.

Chapter 12
Midsummer Madness

There must have been something magical in the air or in the water in Beaver Valley that enchanted summer of 1974. You could see it in the darting eyes of Mayor Mirkin, as he glanced suspiciously at every person he met, wondering if he or she was the person who had retrieved the $10,000 he had left behind a specified bush in Beaver Green Park. You could hear it in Minge's voice every time she began a sentence to Odette Snype with, "Tallulah said the *wittiest* thing at dinner last night..." even though Tallulah avoided eating with her, and on the rare occasions she did say something witty to Minge, it was usually a withering insult.

You could see it in the loopy grins on the faces of Merle Mirkin and Snake Bendix when they sped out of The Pay Ten Place Motel in the dead of most nights. You could see it in the bloodshot eyes of Moondog Hickox and Sandcrab as they paddled their surfboards into the water, giggling.

You could see it in the inspiringly bizarre choreography Floradora Windwillow was creating fresh each day because she could never remember what she'd invented the day before.

You could hear it in the odd, piping cries that came from Darien the Librarian's bedroom windows most nights, about twenty minutes before Henrietta Shemp would sneak out his back door wearing a trench coat, sunglasses, and a straw hat with an enormous, drooping brim she had forgotten had "Henrietta" stitched across the back.

You could see it in the fresh smiles on Fanny's face as she and Shirley rehearsed, played, and romped about town, with Fanny's taciturn nature seemingly banished.

You could see it in the new, unfamiliar joy infusing Phil Rains, as he took to hiking up to remote spots with a fat backpack that was always lighter on the way back.

And you could see it in the proud staggering of Tallulah's acting pupils, as they slurred the dialogue in the acting scenes Tallulah assigned them, scenes that almost always involved them passionately making out with her. It was a summer of joy for most, even if it wasn't so hot for Richard Nixon on the other coast.

One place you could not see it though, was in the increasingly frustrated look on Susan Mirkin's face as her fiancé found more and more reasons to dodge her, and spend time elsewhere. Eventually, she decided to do a little investigating into his disappearing act for herself.

Wednesday July 10th, Susan rented herself a car so that Dick wouldn't recognize her usual one, put on a cheap blond wig, and parked across the street from Alta Caca High School at 6 p.m., just before rehearsal let out. When she saw Dick Rockwood come out of the auditorium, she sank down a bit in her seat, waiting until he was in his car and had pulled out of the parking lot. Susan, feeling like a private detective on TV, followed him for a few blocks, the James Bond Musical Theme playing in her head all the way, until he pulled into the alley behind The Pay Ten Place Motel. She stopped at the entrance to the alley, and watched him pull into the motel's parking lot, accessible only from the alley.

Susan bit her lips. *Oh Dick*, she thought, *Why? Who?* However, there was no way to tell from outside the motel which room anyone went into. She got out of her car and walked down the alley to see if she recognized any vehicles that were parked there.

There were several cars, and a motorcycle she didn't know belonged to Snake Bendix. None of these vehicles were familiar to her. Susan walked back to her car, got in, sat and waited to see who else showed up to see if she could tell who the hussy who was stealing her man was.

Tallulah's Rolls arrived next, driven by Rudy, with both Tallulah and Rita Morecombe in the back. Then she saw her brother Merle come down the sidewalk on foot, and stroll down the alley and into the motel.

Susan sat there for three hours, but no one else arrived. Finally Tallulah emerged, looking severely disarrayed, even for her, and got into her Rolls and waited. Susan smirked, wondering who was so desperate as to be making it with that smelly old hag. A few moments later, Rudy and

Merle came out, each with an arm around Dick, whom they were basically carrying into the car as he appeared to be too drunk to stand.

Susan sucked in her breath. *It couldn't be!* She'd known her brother was a fag ever since the day three years before, when she found a *Playgirl Magazine* he had hidden under his mattress. A person didn't have to be that disgusting Doctor Kinsey to figure out that that Rudy person was a queer, too. But Dick Rockwood? *Oh Susan, you should have known better than to fall in love with a man who owned Broadway show cast albums.* How could Dick be cheating on her with a man? And *which* man?

Or? Could it *be?* She'd once heard something repellant whispered by one of her sorority sisters, about a disgusting practice some fags were said to indulge in, that involved *three* men! She hadn't actually believed that anything so revolting was actually performed by Americans. Russians perhaps, or more likely The French, who were all fags anyway, but not here in Alta Caca. Could it possibly be that her husband-to-be had just been - well - the term she'd heard was "Spit-Roasted"? It couldn't be, although it would explain his difficulty walking. Tears flooded Susan's eyes as she followed the Rolls back to her parent's house.

At her home, Susan saw the four people get out of the car. Dick was able to walk a little better now, but Rudy was still supporting him as he went into the house. Susan waited outside. She saw lights go on in her parent's bedroom, where she knew Tallulah was sleeping, then in her brother's bedroom, and finally, in the downstairs servant room where Rudy slept.

Susan crept up the driveway and up to Rudy's ground-floor window. The shade was up just a fraction of an inch, but it was enough for her to see that Rudy was alone in his room.

Susan sat down suddenly in the flowerbed. She hadn't intended to sit, but her legs just gave out on her as the truth hit her like a ton of feathers. Dick Rockwood, her fiancé, the man she intended to spend her life with, was cheating on her *with her own brother!* The depth of the double betrayal was too much to take in, so she just sat there, in a daze.

Meanwhile upstairs, still high on the Quaalude he'd taken back at the motel, Dick was making loud sloppy love to his wife, the 'Lude still helping him pretend Tallulah was fifty years younger, while he thought about the career that awaited him as a Hollywood star once this summer ended. On the other side of the bedroom wall, in his room, Merle listened to them, imagining himself in Tallulah's place, and pleasured himself as he listened.

It was Concepcion who found Susan sitting in the flowerbed the next morning. She brought her inside and gave her a nice hot cup of tea. Then she led her upstairs to her bedroom and tucked her into bed. Susan didn't speak. She stayed in her room for the next few days. The official story was the flu.

***

Thursday's rehearsal was to be the first rehearsal off-book, when the cast was required to know their lines by heart. This, of course, was why Tallulah had spent the evening before cavorting with her secret husband at the motel and again back at the house. It somehow hadn't penetrated into her head that Iris couldn't memorize her script for her.

For various reasons, they weren't beginning the session at the top of the play, but rather were beginning at scene 12, where Baby Jane serves her sister a roasted rat for dinner. Monica, in a display of professionalism that Tallulah considered "show-offy," had actually already been off-book for a week. Tallulah had explained that she was only still working from her script so that the rest of the cast "wouldn't feel their inferiority to me," despite the fact that she was, in fact, the only person still using a script.

"Well, she does have the largest role," sighed Cyril Savoy, when Monica complained about Tallulah's "relaxed work ethic."

"A mistake I'm more than willing to help correct," Monica contributed helpfully, "We could switch roles anytime. I know all of her lines, too, and I'd be far more believable in the role than she is. Hell, the drunken slut might even prefer playing Blanche. It would be a lot easier for her to play the whole show in the wheelchair. She has a hard enough time standing up dead drunk as it is."

"That is not going to happen," said Cyril, "even if Tallulah suggests it. She is the bigger box office name." Monica flinched, and her lip curled, "She retains the bigger role. That's how show business works."

"But she has no talent!" Monica sputtered, "I couldn't get Thalberg to understand that in the old days, and you don't seem to grasp it now."

"What does talent have to do with stardom?" Cyril replied.

"That's just what Thalberg said," Monica spat out venomously.

"She's bigger box office than you are. She was back at PMS, and she still is. Talent aside, she has something that audiences have always connected with. Maybe it's charisma. Maybe it's charm. Maybe it's just a campy fun time. But good or bad, audiences have always loved her."

"But...she...*stinks!*" Monica screamed.

"Movie audiences can't smell her. And for Baby Jane, it will just seem like she's intensely in character."

"I mean she's lousy. I'm three times the actress she is."

"Nonsense," said Tallulah, who had wandered in behind Monica, "That diet you've been on is almost working. At worst, you're only twice my size."

"Places, scene twelve!" Cyril called out to prevent a confrontation from growing.

Monica took a seat in the wheelchair, but immediately sprang back out of it.

"What is this rat doing here?" She shrieked, pointing to the prop rat on her chair's seat.

"Trying to plump itself back up after being squished by your petit-sometime-in-the-future ass, I imagine," said Tallulah, retrieving the prop and putting it under the cover of the serving dish she would be carrying in on a tray. "I wondered where I'd left this. Hey, Cyril, isn't there some sort of law against cruelty to fake animals?"

"There's a law against cruelty to actresses," Monica snarled.

Tallulah laughed and said, "Yes, and you're the exception that proves the rule."

"Places, please. Take it from Baby Jane's entrance," said Cyril, "Tallulah, are you ready to do it without script?"

"Absolutely. Unlike some of us," she shot Monica a look, "I am a professional."

"Then start the scene please. Very quiet everyone."

Tallulah entered carrying the dinner tray, set it beside the lunch tray, lifted the cover off the lunch plate, saw the fake dead parakeet, snorted, and covered the plate again. Then she picked up the lunch tray and headed for the door. Monica spoke, "Did you have a nice drive?"

Tallulah bowed her head forward and said, "What are you talking about?"

"Nothing dear," said Monica, "I was thinking. It's ever so long since we had a nice talk. You know, a real talk about the future and everything. Jane, I don't want you to have to worry about the house. We'll still be together, even after I sell it."

Tallulah bowed her head again and said, "Blanche, you're not going to sell this house. Daddy bought this house, and he bought it for me."

"Head *up*, Tallulah," said Cyril.

"You're wrong, Jane. I bought this house, with money from the studio."

Tallulah bowed her head again, "Oh, you're a liar. Baby Jane Hudson made the money that paid for this house, that's who."

"Head up please, Tallulah," snapped Cyril.

"You don't know what you're saying," said Monica.

"I do too. These are the right lines, aren't they Cyril?" said Tallulah.

"That was Monica's *line*," said Cyril.

"Oh, right. I forgot she knows some of her lines."

"Monica, again please."

Monica said, "You don't know what you're saying, Jane."

Tallulah set the tray down, bent her head forward, stared at it, and said, "Blanche, you aren't ever going to sell this house." Then she lifted the cover off the plate with the parakeet, and stared into the inside of the cover, adding, "And you aren't ever going to leave it, either." Tallulah did the dramatic point-at-Blanche gesture she had been doing at this spot, only now, since she was holding the silver plate cover, she misjudged the difference, and smacked Monica in the forehead with it.

"Tallulah," asked Cyril, "Why are you holding that dish cover?"

Monica, holding one hand to her bashed forehead, snatched the cover from Tallulah and held it out, "Because she's got this page of her script taped to the inside!"

Sure enough, there was a page of Tallulah's script on the inside. The previous page was taped to the tray, beside the plate.

Cyril sighed. He had directed fifteen-year-olds in plays, but it hadn't prepared him for these two.

"Let's go on, shall we please?"

Tallulah crossed to the window as Monica said, "Jane, do you remember when I had my accident?"

Tallulah stared out the window and said, "You promised you would never talk about that again."

Cyril said, "Tallulah, I think it will work better if you look back at Blanche on that line, as you were doing before."

"No, it won't," she replied.

"Yes, it will. Do it again, and this time, look at Blanche when you say your line."

"But I won't be able to see my lines taped to the back drop."

"Just do the scene from memory," Cyril was so annoyed, his fake British accent was disappearing.

Monica again said, "Jane, do you remember when I had my accident?"

Tallulah turned to her, stared for a moment, and then bellowed out, "Line?"

Iris, holding the script near Cyril, read out, "You promised you would never talk about that again."

Tallulah said, "You promised...ah...you promised...line?"

Iris said, "You promised you would never talk about that again."

Tallulah said, "You promised you promised you would never talk about that again."

"No," said Iris, "just 'you promised' once."

"No," said Tallulah, "just you promised once."

"Stop!" yelled Cyril, "Tallulah, your line is 'You promised you would never talk about that again.' Okay?"

"I'm fine. Let's do it."

Monica once more said, "Jane, do you remember when I had my accident?"

Tallulah stared at her and said, "You...line?"

Iris inhaled deeply and read, "You promised you would never talk about that again."

Tallulah stared at Monica and said, "What she said."

"Just go on please, before I *die!*" said Cyril.

Monica said, "I know I did, but after all these years, I'm still in this chair. And it's your fault. You wouldn't be able to do these awful things to me if I weren't still in this chair."

Tallulah gave Jane's evil smirk and said, "Line?"

Iris read out, "But you are, Blanche. You are in that chair."

Tallulah said, "But you...line?"

"But you are, Blanche. You are in that chair."

"But you are...line?"

"Blanche. You are in that chair."

"Blanche...line?"

"You are in that chair.."

"You...line?"

"Are in that chair."

"Are...line?"

"In that chair."

"In...line?"

"That chair."

"That...line?"

"Chair."

"Chair...line?"

Monica said, "Maybe it would be easier if you just taped your script to my face."

Tallulah replied, "It certainly would be, and you'd look better, too."

"Why you drunken, unprofessional bitch!"

"Ladies!" called out Cyril, "Let's just skip the scene for now, and try the musical number it ends with. Butch, music please."

Butch Miller began playing Phil's Irving Berlin-knock-off melody and Tallulah and Monica began singing together:

"Sisters, Sisters,
There were never such malicious sisters."

Tallulah launched into her solo line: *"Thought my sister Blanche was looking way too fat. That's why I made her lunch a rat.* Line?"

Cyril looked to Heaven, but there was no help for him there.

***

On Saturday, Tallulah had the day off from rehearsal. She, Rudy, and Rita went boating out on Swan Song Lake; Rudy rowing while Rita and Tallulah drank.

"I don't understand this." said Tallulah, "Why the hell did the city build such a tremendously large swimming pool when no one swims in it?"

"Why would people swim in this reservoir," asked Rita, "when they have the beach nearby?"

"They told me," said Rudy, "that a giant squid lives in this lake."

"Rudy," said Tallulah, "don't be silly. That's completely absurd. Everyone knows that giant squids cannot live in fresh water any more than I can." Tallulah seemed to drift off with a dreamy look on her face.

"Tallulah, dear," said Rita, "I had no idea you were an expert on giant squids."

"What is that creepy expression on your face, Tallu?" asked Rudy, stopping rowing and letting them just drift.

"I was just reminiscing," Tallulah said. "I always wax nostalgic when I remember that one unforgettable night in the raging surf of Lunada Bay, naked under the sequined lights of The Milky Way, taking a cruise to Heaven in the tentacles of the giant squid from *20,000 Leagues Under the Sea*. That libidinous mollusk could suck *all* of my erogenous zones at once! Oh Squiddy, Squiddy dear, you aren't *in* Heaven. You *are* Heaven!"

"You made love to a giant squid?" Rita Morecombe thought she'd seen every depravity imaginable through her motel's one-way mirrors, but this was a new one on her.

"Indeed I did. He was all tentacles, but fortunately I had dated Errol Flynn, and next to Errol, Squiddy was a piker."

"How on earth did you ever hook up with a giant squid?"

"Darling, when you meet a giant squid, the tricky part is *not* hooking up."

"Then how did you *meet* a giant squid?"

"Peter Lorre introduced us. They were working together at Disney at the time. Squiddy had a romantic scene with James Mason, where he caressed and sucked him until a jealous Kirk Douglas thrust his massive harpoon into him, and reclaimed James for himself. James told me later that, after a night with Pamela, Squiddy was a welcome rest. Anyway, I had had a brief affair with Peter Lorre..."

"I didn't know that," interrupted Rudy.

"Of course not, darling. I was still married to you at the time. I would never have humiliated you by rubbing your nose in the fact that I was having an affair with Peter Lorre. There are so many other, more creative ways to humiliate a husband."

"Like an affair with a giant squid?"

"Wait a minute," said Rita, "you used to be married to *Rudy*?"

"For ten years," said Rudy looking smug.

"Rita, darling," said Tallulah, "you name him, I've married him. We never publicized our marriage, to protect Rudy's public image."

"And we never spoiled it by having sex," Rudy chirruped happily.

"Why do you think I was driven into the arms of Peter Lorre? A woman had to be pretty desperate or awfully damned horny to do Petey. We broke every third commandment together under the silvery light of a full moon on top of mighty Half Dome in Yosemite National Park. I turned those poached-egg eyes into a cheesy omelette before I was through."

"But when I asked him for a second date, Peter said, 'No, I think once was more than enough. You'd be better off matched up with our squid.' How typically unselfish of him. Squiddy and I had 20,000 orgasms under the sea. Thank Heaven Walt Disney never found out. He'd have fired Squiddy in a second, and replaced him with any old unemployed calamari. Ever been to The Actor's Studio? They're *all* calamari. That Brando kid was all tentacles. Squiddy was terrified of Walt. But Walt not only kept him on the film, but he then hired him to appear personally at Disneyland for ten years. His exhibit was an 'A Ticket' attraction, but believe you me, Squiddy was a genuine 'E Ticket' ride!"

Rita looked over at Rudy with a bemused look, "Rudy, is even one word of that true?"

Rudy rolled his eyes and said, "Honey, I was putting makeup over her 20,000 hickeys for weeks!"

Rita laughed, "Oh, you two are quite, quite mad."

"Isn't that Phil Rains?" asked Rudy. The two ladies turned and saw Phil in another small rowboat, in an inlet that had been hidden by a point of land they had just drifted by. Phil had a large brown parcel in his hands, and he was lifting it over the side of the boat, to hold over the lake.

"Phil darling!" Tallulah yelled out, "How the hell are you?"

Phil was so startled he almost leapt out of his boat, fumbling to hold on to the package, which he quickly stashed back in the bottom of the boat, next to several similar boxes. "Tallulah, Rudy, Rita. Imagine running into you at this remote spot."

"What's in the box, darling?" Tallulah asked, "Champagne?"

"Why would you think he has champagne in a hat box?" asked Rita.

"I saw he was preparing to dip it in the lake, I assumed to chill it."

"And besides," chipped in Rudy, "she thinks every parcel has champagne in it."

"It's nothing important," said Phil, trying to toss a tarp over the boxes in the boat.

"Is it a sandwich?" asked Tallulah, "I ask because there looks to be catsup leaking out of the bottom."

Phil turned a pale green and said, "Oh dear. I better get back before the - ah - catsup stains the hull." He began frantically rowing away.

"Wait, darling!" yelled Tallulah, "We'll help. Rudy, follow that skip."

Rudy began rowing frantically in pursuit of Phil's boat. Phil tried rowing harder, but Rudy kept up with him. Tallulah sipped a martini and said to Rita, "Isn't this fun? One moment we're drifting aimlessly, and now we're suddenly embroiled in a pointless rowboat chase. This would make for a crummy B movie if I weren't an A-list star."

Phil beached his boat on the shore by his car and began frantically offloading the boxes. Tallulah's boat beached beside his thirty seconds later. "Rudy, darling," said Tallulah, "load those boxes for him. The man's still prostate with grief over his marital desertion."

"That's okay." said Phil, "Thanks anyway, but I can handle these."

"I insist," she said. Rudy bounded up and tried to take the hatbox, now dripping catsup, out of Phil's hands. Phil refused to let go of it, and a small tug-of-war ensued.

"No, Rudy," said Phil. "Please leave these alone. I don't need any help."

"Rudy," Tallulah helpfully hollered, "let go of that one, and get the others."

"*No!*" screamed Phil. He tossed the box in his hands into his car trunk, and scrambled to try and prevent Rudy from picking up the other boxes.

"Phew!" said Rudy, wrinkling his nose, "Something has spoiled in one of these."

"Yes," said Phil, trying to pick up all the boxes at once, and failing to keep even one in his arms, "Something is definitely rotten in here. Don't bother yourself with them. They're my responsibility."

"That's okay," said Rudy, scooping up each box that slipped from Phil's increasingly frantic grip, "I take care of Tallulah, remember? This stench is perfume next to the way she can reek on a Monday morning."

"Flattery will avail you nothing," said Tallulah.

"Boy," said Rita, now also sorting through the boxes, all seeping a red liquid, "you aren't kidding about the reek. What have you got in here, Phil, a dead wildebeest?"

"Something like that," said Phil, trying to thrust himself between Rita and the packages he was still trying to transfer out of the boat and into his car.

"You should try wrapping these in plastic," suggested Rudy, as he loaded a couple boxes into Phil's trunk.

"Thanks, I'll try that," said Phil, struggling up to the car with five boxes in his arms. Phil saw Rita picking up the last three boxes in the boat, gave a little screech, dropped the boxes he was carrying into the trunk, and ran back down to Rita to grab them away from her.

"Phil darling," said Tallulah, still reclining in her boat, sipping her martini, "the way you're running around is wearing me out. Take a load off. Have a drink."

"No time, Tallulah," said Phil, slamming the car trunk closed on the last of the boxes. He walked back down to the boat carrying an axe, "Oh look at the catsup stains in this boat. I need to scrape these off." Phil raised the axe and slammed it into his boat's hull.

"That doesn't strike me as a prudent cleaning technique," Tallulah said. "Rudy, you're an old hand at scrubbing my stains out of all sorts of substances. Is an axe the way to do it?"

"Well, I sometimes think about taking an axe to you, but only as a preventative measure, not as a means of cleaning. If I have to clean you, I just slam you against large rocks."

"How thoughtful, Rudy darling. And how I love the feel of a fine pair of rocks slamming repeatedly against me."

"Perhaps you are right," said Phil, trying his hardest to look dismayed at the hole he had chopped into his boat's hull, "Well, I guess this boat is ruined. How careless of me. Rudy, could you do me a favor?"

"Certainly," said Rudy, "drop your pants."

"Not that. Could you tow this boat back out with you, and just let it sink in the deepest part of the lake?"

"If you'd like. But I am from Manila, you know. I grew up on an island. I'm sure I could repair this boat for you."

"No, no. Too expensive."

"Let it be my gift," piped in Tallulah.

"Nonsense."

"It's no trouble, really," said Rudy, "I'd enjoy doing it. I used to help my father build boats when I was a boy."

"*No!*" Phil yelled. Then more quietly, "I mean, thank you, no. Just sink it into silence."

"If you insist," said Rudy. And so, as Phil hastily drove off, Rudy rowed Tallulah's boat out into the middle of the lake, towing Phil's rapidly swamping boat behind, until it sat too low in the water. Then he let it go, and it sank out of sight.

"Another martini, Rita dear?" asked Tallulah.

***

While Tallulah, Rita, and Rudy paddled aimlessly around Swan Song Lake, slinging back cocktails, Monica Montana and Odette Snype were having tea at Odette's house. Their topic of conversation was: *Tallulah*

Morehead, The Humiliating Of. Monica put her finger right on the primary problem, "She's almost impossible to successfully insult. She has some sort of emotional Teflon. No matter what you do or say to her, it slides right off her without making a dent. There's nothing she can't take as a compliment."

"Well then," said Odette, "we'll just have to find something that will sink in. Let us put our minds to it. I'm sure we can come up with something. And if we can't find something, I know someone who can."

***

On the evening of Monday the 15th, the Mirkins were celebrating their wedding anniversary with a few friends. They had made a formal request to Tallulah for the use of their own living room for their anniversary party, to which Tallulah had graciously replied, "You really think your anniversary is cause for celebration? Well, to each his own. As for the living room, I was planning on using it that night myself, for the purposes of passing out naked and drunk. Oh all right, if you're going to pout about it. But don't think you can make a regular thing out of using your own home. I'm only allowing it this time because your anniversary is even more depressing to me than it must be to you."

So after Monday's rehearsal and acting class (During which the 19th century melodramas *Ten Nights in a Bar Room* and *The Drunkard* were discussed as Great American Comedies and boilermakers were served. "Playing a drunk when sober is so fake," she told her students, "The audience can always smell the difference, even in a movie"), Tallulah went off to an ocean side campfire with Moondog, Sandcrab, Floradora, Rita, Rudy, and Merle. Dick was stuck attending The Mirkins' anniversary party. Merle was supposed to attend his parents' party also, but was playing hooky.

"Where's your Snake tonight, Merle dear?" Tallulah asked.

Merle flashed a shaky sneaky look that would have looked at home on Nixon's face as he claimed that he was not a crook. "*My* Snake? I don't know who you mean?"

"Merle," said Tallulah, trying for severe, "I didn't just fall off the turnip truck yesterday." Rudy leaned forward and whispered in her ear for a moment, then she continued, "Oh, right. Rudy reminds me that I *did* fall off a turnip truck yesterday. They should really install seatbelts on those things. Those poor little turnips could fall off and sustain head injuries that could turn them into *vegetables!* However, my point is, I can smell man-juice on a person from twenty yards away, and you're barely one yard away. Honey, I've known snake oil salesmen that reeked of snake-milk less than you do. Besides, do you think I've never noticed how his cycle is always at Rita's Pay Ten Place when you are? But for the sake of argument, let's say you're meeting there every evening to play nude Scrabble, although those little wooden tiles can get lost up all sorts of intimate crannies. So where is he this evening?"

"Well, we're hanging here with surfers..." began Merle.

"Whoa! Righteous, dude," said Moondog, who was trying to hyperventilate an entire joint all at once, as he'd seen Tallulah do.

Merle continued, "...And bikers and surfers don't mix well. There have been incidents."

"They hate us, man," said Sandcrab.

"That's silly," said Tallulah, and then she began singing:

"Oh, the surfers and the bikers should be friends.
Oh, the surfers and the bikers should be friends.
One group likes to ride big curls,
The other likes to gang-bang girls,
But that's no reason why they can't be friends.
Alta Caca folks should stick together,
Alta Caca folks should all be pals.
Surfers ought to get tattoos;
Bikers ought to rape their gals."

Rudy said, "What are you babbling about?"

"Sorry darling. An attack of *Oklahomo.*"

Moondog's eyes were wide, "Wow, Tallu, that was like, deep."

"It was, darling, wasn't it? In a shallow kind of way of course."

Suddenly they all heard a clear yell of "Ow!" echoing down from the small hill behind them.

"Man, what was that?" asked Sandcrab, "A ghost?"

"Nonsense," said Tallulah, "One of my closest friends is a ghost, and they never feel pain."

"Well let's check it out," suggested Moondog.

Taking pieces of the burning wood from the campfire to use as torches, the little band walked up the hill. Upon cresting it they saw Phil Rains in a small hollow below digging a shallow hole with a shovel. His stack of catsup-stained boxes sat in a wheelbarrow beside the unfinished hole. A Coleman lantern also sat on the ground, illuminating his dig.

"Phil darling," said Tallulah, descending into the hollow. Startled, Phil fell into the hole he was digging, "What are you doing, darling? Trying to vacation in China?"

The men hurried down the hill to help Phil out of the hole. Phil's head popped up over the mound of freshly dug dirt. "Tallulah. Hello. I can't seem to go anywhere, no matter how remote, without running into you."

"Of course not, darling. I am ubiquitous."

"Holy Mother," said Rudy, scrunching up his face, "your wildebeest has really gone off now. What a stench."

"What are you up to my dear?" asked Tallulah.

"Fossil hunting?" said Phil, with a hopeful look.

"Why do you need rancid wildebeest to hunt fossils?" asked Rudy.

"Are you burying leftovers?" asked Floradora, who was keeping a good distance from the reeking boxes.

"Leftover *who*?" snapped Phil, "I mean 'what'! No. I'm not burying anything. And I'm done now anyway." Phil scrambled up, grabbed the lantern, and tried to push the wheelbarrow back up the path he'd clearly come down in the first place.

"Hold it there, Mister Rains, sir," said Moondog. "Aren't you going to fill in your hole?"

"Or better yet," said Tallulah, "why don't you fill in *my* hole?"

"You've ripped open a wound in Mother Earth," said Moondog as seriously as a severely stoned teenaged surfer could, "You've torn open her hymen, and spoiled her virginity. The least you can do is heal the wound you've made."

"How can a mother be a virgin?" asked Tallulah, "And why would she want to be? Hymens are overrated."

"Could you do it for me, Moondog?" asked Phil, "I'm in kind of a hurry here."

"Hey, man, I didn't wound Ma Earth. She wouldn't accept it from me. She'd vomit the dirt back in my face. I *hate* when she does that. You have to do it."

"That's right," said Sandcrab, "You dug it. Now, you gotta plug it."

"I'll give you twenty bucks to do it," said Phil.

"Each," said Moondog.

"Done," said Phil. He handed the three boys a twenty-dollar bill each, grabbed his wheelbarrow and ran off up the path.

Moondog hollered after him, "Hey, what about your shovel?"

As he disappeared in the distance, Phil yelled back, "Wipe my fingerprints off of it and keep it. My treat." And he was gone.

Moondog said, "Gnarly, man," and then began shoveling the dirt back into the hole.

"Aren't you good boys?" said Tallulah, "When you're done, we'll get to dinner and some oral sex."

"I'll go make popcorn," said Floradora, and she headed off back towards the beach.

Rita was still looking in the direction Phil had run off in. "You know, Tallulah, something is up with that man. He seems awfully intent on disposing of those boxes secretly."

"He's probably just hiding Christmas presents," said Tallulah. "More importantly, did you bring the vodka?"

"No."

"Then back to the beach!"

***

There were simply too many people in the Mirkins' home, making too much noise for the Headless Indian Brave and his headless girlfriend to enjoy themselves at the house so they decided to go out. As he was supernaturally tied to Tallulah, they followed a trail of her essence that led up into the mountains to the north, and brought them to the giant crevasse in which dwelt the Imawankah Indians.

When the Headless Indian Brave had appeared to The Mirkins, those sophisticated European descendants had run screaming from their house, unable to summon up any response to the horny headless paranormal manifestation beyond a horror movie cliché. But when the Imawankahs found two transparent shades making The-Beast-With-No-Head in what was now their holiest spot, where the Sky Goddess Tallulah had come to them to offer Her Blessed Sacrament, they felt no fear, only awe at this additional miracle.

As it happened, the Imawankahs were sufficiently related to the Headless Indian Brave's own people, for he was from a California tribe as well, that he understood their language and was able, by sign language, to communicate with them. When they learned, as indeed they had at once suspected, that he was an associate of their Goddess Tallulah, they had but two questions: what was the meaning of the words She had used for Her Blessed Sacrament, "giving head," and what had she meant by her departing words, "Come up and see me sometime"? The Headless Indian Brave was able to get across to them the meanings of the word *give* and the word *head*.

The Headless Girlfriend however was not an Indian, and felt left out of the conversation, understanding neither her brave's hand signs, nor the words the Imawankahs spoke. Like many women, she disliked not being the center of attention, and so she began tugging at the Brave to take her away.

Thus it was that they departed again, without explaining exactly how the terms for *give* and *head* related to the act Tallulah called "giving head," and leaving him time to give only the most literal translation of "Come up and see me sometime."

Few things are more dangerous than leaving priests or theologians to figure out something for themselves, particularly with only the literal meanings of the words to go by. If priests and theologians were any good at figuring out things for themselves, they would not be priests and theologians. On that night, a schism erupted in the formerly united Imawankah Tribe. Some believed that "Come up and see me sometime" was a promise that they would, when they died, be united with the Goddess Tallulah in the sky. But others took it as a command that they must at last find a way to ascend from their pit and follow after their goddess, to seek Her out.

And, more sinisterly still, while many believed that the gift of pleasure-by-head was The Sacrament of Tallulah and their most holy act, others, after noting that the Great Spirits sent to them by Tallulah to explain Her words were themselves headless, believed that "giving head" should be interpreted far more literally, and that Sacrifice must be made as offerings to their goddess.

By morning, both sets of believers counted the other ones as heretics, and the inevitable Product of Faith became inescapable. A holy war was about to erupt in the Imawankah crevasse, all in the name of The Goddess Tallulah.

Chapter 13
Do I Dare to Eat Impeach?

When Harry Mirkin left $10,000 in an envelope behind a bush in Beaver Green Park, he was too terrified of anyone learning the contents of the mysterious envelope he had received to enlist any help in ascertaining who retrieved the money. However, when Snake Bendix left $1,000 (the blackmailer apparently made realistic allowances for each victim's ability to pay) behind that same bush he was less fearful, and had stationed several of his biker gang members about the park, to keep an eye out for the blackmailer or his accomplice.

The bush had been well chosen. It backed into a thicket, which made actually viewing the envelope impossible to anyone not standing right beside it, and Bendix reasoned that anyone who had the intellectual wherewithal to have snapped those pictures would not be dense enough to retrieve the money with someone, let alone a heavily-tattooed member of Heck's Seraphim, standing beside it.

Half an hour after Snake left the money, one of his pals, a mildly subhuman fellow named Deathspewer Jones, strolled by close enough to take a glimpse. The envelope was gone. (*Deathspewer* was not a nickname. It said *Deathspewer* on his birth certificate. His parents were - ah - unusual. He did, however, adopt the nickname *Jones*. His full birth name was Deathspewer Herkamer Rabinowitz.)

Jones blew a whistle, and the other bikers converged on the thicket. There was no one there. The gang was flummoxed. No one had been seen to come or go from that thicket but a few children, and all of those kids were still visible, playing in the park. No one had run off, as a child being used as a courier might be expected to do. Who was this blackmailer? The Invisible Man?

Additional bags left there over the next two days, first by Floradora, the next by Moondog, were bulkier, because they didn't contain cash, but were instead herbal in nature.

For Iris Cole, it had been a pleasant summer so far. Since she was staying all by herself in The Presidential Suite of The God Dam Hotel, she wasn't weighed down in Tallulah's day-to-day insanities, happily leaving those in Rudy's capable hands. She went to rehearsals, where she coached Tallulah in her lines and lyrics, took Tallulah's notes for her, and in the mornings, typed up the tapes of her boss's adventures Tallulah dictated in her free time.

Thus Iris was among the very few who knew that Tallulah and Dick Rockwood were secretly married. She was surprised that they weren't meeting up at the hotel suite, where Dick would have an easier time dodging his fiancé, but apparently once Tallulah had taken over the Mirkins' house, her hotel suite completely slipped from her notoriously slippery mind. Iris could not imagine why Harry Mirkin hadn't evicted Tallulah yet. Iris kept her own travels limited to the hotel, rehearsals, and the hotel restaurant. Avoiding the dramas and farces that always swirled around Tallulah was her primary ambition for the summer.

At 3 a.m., on the morning of Wednesday July 24th, The Mirkin household was awakened by high-pitched screams of terror emanating from Tallulah's bedrooms. The entire family burst into the room, followed a moment later by Rudy and Serge, a friend Rudy had made at *The Salty Seaman* a few hours earlier. They were confronted by the sight of three people in various states of undress. Tallulah, Sir Ludwig Von Isherwood, and a gentleman Tallulah had never seen before. The screams still issuing from one of them wouldn't be the last scream to echo through the house before the 24th ended.

Minge Mirkin had been born Minge Johnson of Fresno, California. She had one sibling, a younger brother named Hugh, who was a ranger at Yosemite National Park. Hugh Johnson fancied himself something of a prankster, and so he'd chosen not to phone ahead to tip off his sister that he was coming for a visit, planning to spring a surprise on her. Thus, when he had rolled up in front of the Mirkin household around 2:50 a.m., no one knew he was coming. Hugh had let himself into the house, tiptoed up the stairs and, thinking to give his sister a laugh, had slipped into the master bedroom.

In the very dim light from the window, he saw a man and woman whom he naturally took to be his sister and her pompous husband sleeping in the bed. Hugh liked taking the wind out of Harry's enormous sails. Silently, he took off all his clothes except for his boxers, intending to pretend he had drunkenly wandered into the wrong bedroom. He crept over and slipped under the covers next to his sister.

Tallulah was asleep and drunk, but she was seldom too drunk or too unconscious to be utterly unaware of a warm male body arriving beside her. Operating almost on automatic instincts alone, Tallulah rolled over, took Hugh in her arms, and began kissing him, as her legs clamped around his.

Hugh Johnson, for his part, quickly became nonplused when his "sister" rolled on top of him, showing more passion than he could ever believe Harry was capable of arousing. He tried pushing her away, saying, "Sis, Sis, it's me. Hey! Stop that! It's me, Hugh!" But the woman on top of him wouldn't let go, and instead straddled him, fumbling at the opening in his shorts. Hugh's joke was now seriously out of hand. And judging from the fumes oozing out of "Minge," she was seriously drunk. Although he had never known his sister to be a problem drinker before, he suspected that living with Harry could have made a drunk out of Brigham Young.

But his struggles to get free were only making his sister grind down on him more aggressively, grappling at him with what seemed to be extra arms. *So this is what women meant when they call men octopuses*, he thought. He managed to get an arm free and switched on the bedside lamp. It was when he saw Tallulah's face illuminated an inch from his, suffused with sleep-lust, tongue out and plunging for his mouth, that he let loose the high-pitched, girly scream that had aroused the household.

Startled awake, Sir Ludwig saw Tallulah dry-humping the near-nude screaming man beside him, and said, "Blimey. Well two's company and three's an orgy." He was just rolling over and reaching for them both when the door opened and the Mirkin Family burst in. They all froze, unable to process the weird, kinky scene in front of them. Sir Ludwig looked back at the Mirkins and said, "I say, luvs, how about a lit'le privacy, eh what?"

Then Rudy and Serge burst in and saw the screaming man throw Tallulah off of himself. Rudy launched himself forward screaming, "***Leave Missy alone!***" as her slammed into Hugh just as the confused man reached a sitting position. The two of them went off the side of the bed, Rudy quickly pinning Hugh on the floor beside the travel-wet-bar, twisting his arms up behind him, and yelling, "*I'll teach you to attack women in the night, you bastard!*"

That was just enough to awaken Tallulah from her sleep-lust in time to say, "He already knows how. Let him go, Rudy. We were just getting warmed up." Then she looked about, saw the crowd in the room, and said, "Well, if we're having a pajama party, Rudy, make some cocktails."

Fanny looked over at Serge standing next to her and said, "My name is Fanny. What's yours?"

Minge decided the prudent response was to faint, so she did.

***

(From the personal journal of Tallulah Morehead.)

Tuesday's rehearsal was more pleasant than usual, because Monica Montana was out of town, having a face transplant or something. We are two weeks away from opening night, hardly the time for a vacation.

Sir Ludwig came in her place and walked through her part for her, or rather I should say, *rolled* through her role for her, since Blanche spends the show in a wheelchair, which severely impacts her dancing.

When I arrived, one of Sir Ludwig's little hand-written notes was stuck in my script. It read:

> *A horrible bitch named Montana,*
> *Refused ever to eat my banana.*
> *Till a lass named Tallu,*
> *Made me fire off my goo,*
> *And I found myself singing "Hosanna".*

I must admit, having such timeless poetry written for me by the Bard of Alta Caca brought tears to my eye. Later, during the intermission (which requires as much rehearsal as the acts) that comes after the Act One closing number where I musically kick the crap out of Blanche, everyone's favorite moment in the show except for Monica, Sir Ludwig slipped me another note:

A theatrical baby named Jane,
Was to her big sister a pain.
When Blanche phoned out for help,
Jane caused her to yelp.
And kicked her again and again.

I laughed. On the reverse side was written:

You have so many years in the biz,
It's no wonder your acting has fizz.
My wife is away,
And you know I'm not gay,
So why don't I shoot you some jizz?

I was deeply moved. When a proposition comes in the form of such touching, world-class poetry, what woman could resist?

After rehearsal, I ran my pupils through a Drink System rendition of *Our Town*, which, by Act Two, given the severity of the bourbon highballs I was serving, pretty much consisted of the boys wandering around slurring "Why is there no set?" and "My God, this play is *boring!*" In defense against those whom would say that the boys' inebriation inhibited their appreciation of the finer points of classic American theatrical literature, I would point out that they weren't too drunk to notice how boring *Our Town* is. At the previous class session, I had had each boy in turn play the rape scene from *A Streetcar Named Desire* with me, slightly rewritten so that there was less yakity-yak and more rape. *Our Town* could hardly be expected to follow *that!*

On the other hand, *Our Town* was a good choice for The Drink System because Act Three, by which time the boys were usually deep into The System, was mostly played sitting down. The time we'd tried doing *Hamlet*, the fifth act sword duel had resulted in one boy losing a finger, and a stage floor littered with seven corpses that belched and giggled, especially the boy in drag playing Gertrude.

Rudy's group of pre-teens was rehearsing their presentation, which would be performed for their parents, and anyone their parents had a passive-aggressive grudge against, the night before *BJ!* opened, so they had exactly thirteen days left. Rudy said they were all off-book, and that the play was jelling well, although he still allowed no one to see any of it until the performance.

After class, I met up with Sir Ludwig at *The Wet Spot*. Around midnight Rudy drove us back to Mirkin Manor, along with a guy named Serge, with whom Rudy had been deeply in love for the better part of forty-five minutes.

Sir Ludwig, as I've noted before, was quite well-equipped, but his enthusiasm exceeded his stamina, making ours a short session, followed by a quick descent into slumber. In fact, I'm afraid I may have fallen asleep before it was quite completely over, not that that stopped Luddy.

When someone whom I assumed, in my groggy state, was my husband joined us in the bed, I'm afraid I started up again while still on autopilot. I'm a medically diagnosed somnacopulist, a sleep-fucker.

It was his shrill scream that snapped me back to what passes for reality, and I found myself mounted on a handsome man of thirty-five or forty whose concept of passionate arousal consisted of doing a full-throated impression of Evelyn Ankers in the climax of *The Wolf Man*.

Getting a good look at the rather well-set-up young man who was trying to start a three-way with Luddy and I (something I *never* indulge in unless there are a minimum of three people present), I was all set to say "Fine, just stop the shrieking," and Luddy was even positioning himself to take a - ah - back seat (He is so British!), when the bedroom door was whipped open and the entire Mirkin clan burst in, uninvited I might add.

Harry, Minge, and Susan all looked appalled (as though Luddy's too-ample behind was somehow *my* fault!), Merle looked like he regretted not bringing his opera glasses, and tiny Fanny clicked a quick snapshot with her little Brownie Flash Camera. No sooner had I rolled onto my back to present the camera with a more-flattering angle (an actress's instincts are always on duty) than the stranger sat up, showing lovely, rugged pecs with a light dusting of fine brown hair surrounding dime-sized maroon nipples, not that I noticed, and Rudy rushed in and tackled the stranger as he shouted something in his incomprehensible, quaint native tongue *[English]* as he did so.

Given that Rudy's One True Love of the evening was standing in the doorway, exchanging phone numbers with Merle, I felt that this behavior was a tad rude. Besides, whomever this man was, he'd made his choice of me quite clear, although his willingness to engage in a bisexual *ménage* with Luddy and me may have indicated an ambisexual nature.

Luddy's willingness to engage in a cross-gender, bisexual romp was no shock. He is English, after all. The British are all bisexual, by order of an Act of Parliament, in fact, by a large number of Acts of Parliament, all of them obscene.

"Rudy," I said, "un-gland that guy and make us all drinks. When I need protecting from a man, I'll write you a letter."

"Sorry, Tallulah," said Rudy, getting to his feet and helping the man up, "but this one is in really good shape. No body fat at all."

"Uh, thank you?" the man asked, adding, "Could I ask who you people are?"

"Are you in the habit of ravaging strange women, young man?" I asked.

"Believe me, Hugh," said Harry as he tried to revive Minge, who had chosen this rather odd moment to take a quick nap in the doorway, "women don't come any stranger than Tallulah Morehead."

"Tallulah Morehead?" the man asked, "The old movie star? I thought she was dead."

"Do I smell dead?" I asked.

A chorus of voices replied, "*Yes!*" I think Rudy's was among them.

"Well, I'm nearly eighty percent certain I'm not dead," I continued, "and now that you know who I am, who the Hell are you?"

"That's Uncle Hugh," said Merle.

"Hugh who?" I asked.

"Yoo hoo," answered Luddy, giggling. I'm afraid he was still a bit drunk. Rudy handed him a martini to sober him up.

"No." I said, "Hugh who?"

Rudy and Luddy together sang, "Hugh made me love you."

"That's Hugh Johnson," said Harry.

"I can see that for myself, but who is he?"

"His name is Hugh Johnson," said Harry. "He's Minge's brother."

"Really? I had no idea Mange was related to people. Well, Hugh," I said, casually slipping my heels behind my earlobes, "shall we pick up where we left off before being so rudely interrupted? In the immortal words of Bud Abbott: 'Hugh's on first!'"

Minge opened her eyes at that moment, so she and her brother were able to scream in unison this time, before Minge fainted again.

"Harry," I said, "if your wife is so tired that she is unable to stay awake for more than five seconds at a stretch, perhaps you should bundle her off to bed, and give the rest of us some privacy. Your brother-in-law is trying to get some movie-star poontang, and you know what they say, 'Three's company and ten's a crowd.'"

"No, I'm *not!*" said Hugh, struggling unnecessarily into his pants.

"Well, you're not 'aving me one-on-one, old bean," said Sir Luddy, showing tremendous loyalty for a man cheating on his wife.

"Really," added Rudy, "why would you want that old man when you could have me?"

"I'm not having sex with **anyone!**" Hugh nearly screamed.

"Come on, Fanny," said Merle, "The good part is obviously over," and the two of them left the room.

"Well, if you weren't trying to ravage me, why did you take off your clothes and get in bed with me?" I asked.

"I thought Harry and Minge were in this bed," Hugh cried.

"So your reasonable explanation is that you were trying to commit incest with your sister and Harry?" I pointed out helpfully. "Then you should be ecstatic. Over them, Luddy and I are a vast improvement, Hugh."

"She has a point there, old boy," said Luddy.

"It was supposed to be a *joke*," said Hugh, "Isn't this their bedroom?"

"Not at the moment," I said. "It's been upgraded. But there's still room for three in this bed, if you're willing to cram."

"Come on, Hugh," said Harry, leading Minge out of the room. "We'll find you somewhere else to sleep."

"Uncle Hugh can sleep with me!" I heard Merle call from the hall.

"Serge and I have room for a guest," said Rudy, following them out.

"I'll just go to the hotel. Think I could have a room on the house, Harry?"

"Sure thing, Hugh."

Harry stuck his head back in the door for a moment and said, "Oh, and Ludwig, get the hell out of my house before I tell your wife where you are."

"Must dash, Tallu doll," said Sir Ludwig, gathering his togs, "It's been fun."

And with that, I was alone...corporeally at least. The Headless Indian Brave and his cranium-free girlfriend floated out from under the bed, made the sign for "too much traffic," and floated off through the door. I had no idea where my husband was. That left me just one alternative, so I helped myself to a martini and then to my industrial strength vibrator, which Rudy had made for me out of a rubber truncheon and a jackhammer. Soon, visions of sugarplums danced in my head, although the noise woke up the neighbors as usual.

* * *

Around one this afternoon, I had Rudy take me by the Alta Caca post office, where they were holding a package for me: a crate of Russian caviar and the finest Russian vodka, sent to me by a longtime Soviet admirer who prefers to remain anonymous. Let's just say his initials are L. B. Ah, darling Leonid. Is there a sexier unibrow anywhere behind the iron curtain? He may have been a cold warrior, but when it came to the battle of the sexes, he was hot.

Leonid had sent the crate to Morehead Heights, and Mona, my cook and housekeeper, had forwarded it up to me here. Since Mona felt Mayor Mirkin might be mildly embarrassed to be receiving parcels at his house from the Secretary-General of the Russian Communist Party, she'd had it sent to the post office marked "Hold for Pick-up." Honestly, the woman needs priorities. What is more important? That I should receive my vodka in a timely manner, or that Harry Mirkin should avoid being investigated as a communist?

As I got into line, Rudy poured me a double-strength martini (the only way to face postal employees). Sipping it I heard a familiar voice tell the overworked fat woman behind the counter, "This one is going to Zanzibar, and this one goes to Detroit."

"You've forgotten to include a return address on them," said the woman waiting on the man.

"And your point?" said the man.

"Phil darling!" I hollered out.

Phil Rains turned and saw me, looking overcome with that rare form of joy which can so easily be mistaken for horror. "Tallulah," he said, in a choking tone, "How nice to see you yet again."

"Darling," I said as I dashed over to his side, "How lovely to see you, too. Whatever are you shipping out in these large, smelly packages."

"Whew!" said Rudy, joining us, "Are you sending out mail order dead wildebeest? I'd recognize that stench anywhere these days."

"No..." Phil stammered. "Just some gifts. Surprises."

"Look Tallu, the one going to Zanzibar is the exact same size and shape as his catsup-stained hatbox."

"Headgear for a headhunter?" I asked.

"You know," said Phil, "I've changed my mind. I don't think I'll ship these at all. Thank you very much, miss. See you at rehearsal, Tallulah."

"And probably anywhere else you go, too," I chirped.

"Apparently," said Phil, looking pale for a resident of a beach town in late-July. He grabbed his packages and scooted out the door. I'd have followed him out, but here I was at the counter, and there behind it was the finest-quality Russian caviar and vodka waiting for me, so I just gave the woman my delivery slip while Phil and his parcels gave me the slip as well. At least I had my priorities straight.

***

I returned to the house shortly after 5:30 p.m. that afternoon. Rehearsal had been so taxing that I'd had Rudy send my pupils home. Monica Montana was back at rehearsal today, with some pathetic excuse about having had to attend her mother's funeral. For Heaven's sake, I understand wanting to go out and party when your mother dies. I probably did when my mother finally did the world a favor and popped off. (I can't be certain. I retain no memories of events for most of a year on either side of my mother's death in 1944. I suspect this is the aftereffect of my celebrating like crazy.)

But we are now exactly two weeks from opening night, about to launch into dress rehearsals. You'd think Monica could have held off on the celebrating until after we opened. It's not like her mother was going to get any deader. The work needed to catch Monica up had left me exhausted, so I decided to just spend some quality time at home for an evening. There was plenty of liquor there, and I could always send out for a man if my husband failed to show up.

Hugh Johnson had come by rehearsal just as it ended, to pick up little Fanny for a ride to her job, and to take my assistant Iris to dinner. Apparently they had met that morning in The God Dam Hotel's restaurant, and hit it off. What a man who had nearly had sex with me could see in mousy Little Iris, I have no idea. I suppose the operative word was *nearly*. If we'd had time to consummate our late-night surprise (to both of us) rendezvous, Iris wouldn't have stood a chance.

When I walked in the front door. I was horrified by the obscene spectacle that met my eyes. Harry and Minge were sitting in their own living room, watching their own television. Where on earth had they gotten the nerve? True, I was not in the habit of returning that early in the evening, but they had taken that fact as license for this unbridled violation of my rule over their home. It was nothing less than anarchy! Thanks heaven I hadn't found them making love on their living room carpet. Fortunately, there was very little chance of that! The carpet was white. I shielded my eyes from the grizzly sight of them as I passed the doorway and made my way up to my bedroom.

I was upstairs, drinking my dinner at 6 p.m., when I heard a shriek ring through the house, one that dwarfed the screaming of the morning hours. I stumbled downstairs to find Harry shrieking at his TV, which had just gone to the news.

"*WHO THE HELL DOES THAT TRAITOROUS SUPREME COURT THINK THEY ARE? HOW DARE THEY? HOW DARE THEY?*" Harry shrieked.

"What on earth is all this racket about?" I asked, "I can barely hear myself drink."

Harry was now blustering nonsense syllables, too enraged to muster words. Minge replied for him, "It's the Supreme Court. They've decided the case of The United States v. Richard Nixon."

"What is this," I asked, "*Perry Mason?*"

On the TV screen, Walter Cronkite was saying, "To repeat our headline, by a vote of eight to nothing, with Justice Rehnquist abstaining, The Supreme Court has ruled that claims of executive privilege over the so-called White House Tapes are void, and they have further ordered the President to surrender them to Watergate Special Prosecutor Jaworski. The Congressional House Judiciary Committee has announced it will take steps towards impeaching the President for obstruction of justice, abuse of power, and contempt of congress."

Harry's face was swelling up purple, and he looked ready to explode. "It's - it's - it's - treason! *Treason!*"

"Good heavens," I said, "Is this all it is? A few of Nixon's crimes catching up with him? Did you think he'd get away with it forever? Honestly. I thought it was something important. For this triviality you interrupted my drinking?"

"*TRIVIALITY?*" screamed Harry, "The very foundations of the republic are crumbling! If the President has to be accountable to The People, how can he be expected to govern? Do you think I could run this God-forsaken town if I had to let the citizens know what I was up to?"

"I don't think you could run a church picnic if you had to do it honestly."

"Exactly! And I...*What?*"

"Harry, I don't doubt for one second that you're robbing this town blind, and I could not care less. Any town that elects you deserves what they get. I am going to assume that you're not as stupid as Nixon, and that you don't have a bunch of tapes or incriminating photographs floating around, to send you off to share a cell with Tricky Dick."

"You have some nerve lady! I..." Harry's face went all funny, though it wasn't making me laugh. (Well, maybe just a little.) "Pictures, you say? What do you know about...?" He glanced at Minge, who was her usual uncomprehending self, and then said, "Never mind. Nixon will beat this. You'll see. You can't beat our Dick."

Just then Fanny came running into the house from outside, clutching what looked like her life-size double, freshly emerged from its seed pod.

"Mommy, look!"

"Fanny," said Minge, "I thought you were at your little job."

"My boss gave me the night off when she saw that these had arrived. I was going to quit tonight anyway. But look, Mommy; it's me! *It's me!*"

Fanny, who had changed over the summer from the sullen, taciturn little girl she'd been when I arrived, into a sunnier, happier child, now seemed transported with joy. There was no question what she was holding. It was one of the several Baby Jane dolls made as props for the play, each an identical double of Fanny herself. The original had been sculpted by a local artisan, and now the prop versions to be used in the show had arrived from a custom doll manufacturer. Fanny seemed wildly happy to have been given one of her creepy *dopplegangers*.

It was quite the family portrait: Fanny cooing with joy over her effigy, Minge looking at her happy child with tears in her eyes, and Harry looking at his disgraced idol with tears of rage in his. I left them to Walter Cronkite and went back upstairs to finish drinking my dinner, now knowing what The Sandals meant by *The Endless Summer*.

Chapter 14
Ship of Tools

On Saturday, July 27, as Harry Mirkin was going ballistic over the news that the House Judiciary Committee had voted twenty-seven to eleven to recommend the first article of impeachment against Richard Nixon for obstruction of justice, a private detective named Joe Lanchester, hired by Odette Snype and Monica Montana to find something - anything - they could use against Tallulah, discovered in the Nevada public records the wedding license and marriage certificate that proved she was currently married to Dick Rockwood, Mayor Harry Mirkin's son-in-law presumptive.

At the same time, Tallulah was strolling out onto the Alta Caca Marina dock, to join Rita, Dick, Rudy, Serge, Floradora, Moondog, Sandcrab, Merle, Snake, Iris, and Hugh on *The Bawdy Strumpet*, a sleeps-twelve yacht she had rented for a relaxing overnight, drunken-and-drugged cruise up the coast. As she stepped onto the pier, she saw Phil Rains get out of his car, carrying some now-familiar-looking parcels. He started down the walkway, saw Tallulah, and without even pausing to say *hello*, reversed course back to his car, dumping the parcels into the trunk again before getting back behind the wheel and driving off. As he drove off, it occurred to Phil that, even if drove straight up into the mountains right this very moment as she was sailing away, no matter where he went, he would still run into Tallulah. Jehovah was less omnipresent.

Tallulah had been a tad annoyed when Iris mentioned that she was bringing Hugh on the cruise, since he was Susan's uncle, and worse, was going to be sleeping with Iris instead of Tallulah, a concept Tallulah found inexplicable. However, Iris assured her that Hugh had been sworn to secrecy, and given a choice between keeping his niece in the dark and getting laid, or spilling the beans and not getting any, he had made the traditional male choice.

Merle had also been a bit miffed to find his Uncle Hugh on the cruise on which he was sharing a cabin and pretty much everything else with Snake Bendix, but Hugh himself had taken Merle aside to tell him that it was okay; he wouldn't tell on Merle if Merle didn't mention to Minge that her brother was cruising overnight with a woman he'd known less than a week. Merle didn't understand why a grown man cared what his sister thought. Hell, he was seventeen, and he didn't give a fig what his older sister thought about anything. Frankly, she hadn't even spoken to him in a couple of weeks now; he had no idea why not. In fact, Merle thought his sister's fiancé being married to Tallulah was hilarious.

The Marina was located just below a large, rounded hill at the southern end of *Beaver Valley* called *Bubble Butte*. As The *Bawdy Strumpet's* passengers boarded, and prepared to set sail for its twenty-four hour voyage, two sets of eyes were watching from atop *Bubble Butte*.

Susan Mirkin was on one of *Bubble Butte's* knolls, with a pair of binoculars borrowed from her father's hotel, intended for guests to use to peruse the scenic wonder that was The God Dam. When Merle announced he was going on an overnight cruise with Tallulah, and then simultaneously Dick had explained that he had to visit his sick aunt in Santa Barbara over the same night, Susan had put two and two together and come up with four, never thinking for a moment that there might be more to the equation, and that once again she had gotten her sums a bit wrong. Now she was watching the passengers board. There was her brother, and there was her fiancé. Sure enough; her brother and Dick *were* betraying her, and Tallulah was their accomplice.

Deathspewer Jones was on the next knoll, watching the party board the yacht through the telephoto lens of a camera. Deathspewer was second-in-command of the Alta Caca chapter of Heck's Seraphim, and he had ambitions of being number one. When he'd aided his leader Snake in paying off his blackmailer, he'd grown curious as to just what the blackmailer had on him. Was it something Deathspewer should be worried about? Despite his peaceful name, Deathy, as his friend called him, had committed the occasional illegal act, sometimes with Snake. Was this something that implicated them both? Or, looking at the bright side, was it something he could use to usurp his superior's position?

So Deathy had slipped a mickey to Snake in a beer a couple nights before, and then gone through his saddle bags until he found the envelope with the incriminating pictures. He couldn't believe it. Snake Bendix, the butchest, meanest, badass, butt-kicking biker in all of Alta Caca had been photographed committing a number of sex acts with the mayor's faggot son in a room at The Pay Ten Place Motel. This was gold. The other members of Heck's Seraphim would never put up with being led by a queer.

But he needed proof. He had had to put the pictures back, since, if Snake noticed they were missing, he would become very suspicious. Secondly, it only proved it had happened once. Snake could argue it was just a one-time rape. Raping queers was okay; you just weren't supposed to get emotionally involved with one.

So when Snake took off, saying he was going on a dope run by sea, Deathspewer decided to follow him. Sure enough, there he was getting on this yacht, holding hands with his boyfriend.

But then even worse, he saw Moondog and Sandcrab boarding also. It was bad enough Snake was having an affair with a homo, but here he was fraternizing with *surfers!* Deathspewer knew Moondog of course. He sold him his pot. Heck's Seraphim's primary sources of income were selling marijuana and doing "charity" car washes. Surfers, tourists with dirty cars, and that Windwillow woman were their best customers. You don't take your customers along on a product run. If the customer knows where you get it, they won't need you. Besides, that grotesque old movie star was on board, too. Who takes famous old ladies on a dope run?

No one. This was a pleasure cruise. Snake had turned homo and was fraternizing with surfers. This was very bad for Snake, but could be very good for Deathspewer; he started snapping photos. He would need proof to show the other bikers when he made his move.

The cabin assignments placed Tallulah and Dick in Cabin 1, Rudy and Serge in Cabin 2, Rita and Floradora in Cabin 3, Moondog and Sandcrab in Cabin 4, Merle and Snake in Cabin 5, and Iris and Hugh in Cabin 6. This put Rudy next to Tallulah in case he was suddenly needed, and put Iris directly across the hall from Tallulah, in case she needed "Personal Assisting." Rita and Flora flipped a coin, and Flora ended up trading cabins with Moondog.

The stewards and other crew who waited on the passengers were used to all sorts of peculiar behavior from the rich folk who chartered the boat, so they were unfazed by the fact that Moondog, Sandcrab, Floradora, and Tallulah were all soon all up on deck naked, and that there was nearly as much pot being passed around as there were drinks. Since Rudy didn't have to mix Tallulah's cocktails, he and Serge didn't even emerge from their cabin until dinnertime. And Merle and Snake were locked in theirs all afternoon as well.

***

(From the personal journal of Tallulah Morehead.)

The last weekend of July is to be our last free weekend all summer. Starting Monday we are going into what the foul-mouthed call "Hell Week," a week of tech and dress rehearsals, during which our slave-driving director Cyril *insists* I actually commit all my lines to memory, culminating in a preview performance on Monday the 5th. Then on Tuesday, *BJ!* will have a night off while Rudy's prepubescent pupils perform their little playlet.

Then, opening night on August 7, after which we will be running Wednesdays through Saturday nights, with matinees on Sundays, through Labor Day weekend. Gad, how tiresome. In Hollywood, we did things *once!* In primitive Alta Caca, we have to do them over and over.

I decided to spend my last days away from Monica Montana and repetitive performing by chartering this cruise with the handful of people I've met in this hellhole whom I like, and also my husband.

Much as I would like to have taken Martin Lewis, my handsomest student, along on this cruise the fact is that the boy is hopelessly ageist and apparently exclusively prefers girls in his own age bracket. If only he knew what a truly experienced woman could bring to a bed besides vodka and regrets. Not surprisingly, he also displayed no acting talent in class, despite embracing The Drink System with both fists, to the point that he was currently in jail on his third DUI arrest this month alone.

I had invited Moondog and Sandcrab because, although also showing little promise as actors, they had both shown a willingness to submit to the attentions of more mature women.

Moondog eloquently complained that: "Beach Bunnies all want 'relationships.' You have to convince them you *love* them, when it's all I can manage just to remember their names. Man, I just want to get off between waves."

Such wisdom. Plus, their abundant pot use has reminded me that there is more to Life than just sex and booze; there are also drugs. Who says Youth has no lessons to teach Maturity?

Iris has thoughtfully brought along Hugh Johnson for me, knowing that he has been avoiding my bed under the absurd misapprehension that my secret marriage would mean I am sexually unavailable. Honestly, where do these urban myths come from? Since Dick is onboard, Hugh is maintaining a fiction that he is "dating" Iris, even though the very idea of someone preferring Iris over me is about as believable as a Nixon speech. No one knows this better than Dick, who has married me while continuing to pretend to be engaged to the drab Susan.

So I have worked out a simple plan and brought Dick in on it. He will - ah - *distract* Iris, while I make Hugh's dreams come true. Dick is very enthusiastic about his part of the plan.

That is good, because his is the hardest part. He has to convince Iris that he desires her, even though she knows he has full access to me. Iris is more than smart enough to know that no man in his right mind would prefer her over me. It is true that Iris is mildly attractive, in an Olivia De Havilland-on-a-bad-day sort of way, and *claims* to be a bit younger than I, but she's just a personal assistant. I am a *Movie Star!*

Our plan kicks in after dinner tonight. Meanwhile, I intend to relax on deck with my nudist surfer boys, and see how well pot, vodka, and sea air mix.

***

It would have been easier if Iris drank. Getting her good and sloshed would have made our little subterfuge simpler, but among her many other vices, Iris doesn't drink. Sometimes I despair for this younger generation. What virtues won't they sink to?

Merle and Snake joined us at the table. Merle had fresh red welts on his wrists, ankles, and back, and seemed in a tremendously cheerful mood. Snake seemed unaccustomed to eating with utensils other than a knife, and tended to stab his food. He wasn't much for conversation either, but he snarled and grunted at folks in what was for him a genial manner.

Rita, Floradora, Moondog, and Sandcrab all had unhealthily healthy appetites, something they called "The Munchies," although what it has to do with singing dwarves I cannot decipher. Frankly, Rita and Floradora had been cramming meat in their faces all afternoon, but somehow they were still peckish. As for the boys, well, perhaps they enjoyed the change of having a meal instead of being one, not that I've ever known a man to complain about it before.

Hugh found a note from "Iris" under his dinner plate, telling him to meet her in the game room after dinner but to say nothing to anyone, even her, as they were going to engage in a bit of make-believe role-playing. Iris found a note under her plate, telling her to come to my cabin after dinner to go over her typed copies of this journal. Everyone else had been invited to the main ballroom after dinner, for a formal orgy. ("Formal orgy" means black ties and nothing else for the boys, and gownless evening straps for the girls.)

I slipped out of the dining room during dessert, and scurried on down to the game room, where I changed into one of Iris's dresses I had had Rudy "borrow" for me from her luggage without actually bothering her about it and then waited in the dark. Ten minutes later Hugh entered the room, leaving the lights off, as per his instructions in the note. "Iris?" he whispered, "Are you here?"

"Yes, darling," I said in my finest Iris Cole impersonation, "don't speak."

"What's wrong with your voice? Did you catch a cold?"

"Sure. Why not? Ravage me."

"Wait a minute. I know that stench. That's Tallulah's stink."

At this point the door flew open and the lights snapped on. Iris stood in the doorway, glaring down at me on my knees, trying to fumble Hugh's pants open to determine if he lived up to his name. Hugh looked down at me and let fly with another of his high-pitched screams. What on earth did Iris see in a man who turns into Janet Leigh taking a shower every time the lights snap on?

Iris was glowering, and said, "Tallulah, get up."

"Iris darling, whatever are you doing here?"

"Extracting my fiancé from your gin-soaked clutches."

"My 'gin-soaked clutches'? That's absurd. I've been drinking vodka and bourbon all day. I haven't touched any gin since breakfast. And what do you mean by your 'fiancé'?"

"Hugh asked me to marry him. I've accepted. When we leave Alta Caca, I'll be leaving your service and moving to Yosemite with him."

"But you've only known him a few days. Aren't you rushing things?"

"Oh please. You didn't really meet Rudy until *after* you'd married him."

"And look how that turned out."

"You were married for a decade. It was your longest lasting marriage. And you hadn't known Dick a full two weeks when you married him, had you?"

"But that's *me!* I'm a *star!* People want to marry me before we even meet. Hell, I've been married to men I still haven't met. But you, you're *nobody!* Hugh, why would you marry her when you could fool around with me?"

Hugh had slunk over to Iris with a scared, horrified look on his face. "I'm crazy about Iris. It was love at first sight."

"That makes no sense at all. You're clearly insane. Iris, I won't have you marrying a mad man."

"You don't get a say in it."

"Wait a moment. How did you know what was going on down here?"

"Tallulah, I type up your journal tapes, remember? You laid out your plan for this evening on the tape you asked me to type up this afternoon."

You mean you've been listening to my personal memoir tapes? What an invasion of my privacy!"

"How could I type them up without listening to them?"

"But you assured me that you paid no attention to them."

"Tallulah, when you go on and on about how unattractive you think I am compared to you, and lay out your plans to seduce my boyfriend on the tapes I am typing up, obviously I am going to hear them."

"How rude. Where's Rosemary Woods when I need her?"

"Oh, expletive delete yourself, Tallulah. Come along, Hugh. The smelly woman won't hurt you."

Iris and Hugh left the room. I went out into the hall, where Dick was lurking.

"Dick, you were supposed to be seducing Iris. What happened? I make one teensy little request of you, that you screw my assistant while I get into her boyfriend's pants, and you can't even do that."

"Sorry, Tallu, but she wasn't interested, at all. I don't understand it. I mean she didn't even say 'no.' She just laughed in my face and walked out. I think we should clearly consider sacking her when we get back to Hollywood."

"She just said she's quitting when we get back anyway. She's marrying that adorable boob with no taste. It was 'love at first fright.' He's a screamer. Honestly. He's Minge's brother. She'll be giving her children Minge genes. Oh, well, let's get a drink or five and join the orgy in the ballroom."

The rest of the cruise was uneventful. Rudy and Serge managed to get two of the waiters to join in the orgy, but they both turned out to be gay, so the gay men outnumbered the straight ones by six to three, which left the three straight males in the room more work than they were actually up to.

And then Sandcrab turned out to be willing to "experiment," which dropped the percentage even lower. Oh, Snake kept saying how straight he was, but his idea of straight is having sex with gay men while verbally and physically abusing them. Next time I book an orgy I've got to remember to invite more straight men. This orgy was turning gayer than my first, fifth, and sixth honeymoons.

***

When we docked back at the Alta Caca Marina late Sunday afternoon, Harry, Minge, and Susan Mirkin were all waiting for us on the boardwalk. You'd have thought that their having free run of their own house for a whole weekend would have cheered them up, but Harry and Susan were glaring with rage, while Minge was weeping.

Merle, seeing his dad on the shore from onboard *The Bawdy Strumpet*, dropped Snake's hand and quickly distanced himself from him. Then, seeing his mother crying, he had a very peculiar reaction. Instead of responding how any normal person would to seeing their mother in tears, you know, cheering, laughing, pointing, mocking, Merle got upset, and ran down to her, yelling, "Mommy, what's wrong?"

But before he could embrace his mother, Susan hauled off and slapped him hard, and then slapped Dick, who was coming up just behind Merle and feigning pleasure at seeing her.

"*You bastard!*" Susan screamed, "*I know! I know what you've been doing behind my back! Our engagement is OVER!*"

Dick turned pale.

"Snookums," he began, "I don't know what you're talking about. I was just..."

"Oh, *save* it!" Susan snapped. "Was your 'sick aunt' on that boat?"

"It's a yacht," I pointed out helpfully.

"*You've been cheating on me!*" Susan shrieked in a ladylike manner, "I know everything. I've known for a couple of weeks now. How could you?"

Dick changed tactics, "I'm sorry, Snookums. I couldn't help it. She is just so..."

"Don't call him '*She*'!"

"What?"

"How could you do it? How could you cheat on me **with my own brother?**"

Merle, Dick, Snake, and I all said, "What?" in unison.

"I told you, *I know everything!* I saw you! I saw you go into **HER**," pointing at Rita, "filthy flesh pit and come out again with my brother. I saw you come into my daddy's house and go upstairs to have sex with him right next to my bedroom, the bedroom where I have been saving myself for *you!*"

"Snookums," Dick began sickeningly, "you've got it all wrong."

"Good heavens!" I said, "*Another* gay husband? Was Moondog the only completely straight man on this voyage?"

"Well, actually," said Moondog, "I let Serge blow me this morning. He's really good at it. But it was just, you know, getting off."

"*You whore!*" shouted Rudy, shoving Serge off the pier into the water.

But now Snake entered into the fray, turning to Merle and saying, "You've been cheating on me with this stiff? You little slut!"

Merle, who was now utterly bewildered by the accusations being showered on him, said "No. I never did. I love *you*, Snake."

"So it's *true!*" hollered Harry, entering the family dustup. "My only son is a *deviant!* And you've not only been debasing yourself with this - this lowlife scum..."

"Hey," said Snake, "I'm standing right here."

Harry carried right on, "...but you've also betrayed your own sister!"

"No, daddy," Merle cried, "I mean yes, I've been seeing Snake. We're in love." Harry shuddered as Merle said he loved Snake. "But I never touched Dick. He's straight."

Harry didn't limit himself to slapping his son. He punched him hard enough to knock him down. Then he stood over him and said, "You are no son of mine. I have no son. And as I don't need *three* daughters, I disown you. You are no longer a Mirkin. Get out of my sight. My home is no longer your home. Don't come back. I never want to see you again!"

Then Harry turned and walked away, dragging his sobbing wife along with him.

Snake then stepped forward and said, "You've been seeing this creep when I wasn't around? Well I'm through with you, too. Stay away from me, faggot." Snake spat on him and stomped away also. Merle, sobbing, got up and ran off after Snake.

Dick made another shot at getting through to Susan. "Look, Snookums. It's not true. I'm not gay. Don't be absurd. Yes, it's true that I strayed. But that's really *your* fault you know. A man has *needs*. But I never touched your brother. I was sleeping with Tallulah."

"He was," I piped in helpfully.

"Oh, please," said Susan bitterly, "Am I supposed to be so stupid that I would believe you'd have sex with this withered, drunken old hag?"

"Hey," I said, "I'm wobbling right here."

"But I did, bootsie. I - I married her."

"How big a fool do you think I am?"

"May I answer that one?" I asked.

"***Shut up, you drunken old cow!***" Susan yelled in a manner I found verging on potential rudeness.

"But I did. I married her. I married her for us. She'll take me to Hollywood and make me a movie star. She's really old. She can't live much longer, and then I'll be free to marry you, and we'll be rich and famous and living in Hollywood, and never have to set foot in this dead-end burg again."

"*Stop lying to me!*" Susan barked. "I may have been fool enough to think you loved me, but I am not stupid enough to believe you've been sleeping with this ancient old bitch."

"You know, Susan," I said, "I'm *this close* to taking offense."

Susan plowed right on, "It's bad enough you're a closet fag; but that you're a liar as well, who thinks I'll believe anything you say? *I never want to see you again!*" And with that she pulled off her engagement ring and threw it in the sea before marching off in a nice imitation of the huff her father had left in.

"Whoa," said Moondog. "Bummer, man. So, who wants to hit our surf shack and get stoned?"

"Finally," I said, "someone on this dock with some sense."

***

The remaining three days of July were grim ones at The Mirkin Household. Merle was neither seen nor heard from. Susan, still not believing Dick's story that he had married Tallulah, was sulking. Minge was given to sudden bursts of tears, and Harry, troubled enough by the events in his own family, was made even more irritable by the House Judiciary Committee voting on Monday to recommend the second article of impeachment against President Nixon for abuse of power, and then on Tuesday voting to recommend the third article of impeachment for contempt of Congress. Harry snarled that he himself ought to be impeached, as well, as he was *filled* with contempt for congress.

Meanwhile, up in the hillside hideout where the Heck's Seraphim hung out, Deathspewer Jones sprang the pictures of Snake and Merle, both in the motel and on *The Bawdy Strumpet*, on the entire gang. Confronting Snake, Deathspewer presented him with a choice. Give over Merle to the whole gang, to be used as a pass-around sex toy and then discarded, or face expulsion from the gang. Snake refused. He was stripped of his Heck's Seraphim jacket and banished forever from the gang. Snake roared off on his motorcycle, as Deathspewer Jones took the reins of command. He had a plot for a raid on the surfers. It was time they stopped playing at being badasses, and became the real thing.

Moondog and Sandcrab, whom were now known to have been fraternizing socially with Snake, were to be the targets. The following Wednesday, when they would be attending the opening of *BJ!*, was selected for the target date. Deathspewer sat down with his new second-in-command, The Scorpion (born Billy Highsmith), to lay out his plan.

On Wednesday, July 31, deep in the Imawankah crevasse north of town, Holy War finally broke out between the two religious factions that had been inadvertently created by Tallulah's visit and the subsequent visitation of the Headless Indian Brave and his headfree girlfriend.

The brief and bloody battle had been won by the literalists, (what one might consider Imawankah fundamentalists), who interpreted the Sacrament of Giving Head and the command to "come up and see me sometime" literally, while the metaphoricists had been soundly and permanently defeated. Sacrifice had been made. But now the victors' sacrificial offerings must be taken to their Goddess, to be given in person.

The Goddess Herself had left behind the means of obeying her command: the rope ladder Tallulah had ascended to the helicopter. It had been left lying in a heap in the crevasse, too Holy a relic to touch.

But now it would be touched. A strong lead of twine was tied to the top rung. This was then attached to an arrow, and the best Imawankah Fundamentalist archer shot at a tree that overhung the edge of the crevasse. This carried the rope ladder up, and allowed them to pull on the twine until the top rung was securely caught on a shard of rock that jutted out from the crevasse's rim.

The most courageous of the Imawankah Fundie braves then ascended the ladder, becoming the first Imawankah in a thousand years to stand above their subterranean home and see the outside world again. The ocean glimmered to the west, while in all other directions were the jagged peaks of the mountains under which they had lived.

He tied the ladder securely to a tree and then, one by one, the other surviving Imawankahs ascended, until all the remaining members of the tribe stood above their so-long abode. Their Goddess was calling to them.

Although they did not know where she was, their hypersensitive sense of smell, selectively evolved over a thousand years cut-off from the rest of Mankind, told them she was to be found to the south. Miles of jagged mountains lay between them, but those would only hamper, not thwart their journey. The way would be hard and dangerous, as any road to a Goddess should be. Not all would survive the pilgrimage, but they would not stop. They would follow their noses, find their Goddess, and make unto her their offerings.

And so the Imawankahs set off southward, towards where Alta Caca waited, as unaware of them as they were of it.

Part Three

Village of the Darned

(August)

Chapter 15
Heck Week

While we were off cruising the California coast, posters had appeared all over town. They featured a picture of me that was not in the least bit flattering, in my full, grotesque Baby Jane make-up and costume, acting my brains out. (It took almost an hour of removing my normal "street" make-up to achieve the hideous Baby Jane look.)

The best part of the graphic was that Monica Montana was represented as a small, black silhouette in a wheelchair down in the corner of the image. The poster copy read "Tallulah Morehead performs *BJ!*, an all-new musical thriller, with Nelson Baker Eddy, and also starring Monica Montana as 'Blanche.'" It was felt to be wise to keep us apart from each other in our billing as it was to keep us apart offstage.

Apparently, even though the Alta Caca Arts Council had seen the rehearsals, they were nonetheless intending to open the show anyway. Oh well. At least I didn't have any of my money in the production.

No one to my knowledge set eyes on Merle during the week of dress rehearsals. I had no idea where he'd disappeared to, nor Snake either for that matter. My husband Dick was, perhaps wisely, avoiding the Mirkin household. Susan still steadfastly refused to believe that he was married to me. That her fiancé could be gay, she found credible (So did I. He'd married me, after all), but that he might have married a glamorous movie star so beautiful she had once driven Kaiser Wilhelm to try and conquer all of Europe just to make her his love slave she found impossible to believe. I even tried showing her our marriage certificate, but she dismissed it as a crude forgery. Reality and Susan Mirkin had not even a nodding acquaintance.

When I ran into Henrietta Shemp after the first full-dress rehearsal in which she had blacked-up to play Elvira, the black maid whom I murder with a hammer to the skull, I was amazed to see she was still in her full Negress makeup. "Aren't you going to wash off your makeup?" I asked her.

"Oh, Tallulah," she replied in a state of high excitement, "I haven't told anyone else but..." she dropped her voice to a loud stage whisper, "*It isn't makeup!*"

"What on earth do you mean, darling?"

"I've had my skin dyed - permanently!"

"Permanently? But darling, we close the night before Labor Day. I understand not wanting to put all that makeup on every night, but you'll still be black when the show's run is over."

"That's the idea. Tallulah, I'm changing races."

"Really? How novel."

"Can you keep a secret?"

"Do you know how many times I've been married?"

"No."

"Neither do I. That's how well I can keep a secret. I even keep them from myself."

"Well then, we're telling no one until we're ready, but I'm having an affair."

"Get out of town!"

"That's what I'm afraid they'd make us do if anyone knew. You see, I'm having an affair with Darien Littlewood."

"Who? I'm sorry darling, but *Littlewood* hardly seems a promising name for a lover."

"Darien the Librarian."

"Oh, him. Really?"

"Oh, Tallulah, he's the most divine lover I've ever had."

"How many have you had?"

"Well actually, he's the first. But everything you said about black men as lovers is true. 'Once you've had black, you never go back.'"

"I recall going back - for seconds, and even thirds. Wait a minute. You were a fifty-year-old virgin?"

"Fifty-five, actually. And I'm so glad I waited for the right man."

"And you were able to pick up lovemaking at that age?"

"Certainly. Why not?"

"Well, darling, it's just that if you buy a new car, and then lock it away for half a century without ever firing it up, when you do finally slip the key in the ignition and give it a twist, the battery is going to be dead. I had to throw that *Isotta Fraschini* of mine out unused, simply because I forgot to drive it for forty-five years, and that damn thing cost me 25,000 bucks in 1925 dollars. Do you have any idea how much vodka that much money could buy? The better part of an entire week's supply. Anyway, what has this to do with you dying your skin?"

"It's to show my commitment to our people. I'm becoming a Negro, and we're going to defy 'The Man' together. Right arm, sister!"

"I believe the phrase is 'Right on.'"

"Is it? Let me make a note of that. There's so much to learn when you change races."

"Henrietta, my dear, you're taking Method Acting to a whole new level of insanity."

"Thank you. But after the play closes, I won't be Henrietta anymore. That's my slave name. I'm going to be Taonga. It's a Tumbuka name that means 'we are thankful,' because I am grateful for Darien. I'll be Taonga Shemp, and maybe someday, Taonga Littlewood."

"And Darien is all right with all this?"

"He will be. It's just a matter of finding the right time to tell him."

"In bed, *during*."

"That's right."

"You have learned my lessons well, old grasshopper."

Life back at Mirkin Manor was drearier than usual, impossible as that is to imagine.

Minge was always sobbing, Susan was sour and petulant, Fanny's former cheer had evaporated, and Harry, though seemingly immune to the misery he'd foisted on his remaining family by disowning Merle, was thrown into a state of depression when the so-called "Smoking Gun" White House tape was released, on which Richard Nixon could be plainly heard conspiring with my fellow Christian Scientist Bob Haldeman (though Bob actually practiced the insane religion) to obstruct justice.

Oddly, Harry wasn't downhearted because his political idol was proven to be a cheap, petty felon, but because he'd been caught and

Congress didn't seem to be of a mind to just give him a pass on it. "*It's not a crime when the President does it!*" Harry repeatedly railed, "*Unless he's a Democrat! Why didn't they investigate Kennedy?* I'll bet he was a bigger crook than that father of his ever was!"

"Harry, darling," I added helpfully, "When I met old Joe Kennedy over at the home of that hopelessly plain no-talent Gloria Swanson, he was perfectly charming. And his son went on to have an affair with Marilyn Monroe. How both generations managed to skip me, I'll never understand, although I have had cocktails a few times with Teddy. That man knows how to party, though I felt it advisable to take a cab home."

"This whole supposed 'Watergate scandal' is a Kennedy Family plot," railed Harry, "hatched in the White House itself by John and Bobby, in the event that Justice finally triumphed, and Nixon achieved his rightful place as President."

"But John has been dead for eleven years, and Bobby for six. How could they be behind Watergate?"

"They worked it all out years ago, and left it to Teddy to frame Nixon."

"You're telling me that this whole, huge scandal, with its enormous cast of disreputable characters and its weird permutations, not to mention all these White House tapes that Nixon admits he made, was all secretly engineered by Ted Kennedy, a man who can't even handle a task as simple as driving his secretary home?"

"That's right," Harry was descending into madness at an alarming rate.

"Then why doesn't Nixon denounce Teddy?"

"He's too much of a gentleman to heap further disgrace upon the tragedy-ridden Kennedy Family."

At this point I'm afraid I burst out braying with laughter in Harry's face.

"Harry darling, if Alta Caca ever wises up enough to kick you out of office, you should really try out that routine at *The Comedy Store*. The idea of Richard Nixon martyring himself to protect the Kennedys is priceless."

Rehearsals were little relief. Monica is not a pleasant person. Why a delightful artist like Sir Ludwig ever married that shrew I cannot fathom.

Monica tried to pull a fast one on me. She had talked with Joan Crawford for reasons I cannot fathom about playing Blanche Hudson.

Imagine getting tips from Joan Crawford on *acting*? Is there anything movie star-related on earth that Crawford knows less about than *acting*? Posing? Sure. Twenty-years out-of-date fashion tips? Right up Joan's alley. Getting away with child abuse? She's the go-to girl. But *acting*?

There's a scene in the *Baby Jane* movie where Jane has to haul Blanche out of bed, drag her downstairs, and lift her into the car. Joan has some sort of inexplicable grudge against that shy, sweet, gentle, unassertive little shrinking violet Bette Davis merely because Bette is five thousand times the actress Joan is. So when shooting those scenes, Joan had played a small prank on Bette by wearing a diver's weight belt under her costume, greatly increasing her weight.

Joan told Monica about this, wearing secret weights being Joan's idea of an acting tip. What Monica didn't count on was her husband telling me about this ploy during pillow talk. (Well, it was in the backseat of my Rolls after a cramped but enjoyable quickie, so I suppose it was headrest talk.)

I had a quick chat with our director, Cyril Savoy, in which I made some blocking change suggestions without mentioning the weights Monica intended to wear. Cyril thought my suggestions were just spiffy. (His word.) I promised to tell Monica about the staging changes before rehearsal.

Monica duly strapped on an additional thirty pounds under costume during the intermission of the first full-dress rehearsal, which is often a stop-and-go affair while technical problems not solved at the tech rehearsal are worked out. Monica had forgotten that in movies, Joan could strap on her weights for just the shots where Bette had to lift her, whereas Monica would have no such between-takes break to add the weight, and would therefore have to wear her weights for all of Act Two. Heh. Heh.

Our primary set was a massive, two-story rendering of the Hudson mansion interior, with the kitchen, hallway with stairs, and living room on the stage level, and the upstairs hallway and Blanche's room ten feet above. This huge set was a single unit, which rolled backwards whenever the scene changed to somewhere other than the house.

During intermission, Monica would be strapped into the traction rig over her bed, the same rig I had last seen Claudia Rains so lovingly strapped into. Monica would then hang there until I released her, forty minutes into Act Two, her mouth duct-taped so she couldn't even ask for an emergency bathroom break. (There had been an unfortunate incident at the full-tech rehearsal the day before, the result of which being that at the first full-dress, Monica was wearing a replacement costume and was suspended above a brand-new mattress purchased that day.)

As we were trussing her up (I was being helpful, in the spirit of getting the tech aspects moving quickly. I'm a team player. Just ask the 1972 American Olympic Greco-Roman wrestling team how they all got that identical embarrassing itch), I gave the rig a couple extra twists on the ratchet, so that Monica's ample butt was hoisted three or four inches above the mattress.

And so Monica got to hang there with the extra weight pulling down on her arms, her own private stretching rack, with her mouth duct-taped shut, so she couldn't even demand to be lowered to where the bed held her weight instead of her arms. Meanwhile, the rehearsal went especially slowly. In fact, I was having a particularly bad second act: flubbing lines, screwing up lyrics, stumbling during musical numbers. I can't think why I was so off my game, but the usual forty minutes Monica would normally spend hanging there stretched into ninety. Poor dear.

Finally the moment came where I had to take Monica down. You should have seen the look in her eyes. First, the look of grateful relief as the bed took the weight, then the crafty look, thinking that her plan to mildly inconvenience me for five minutes was now about to bear fruit, albeit after her hour and a half of being stretched out in mid-air. Oops. It must have slipped my mind to warn Monica about the staging changes.

So, after unstrapping her and ripping off the duct-tap, Monica expected me to drag her off the bed, lift her up, and carry her down the stairs and out to the garage set (which slid in from the wings as the house set rolled backwards).

Instead, I rolled her off the bed with a hard shove, allowing her to slam onto the floor. (She made a wonderful "Oof!" sound. Completely in character.) Then I rolled her to the stairs with my feet while she hollered out-of-character remarks like: "*Stop that! What are you doing?*" and "*That hurts, Tallulah!*"

How unprofessional. (And how inaccurate. That didn't "Hurt

Tallulah" in the slightest. In fact, I was having a ball.)

Once at the stairway, I just shoved her off and watched her roll all the way to the bottom. The whole crew applauded at how well Monica handled this new stunt. She even gave a very convincing imitation of being only semi-conscious when she landed in the hall. I then proceeded to kick-roll her to the garage. However, I must admit her performance in the final scene on the beach was subpar even for her. But then fortunately, I'm the one who sings the finale by the shore.

Oddly enough, at the next night's rehearsal, Monica had left the weight belt in her dressing room.

And so the week went by in work, work, work. (Well really: work, work, work, drink, drink, drink, fuck, fuck, fuck, and those usually shuffled into a random order) But after the final dress run-through on the 5th, before an inexplicably enthusiastic invited audience, we were as ready for opening night as we ever would be. We had one free day, so we could be rested and refreshed for the critics and Alta Caca first-nighters. On that free night, we would be seeing what Rudy and my prepubescent pupils had cooked up in their Junior Drink System rehearsals. Rudy and I had prepared a one-hour script from a popular Broadway play. It was bound to be an evening of surprises.

And it did not disappoint.

Chapter 16
Alta Caca's Boys Band

I arrived for the show by cab, with Little Fanny in tow, since Rudy, as the director of the evening's presentation, had been at the theater all day, putting the set together, and handling all the last minute details for his pupils' presentation, while Iris was off Heaven-knows-where with Hugh Johnson, this being his last day in town before he had to return to Yosemite. I was forced to spend the afternoon at *The Wet Spot*, where I had someone to pour my vodka. How I sacrifice for my art.

Around three in the afternoon Rita came by, and she and I retired to her private peeping room where we could watch her Pay Ten Place patrons play through the glass while we drank. It's a vast improvement over daytime television, particularly when there is practically nothing on but coverage of the impeachment debate in Congress.

As we left Rita's private room I encountered Fanny in the motel lobby, I assume looking for me, so we rode back to the high school together.

After being a cheerful, happy child most of the summer, Fanny had turned morose again after the incident at the docks. I tried to make conversation with her in the car, but aside from saying "yes" to an offer of a "Shirley Temple Black," (like a regular Shirley Temple, but made with vodka) she didn't speak a word the whole seven blocks of the drive, just drank and glared.

When we pulled into the Alta Caca High School parking lot, Merle was standing outside the auditorium. Fanny squealed with joy when she saw him, leaping out of the cab before it had even completely stopped moving, and running up to hug her brother. I must confess that I do not fully understand sibling affection. I was an only child, as my mother always said she wouldn't make the same mistake twice. Apparently she feared it would cramp her creativity, which she employed in always finding brand new mistakes to make.

But as I was walking up to them, Harry Mirkin emerged from the auditorium. Seeing his son, he roared at him, "What are you doing here, you disgusting little pervert?"

"I came to see the show."

"I don't want you here with decent people. Get out!"

"No. You can order me out of your house, but this is a public place, and I have just as much right to be here as anyone."

"Since when do perverts have rights?"

"1776," I piped in helpfully, "You know, 'All men are created equal.' If *only* that also applied to their anatomy. Anyway all that inalienable rights stuff that Jefferson knocked out when not knocking up his slaves."

"Exactly!" Harry snarled, "He had slaves. He knew they didn't have rights, and neither do queers!"

"There are two schools of thought on that point, Mayor," I replied. "It turned out the slaves *did* have rights. Gays will have their day as well."

Harry actually said, "Harumph!" and then added, "Well, Jefferson wrote 'All *men*.' Clearly Merle here is not a *man* at all." Then he spat in his son's face. "This is all your fault, Miss Morehead. We were a happy, perfect family until you invaded our lives. You're like - I don't know - you're like Mary Poppins for perverts. Well, we have a little surprise for you tonight. I'll see you inside. Merle, stay away from me." And he turned on his heel and stomped back into the auditorium.

Fanny looked up at me, her little eyes brimming with tears, and said, "I wish you'd never come to Alta Caca."

Merle turned Fanny to face him, keeling down to talk to her face-to-wet-face. "No, you don't, Fanny."

Fanny looked surprised, "Brother, you believe her?"

"I believe everything she ever slurred."

"But she promised us."

"I know what she promised us. And it all happened just like she said:

the lights, the songs, and the drinking."

"Where was all that?"

"In the way every kid in this town staggered around all summer, and acted and smelt. Especially you, and the parents, too. Does Momma wish she'd never come to Alta Caca?"

"No, but that's just because having her in the house helps her show up Mrs. Snype. But you do, don't you? She ruined your life."

"No, Fanny. She was the first person to accept me just as I am. She's an actress, but she showed me how to stop acting."

I joined in, "The critics say I'm far better qualified to teach not-acting than acting."

"But you better go Tallulah, please," said Merle, "I don't know what Dad has up his sleeve in there, but it's bound to be pretty unpleasant."

Fanny, still all teary, hugged my knees. "Go on, Tallulah, you can leave."

"I can't go, Fanny."

"Why not?"

"My driver is inside. Besides, I wouldn't dream of letting Harry win. Shall we all go in?"

The three of us linked arms and walked into the auditorium.

The place was packed. Not an empty seat, in a room that sat 300. The curtains were drawn across the stage. Harry, Odette Snype, Sheriff Hermosa, and a man I'd never seen before were all standing on the stage apron. Harry and Odette were smirking. Fanny and Merle sat in the empty seats held for us in the front row, leaving an empty seat for me between them.

Harry spoke from the stage, "Miss Morehead, would you be so kind as to join us on the stage?"

As this was an invitation I have never turned down, I ascended the steps beside the stage and joined them.

"Miss Morehead," said Harry with a terrible politeness, "we would like to inform you that you are under arrest."

"Arrest? Whatever for? *I was framed! I never even met Don Damfino, so how could I have shot him and tossed him off the Santa Monica pier? I have an alibi. I was in Paris at the time. Or Hemet. Some awful place like that. And anyway, it was self-defense!*"

"I don't know what you are babbling about, as usual," said Harry, actually bragging about his obtuseness, "but you've been contributing to the delinquency of minors, and you alienated the affections of my daughter's fiancé."

"What are you talking about?"

Odette stepped forward, grinning like a Cheshire cougar, and said, "This man is Joe Lanchester, he's a private detective."

"A private dick you say?" I said, "Private privates. How redundant."

"And he found proof that you are married to Dick Rockwood."

"*What?*" screamed Susan from the audience.

"I'm sorry, sweetie," said Harry, "But it's true. He found the proof. She stole your man."

"So what?" I said, "What are you charging me with? Petty larceny? Last time I looked, it wasn't a crime to fall in love, or whatever it was we fell into."

"I should hope you'd at least have the decency to be humiliated by being revealed as robbing the cradle and marrying a man almost half a century younger than you are," smirked Odette.

"I'm only thirty-something."

"Yes, if that 'something' is another forty-seven years."

"Even if it is true that I am a tad more mature than my husband, and it isn't, how is that humiliating? You're no spring vulture yourself, Odette, and I've never seen a man holding your talon."

"Well, it's humiliating to *me!*" screamed Susan, "Dick preferring a man to me I could understand. I prefer men myself, or will when I finally begin having decent, married sexual relations. But to throw me over for this smelly old hag, *how* could he do this to *me*?"

"He didn't do it to you. That was probably the problem. Because I let him do it to me."

"*You're the Whore of Babylon!*" Susan screamed at me, and then the rude little twit ran from the room, wailing.

As she ran out, I called out after her, "Nonsense! I don't charge for it, and I've never been to Babylon. I'm the Slut of Alta Caca."

Harry looked a bit thrown off his game by Susan's exit. Apparently his ambush wasn't going quite as planned. But he wasn't done. "There's still the matter of your acting classes. We have it on the testimony of Martin Lewis that your classes consist of nothing more than getting our kids drunk!"

"He left out the sex? What a selective memory that boy has. Well, never mind. You're telling me that you're taking the word of a teenage alky over that of a Movie Legend?" I asked, amazed and appalled.

"I've asked the Sheriff here to take you into custody."

Sheriff Hermosa spoke up, "Well, Harry, I wish you'd explained that to me beforehand, because the unsupported word of a known trouble-maker like Martin Lewis isn't really sufficient for me to arrest a public figure who can afford better lawyers than we have."

"But I want this bitch in jail!" Harry shrieked.

"Stop this!" a voice from the audience called out. "Stop this right now!" Henrietta Shemp rose to her feet and charged up onto the stage. She was dressed in colorful African robes, and with her new, black complexion she looked like the elderly singer for a Nairobi steel drum band.

"You all know me," said Henrietta, "I am Taonga Shemp, born Henrietta. And I should think some of you could forget your stuffy Republican pig-headedness long enough to remember what this town was like before Tallulah Morehead came here. Do you? Well, do you? And after she came, suddenly there were things to do, and people to do them to you. She didn't stay hidden away like Carol Channing. She came right into our lives, with a vodka chaser, and reminded us to live, live, live. Life is an orgy, and most poor sons-of-bitches are just playing with themselves. She's changed my life for the vastly better. So what if the techniques she uses to impart her art are unconventional? *She's* the artist, not us, and we should learn from her."

"Henrietta," said Harry.

"It's Taonga."

Harry rolled his eyes, sighed, and said, "All right, *Taonga*, you're out of your mind. And the rest of you who are just sitting there like a throng of lemmings, maybe you can remember some other things, like what you paid for acting classes for your kids, with the clear understanding and warranty that your children would be taught to act. Well, where is the show? Where is the acting? *Where?*"

"Well, if you'll kindly move your fat ass out of the way," I said politely, "you'll see for yourself. Folks, listen. A band will do it, my friends, oh yes. I said a boys band, do you hear me? I said Alta Caca's gotta have a boys band, and I mean she needs it today! Well, Tallulah Morehead's here on hand, and Alta Caca's gonna have her boys band, and here they are: *The Boys in the Band!"*

And Rudy, backstage at the controls, plunged the room into

darkness. We cleared off the stage apron. I sat down between Merle and Fanny, and the curtains parted, revealing the stage.

The main set of *BJ!* was, of course, on the stage. But the living room, hallway, and Blanche's bedroom were all decorated with movie posters featuring glamorous screen queens like Judy Garland, Bette Davis, Barbra Streisand, Marlene Dietrich, Barbara Stanwyck, Mae West, me of course, and Delores Delgado. (What was *that* bitch doing there? Oh, wait. Then I saw. She was on a dartboard. Nice touch, Rudy.)

Upstairs, two small boys entered the room. The ten-year-old was holding a small, chi-chi shopping bag in one hand, and a martini glass in the other. The nine-year-old was just wearing a robe, as though fresh from the shower. Under my breath, I said to them almost like a prayer, "Now drink, boys, *drink!*"

The ten-year-old took a swig of the martini he had in hand (for realism, they were using *real* martinis) and said: "This'll cheer you up. I went shopping today and bought all kinds of goodies. Sandalwood soap, your very own toothbrush, because I'm sick to death of you using mine."

The nine-year-old replied: "Well, how do you think I feel?"

And then the ten-year-old said: "You've had worse things in your mouth."

The entire audience gasped as one. The sudden collective intake of breath created a momentary vacuum so severe I thought the room might implode. Honestly, hadn't any of these people ever seen *The Boys in the Band* before? Well, maybe, but not performed by grade school children.

Shock kept everyone riveted to their seats. I would not have been too surprised to have gotten a few walkouts, but they were all so shocked, they couldn't even move. And then, a few minutes later, the ten-year-old playing Michael got to the line: "Well there's one thing to be said for masturbation; you certainly don't have to look your best," and it got a laugh.

Even the people who laughed seemed surprised that they had laughed. And then a woman a few rows back stood up and said with pride and tears, "That's my Billy. That pervert is *my* Billy."

Good job, Billy, I thought to myself.

A few moments later, after singing a few bars of *Get Happy*, Billy/Michael said: "What's more boring than a queen doing a Judy Garland impression?"

The boy playing Donald replied, "Judy Garland doing a Judy Garland impression."

I leaned over to Merle and whispered, "I '*improved*' that line myself. Don't tell Mart Crowley."

A lady in my row stood up and called out, "That's Zachary! That prissy queen is *my* Zachary!"

The audience, to everyone's amazement, was starting to enjoy it. The weird spectacle of little boys saying these lines was holding them, and the play itself was entertaining them almost in spite of themselves. Given how streamlined the script was (Rudy and I had cut the play to almost half of its original length), the laughs were coming fast, so it was only a few minutes later when the boy playing Emory spoke the greatest line ever written in the English Language Theater: "Who do you have to fuck to get a drink around here?", and a woman just behind me stood up, hands clasped to her breasts, and cried out, "Bernie, cuss to me, Bernie, cuss to me."

Merle leaned over and said, "I think they like it. They don't want to, but they do."

I replied, "You've just described every audience I've ever had."

Soon the audience was roaring at the jokes. I saw only one walkout. Unsurprisingly, it was Harry Mirkin. Henry Hermosa was standing off to the side, laughing at the jokes.

When the eleven-year-old "Alan" said, "I've never been to Hollywood myself, but I would imagine it must be awful. Everyone must be terribly cheap." I whispered to Merle: "Please. Try divorcing Zsa Zsa Gabor; you'll find out what *expensive* means."

At one point, the ten-year-old boy paying Harold said: "I keep my grass in the medicine cabinet in a Band-aid box. Somebody told me it's the safest place. If the cops arrive, you can always lock yourself in the bathroom and flush it down the john."

I felt a tap at my shoulder. It was Moondog leaning in from behind me to say, "Wow. What great advice. This is so educational. I'll never say theater is irrelevant again."

"Had you ever said it before?" I asked.

"No, and I won't again, either."

When the play ended, there was a thunderous ovation, people cheering and crying. Of course, it probably helped that, in trimming the play for the kids, I had cut out all the nasty truth games from Act Two.

Still, who says educational theater can't move people?

Henry Hermosa came over and shook my hand after it was all over. "Tallulah," he said, "That was audacious and obscene."

"Darling, that was how Alexander Woolcott *always* described my work."

"I ought to take you in," he said, "I can smell the booze on those tots from here."

"That's just the force of their *acting!*"

"Don't kid a kidder. But we need you on that stage tomorrow night. The Alta Caca Arts Council has a lot of money tied up in *BJ!* And anyway..." he leaned in close and whispered in my ear, "It was worth it to see that old windbag Harry Mirkin's face. You're a scofflaw if ever there was one, but you're okay, Tallulah." And the sheriff kissed my cheek and walked away. Everything was looking rosy. What could possibly go wrong on *BJ!*'s opening night?

Chapter 17
Tallulah's Big Opening

The big night has at last arrived. It is *BJ!'s* opening night. I am as ready as I am ever likely to be.

Harry has been in a foul mood all day over his failure to have me arrested, and over the certainty of Nixon's impending impeachment. He's just glowered around the house, too depressed even to go down to City Hall and accept a few bribes.

A few minutes ago, as I was imbibing a light pre-show dinner vodka, little Fanny ran into the dining room and up to her sullen father, carrying an envelope.

"Daddy, a man at the park handed me this letter, and said it was very important that I give it to you right away."

Harry snatched up the envelope. "Who gave you this letter?"

"I don't know, Daddy. I'd never seen him before."

"What did he look like?"

"Tall, kinda ugly."

"We'll have you sit with a sketch artist later," Harry said, picking an odd moment to decide to try to interest his daughter in art, as they weren't yet finished forcing her into theater. Harry read the letter, his face getting redder and redder, until he exploded. *"No! I won't! This is too much! I've let this boozy slut overrun our house the way he demanded, and she's corrupted two of our children and broken the third one's heart, but this time whoever he is has gone too far! I will not let him come home! I just won't do it!"*

"Won't do what, dear?" asked Minge, standing in the doorway, "And who are you talking about?"

"*Never mind!*" Harry roared at Minge, "It doesn't concern *you!*" and Harry ripped the letter into shreds, stuffed the pieces into his pocket, and stormed out of the room, adding, "Come on. If we're going to see this musical freak show tonight, we better get ready."

"Dear," said Minge, following him upstairs, "It's Fanny's stage debut. It's a very important event."

Fanny stared after her departing parents with a dull, bitter look, moisture glinting at the corners of her eyes. Quietly she said, "So be it, daddy. The show will go on."

"Fanny, darling," I asked, "How about a little pre-show bracer to get you in the mood to play me?"

"Thank you, Tallulah," Fanny replied politely without even glancing in my direction, "but this is one show I'm going to do cold sober."

"What an extraordinary idea," I said. "Where are we, Salt Lake City? Do you really think opening night is the best time to experiment with a radical change of technique? Well, we all have to make our own mistakes, I suppose, not that I ever have. A person who makes other people's mistakes is called a plagiarist or a network executive. Will you be ready to leave for the theater in an hour?"

"Yes, Tallulah. I just have to get a few things together first, but I'll be ready all right. I'll give them a show they will never forget."

"That's the spirit, child. Break a leg." And I toddled off to my room to dictate these last few pre-show observations for the sake of posterity, and then knock a few back. The play's the thing, and our show, like Hamlet's *The Murder of Gonzago*, is a dumb show.

***

Few are the people still living who attended the opening night of BJ! on August 7th, 1974, but for those few, with the exception of Tallulah herself, it was an event never to be forgotten, no matter how hard they tried.

It was a sellout show. The entire Alta Caca Arts Council was there, of course, along with anyone of even the slightest social standing in town. William Randolph Hack was there in his capacity as his own paper's theater critic, smirking, ready to take notes and already composing amusing insults in his head.

Backstage, Monica Montana was slipping into the thick full body padding she now wore under her costume to protect her already bruised body from the onslaught of physical abuse that Tallulah got to rain down happily on her throughout the play. It made her look fairly plump, but it was that, or more broken ribs.

In her own dressing room, which had been wisely located on the far side of the stage from Monica's, Tallulah sat sandpapering off her street makeup to create her Baby Jane look. Impending triumph filled her heart.

In the catwalks high above the stage, Phil Rains lurked, still carrying his stained hatbox. His other parcels had finally been disposed of, one by one, at various, widely separated locales: dropped in the lake here, burned in a furnace there, a variety of shallow graves, all done when he was certain Tallulah was stuck at the theater. But the hatbox he had hung onto. Part of him wanted her to hear his score's triumph, and he'd decided to leave the hatbox forever hidden way up in the theater's highest attics, seldom visited by anyone, stuffed behind boxes and crates that hadn't been opened or moved since Herbert Hoover was president. Maybe it would be found and opened someday, long, long in the future, but by then it wouldn't matter. And in the meanwhile, she could order around the forgotten costumes of high school plays from the depression era.

A block away from the high school, ten motorcycles were parked, as the members of Heck's Seraphim dispersed themselves around the school, waiting for their moment to move in, while a second group of men were lurking about as well, awaiting a different-but-not-unrelated moment to make their move.

Back at the Mirkin residence, the Headless Indian Brave and his skull-deficient girlfriend found they had the house to themselves. Even Concepcion had gone to the play. Like children when the grown-ups are away, they decided to misbehave right in the middle of the living room, regardless of what transparent ethereal stains they might leave in Minge's white carpet. It can be difficult to remove those pesky ectoplasm spots.

Little Shirley Knott, the child who played Blanche Hudson as a child, was carrying a beverage on a platter up the stairs that led to the tech booths. She passed through the booth from which the lighting techs ran the show's lights, the smaller booth where the sound tech ran the audio, and into the projection booth, where a lone audio-visual kid from the high school waited his cue to project a series of slides.

The show would open with an overture, and then Fanny would

sing the opening number on the stage apron in front of a huge screen onto which the production credits would be projected, movie-style, to emphasize the movie's Old Hollywood setting and themes.

"Shirley," said Stan the audio-visual guy as Shirley entered the room, "what brings you up here? You'll be needed on stage pretty soon now."

"Miss Morehead brought everyone working on the show some lemonade for luck. I brought you a glass of it."

"Thank you, young lady. Just set it there. I'll drink it in a bit."

"No, you need to drink it now, while it's cold. Everyone has to have some, for luck. I'll wait to bring back the glass."

"Okay then," said Stan, and he drank the lemonade down. Shirley grinned. She had something else with her, under the platter.

Outside, the bikers snapped to alert all over the school as they saw Moondoog Hickcox's woody pull into the school parking lot. Moondog and Sandcrab got out of the car, but as they approached the auditorium doors Deathspewer Jones and The Scorpion stepped out of a nearby men's room doorway and stood in front of the two surfers.

"Hi, Deathy," said Moondog, "and thanks to you, I am."

"Hello, Moondog. I got a question for you. I hear you took a little cruise recently, with Snake Bendix."

"Well, yeah. We got invited on a cruise with Miss Morehead. She is like this totally cool, boss old chick. She invited Snake, too."

"So are you guys fags also?"

"What?"

"You and Sandcrab here. Are you a couple of fags like Snake is?"

"Wow. Like no. We love the ladies, and the ladies love us."

Sandcrab added, "Lately, older ladies have been loving us like even we wouldn't believe."

"Ladies like Snake?"

"What do you mean, man? Snake ain't no lady. What's this hassle about?"

Sandcrab glanced around and saw that the rest of Heck's Seraphim had emerged from all directions, and were in a ring around them, slowly closing in. "Moondog, I'm starting to get seriously bummed here. We should go in. It's like 'Magic Time.'"

"Oh, you two ladies ain't going nowhere," said Deathspewer, "Well, I mean, you're not going into the show. You're coming with us. You got a hot date tonight, with all of us. You surfing fags are gonna be our bitches tonight."

Sandcrab said, "Ah, we're busy tonight. We're gonna be Miss Morehead's guests in her big opening."

"No," said Deathspewer, "you're *our* guests tonight." He nodded, and the bikers grabbed the surfers. "Scorpion, drive them in their woody up to the camp."

Another voice said, "The only place you men are going tonight is jail." Henry Hermosa stepped out into view.

"*Christ, it's pigs!*" yelled Deathspewer, "*Scatter!*" The bikers let go of Moondog and Sandcrab, and started to run off in all directions, but wherever they ran, a cop waited. In fact, the bikers were outnumbered three-to-one, and all quickly found themselves in handcuffs.

Moondog, nervously aware that he and Sandcrab were both "holding," asked, "Ah Sheriff, are we under arrest, too?"

Henry said, "No, boys. You're the victims tonight. You go on in and enjoy the play."

"Thank you, sir," they both said, well aware of their two consecutive narrow escapes in less than five minutes. As they walked in, Sandcrab said, "Man, the play is gonna have to be really gnarly to be scarier than the parking lot."

The police force of Alta Caca was not a large one. Henry Hermosa had borrowed cops from a number of other California communities for this raid on Heck's Seraphim. He'd been aware of the planned attack on the surfers that night for a week now, having been alerted by the only biker not now in custody, The Scorpion, who was really undercover police officer William Highsmith, who had infiltrated Heck's Seraphim two years before. While the bikers had confined themselves to peddling pot to surfers and washing cars, Henry had been content to turn a blind eye to their activities, but when, with the departure of the essentially peaceful Snake Bendix, their aims had turned to intended violence he felt the time had come to step in. Shortly, the bikers were all loaded into a conveyance to be taken off to the Alta Caca jail.

Henry heard some agitated squawking, and a female voice crying out, "*Let go of me, you honky pig. Power to the people! We shall overcome! I have been to the mountaintop! I have a dream!*" Henry turned, and saw one of the on-loan cops dragging Henrietta Shemp and Darien Littlewood towards him, both in handcuffs.

"What are you doing, Officer – Davis, is it?"

"I found these two niggers skulking around the stage door, obviously getting ready to rob the dressing rooms as soon as the play starts."

"Officer Davis, let them go!"

"But they..."

"She is *in* the play, you blithering idiot, and this other so-called criminal you've cuffed is our town librarian. Let *go* of them!"

"Well, how was I to know?" asked Officer Davis, "Where I come from, you can't trust these people. They're all bad."

"Shut the hell up, officer," Henry barked. Davis snapped his jaw closed. As he uncuffed the desperate criminals, Henry said, "I'm terribly sorry, Henrietta."

"It's Taonga now, Henry."

"Taonga. Do you want to press charges against this officer? I'll support your claims if you do."

"I can't think about that now. I have a show to do."

"All right. Darien, what about you? I'm sorry about this. Do you want to press charges?"

"Thank you, Sheriff, and no. No point to it. My daddy always said, 'Try never to piss off a cop.'"

"Good advice. Too bad Officer Davis hasn't followed it." Darien and Henrietta went off, and Henry turned to Davis, "Where the hell are you from, Officer Davis?"

"Los Angeles. I know about these people. I was in the Watts Riots nine years ago."

"I wouldn't be surprised if you caused the Watts Riots. You're relieved of duty. Get out of my town, and I mean right this second. **MOVE!**" And Officer Davis took off running.

The opening strains of the *BJ!* overture could now be heard coming from the auditorium. Hermosa called over his second-in-command, "Are the prisoners all secured?"

"All except 'The Scorpion.'"

"Good work. Well, let them just sit then. The men deserve a treat. Have four men take the prisoners back to the station and lock them up. The rest can come in and watch the play. We'll process them after the show. I don't want to miss this."

"Yes, sir." And so a force of almost thirty policemen were standing in the back of the auditorium when the overture finished and Fanny stepped out and sang *I'm Sending Mother to Heaven, Where Daddy Wants Her*

Bad, while the show credits were projected behind her.

After her song, there was wild applause. In the catwalk over the stage, Phil leaned into the box he was holding and whispered, "Hear that? Hear that applause? They *love* my music. *My muuuusic.*"

At this point, Fanny was supposed to make a short speech and then introduce her daddy, played by Dick Rockwood, but instead, Fanny departed from the script. She stepped forward and said, "And now, kind friends, I would like to read a poem of my own, called *I've Written a Letter to Daddy.*"

Butch Miller, conducting the orchestra in the pit, and Cyril Savoy and Ignatius Wambaugh in the audience, were both gripped with subdued panic. Not only was Fanny departing from the script, but she was coming dangerously close to stepping on the copyright of the movie song. But you didn't interrupt a show unless things got completely out of control, which they had not, at least not yet. Tallulah joined Dick and Rita, who was stage-managing the show and thus had to deal with this deviation from the script, in the wing, all listening for what Fanny would do next.

Fanny continued speaking,

> *"I've written a letter to daddy,*
> *Because he's so often a baddy,*
> *With a quite strange idea of fun.*
> *I showed him a photo,*
> *Said Tallulah must not go,*
> *And no one will see what you've done.*
> *He said my brother is no more his son.*
> *And our family now is undone*
> *He got up his nerve*
> *To call brother a perv,*
> *Well, Daddy, It takes one to know one."*

And onto the screen was projected a picture of the man Tallulah had seen in The Dungeon Room of The Pay Ten Place motel, locked in the pillory, with the large woman in a black leather hood, mask, and tight-fitting garment, apparently lashing his exposed buttocks with a riding crop. Only in this picture the man was unmasked, and it was unmistakably Harry Mirkin.

Upstairs in the projection booth, Stan was snoozing quietly on the floor, under the influence of the sleeping pills that Shirley had stolen from her parents' medicine cabinet and slipped into Stan's lemonade. After projecting the credit slides, Shirley had switched the slide carousel with the one she had carried upstairs under the platter. The pictures she was now showing the stunned audience were in this second carousel.

Minge shrieked. The audience gasped, and Harry's head was whirling. Even more galling than the public disgrace was the realization that the person who had been blackmailing him all summer was his own little girl.

Tallulah asked Rita, "How did Fanny take that picture?"

Rita, looking very chagrined, admitted, "Fanny has been working for me all summer, as a check-in clerk at the motel. She must have found a way into my viewing room. You can see the pictures were taken from behind that mirror."

Fanny spoke again, once the murmuring had died down enough for her to be heard, "But who is the mysterious woman giving daddy the spanking he so richly deserves? Take a look. Next picture please." And the picture changed to another one. Harry was naked now, tied face up, spread-eagled on the bed. The woman was straddling him, apparently riding his manhood. Her mask was off, and her face, distorted in ecstasy and triumph, could be clearly seen. Every person there recognized the vulpine features of Odette Snype.

"Naughty, naughty, Mrs. Snype," said Fanny.

"*Harry!*" screamed Minge, "*How could you? And with her? With that evil bitch? I want a divorce!*"

"But wait, folks," said Fanny, "there's more." And a series of pictures of Harry and Odette' Sadomasochistic games began flashing across the screen, each one more depraved than the one before. There were gasps and screams. Sandcrab said to Moondog, "Wow, this show is a lot better than I expected. Gnarly, man."

"Most truly gnarly," Moondog solemnly agreed, while realizing who it was he had paid off in pot for the pictures of him and Sandcrab breaking a few drug laws in that same motel.

Harry stood up and yelled, "*Fanny, no! This has to stop!*" He ran for the steps to the stage, but instead of running to Fanny, he ran backstage.

Odette stood and started up the aisle towards the lobby, but Minge stepped in front of her, yelled, "***You fucking cunt!***" and slapped Odette so hard, she knocked her to the ground.

Dick walked out on the stage to Fanny and said to her quietly, "That's enough now. Better go over to Tallulah." Fanny walked over to Tallulah in the wings. The increasingly pornographic slide show continued.

Rita bent down to whisper to Fanny, "How did you get into my viewing room?" Fanny held up a ring of keys.

"Two years ago for Christmas," Fanny said, "Daddy gave me a kit, called *My Little Locksmith*. I can make keys myself. And last year he gave me *My First Darkroom*, so I develop all my own pictures and slides."

Rita said, "Well, aren't you industrious?"

"I better talk to my fans," said Tallulah, and she staggered out onto the stage.

On the other side of the stage, Harry grabbed a fire axe. Along the side of the stage were a series of ropes that controlled the raising and lowering of everything above the stage. "*I'll stop this!*" he yelled, and chopped through the rope marked "Screen." However, it was a large axe, and Harry severed three ropes at once.

The screen plummeted to the stage, the hard wooden bar across its top hitting Dick on the head, fracturing his skull and killing him instantly. The other two ropes held one end of the catwalk Phil Rains was standing on. It dumped him, and his left foot got tangled in a loop of rope on the catwalk as he fell.

The audience saw Phil fall into view only to stop suddenly, so he was dangling upside down by one leg in mid-air. There were several screams from the audience, who no longer had any idea what was the show and what wasn't. It was supposed to be a shocker after all.

The hatbox was jarred from Phil's hands, and fell to the stage where it burst open. The object inside the box flew out and rolled to the edge of the stage, where it came to a stop at Tallulah's feet. Many were the people in the audience who recognized the object as the severed head of Claudia Rains. Tallulah glanced at it and said, "Claudia darling, you've lost weight." She then glanced up, saw Phil dangling above her, and added, "So, the Rains came."

Phil called out, "Claudia! You've been murdered! I won't rest until I find the real killers!"

At the back of the auditorium Henry Hermosa told his lieutenant, "Seal the exits. No one leaves."

But before the police could move all the doors, both the lobby doors and the side exits, burst open and a few Imawankah Indian Braves entered through each one. Almost everyone in the room screamed.

Led by their noses over mountains and cliffs, the Imawankahs had arrived. It had been rough going, and a number of them had met their deaths along the way, plunging off cliffs and falling into crevasses, but there were still fifteen of them who survived to finish their pilgrimage and find their Goddess.

Seeing her standing there on the stage, the Imawankahs swarmed down all the aisles to stand in a row before the stage bowing and chanting "Morehead" over and over. Now many of the people in the audience were convinced it was part of the play, as this just couldn't be real life. One man even yelled at the Imawankahs, "Hey, down in front!"

"Darlings," said Tallulah to the Imawankahs, "how lovely to see all of you again. I'm a little busy right now. I'm *acting!* But I'll be glad to sign autographs for you after the play ends."

"This play has ended now!" Henry Hermosa shouted from the back, but he was drowned out when the Imawankah chief spotted Claudia Rains's head on the stage.

"Head," the Chief said, "Give head. Give head."

And realizing that the time to make their offering to their Goddess had come, each brave reached into the pouch he had strapped around his waist and removed his gift, placing each gift on the stage before Tallulah, until she was standing behind an enormous pile of human heads, the severed heads of the Imawankah apostate metaphorisists, sacrificed in the Imawankah Holy War.

Half the audience screamed in horror while the other half rose to their feet applauding, cheering the most outrageous stage horror effect they had ever seen. Tallulah took her automatic response, and started taking bows, saying, "Thank you, my darlings, thank you. Bless you; bless all of you."

The Imawankahs all prostrated themselves flat on the floor before the stage, chanting their worship, which made it considerably easier for Sheriff Hermosa's men to handcuff them. Rita ordered the curtain lowered, and the aborted only performance of *BJ!* came to its admittedly spectacular conclusion.

Standing behind the curtain, Tallulah said, "What? No encore? They *love* me!" Then, glancing upwards, added, "Hello, Phil darling. How's it hanging? What are you doing after the show? I see Claudia's dead, and as it happens, I'm a recent widow myself."

She kicked a couple of heads out of her way, stepped over her husband's corpse, and said, "How about an opening night celebratory shag?"

Chapter 18
Vodka & Sympathy

At the moment all hell broke loose in the Alta Caca High School auditorium, the Headless Indian Brave and his headless girlfriend were enjoying a bit of post-coital afterglow, which in their case involved actual glowing, in the middle of the Mirkin living room. However good or bad the summer had been for everyone else, it had been the best summer the Headless Indian Brave had had in over four centuries.

But at the moment that Claudia Rains's head had rained down onto the stage, her murder revealed to the world, her murderer caught, the headless ghost lying beside the Headless Indian Brave grew her head back, and the brave discovered he'd been dating the ghost of Claudia Rains.

Dead Claudia sat up and said, "Well it's about time someone realized I was murdered. Talk about a town without brains!"

She looked over at her deceased lover, "Now as for *you!* First off, this ragged loincloth look is *over!* You're going to start dressing like a normal person, start manifesting a nice suit and a sharp tie, and you'll manifest that before you get any more of me! What are we, savages?"

The Headless Indian Brave nodded his neck stump.

"Well *you* may be a savage, but I am *not!* You are going to spruce up. And you will find a way to detach yourself from this hideous drunken old actress. I am not spending eternity haunting a pathetic, oversexed lush. And find yourself an occupation of some sort. If you spend your whole afterlife just hanging around some old booze hound, how do you ever expect to get a head?"

The Headless Indian Brave just sat there, stunned by this sudden onslaught of overbearing orders. Claudia however, was just getting warmed up.

"Now, I have a nephew living up in Merced. Frankly, the boy is practically a hippie, but he's the only living relative I have, except for his mother, and frankly, I cannot stand my sister. It's her wishy-washy mothering that let the boy run to rot the way he has. I mean, he goes to a *junior* college, and he's married a *waitress!* So I have decided that you and I will start haunting him, and we'll scare him into cleaning up his act, that is, once you've cleaned up yours!"

At which point, the Headless Indian Brave, unable to ask her to stop issuing unilateral orders, and coming from a culture where women did not order men around in the first place, lost his patience and lashed out the only way he could, by slapping her face. Claudia's head rolled off her shoulders and onto the floor.

"Are you happy now, you brute?" Claudia's head asked. Her body reached down and picked her head up and set it back in place. "I can see I will have to be more careful. Apparently my head is no longer firmly melded to my body. Now listen to me, buster; if you *ever* strike me again, I will make you wish you were alive. I'll make you yearn for Hell, as Hell would be nicer than your afterlife will be with me! Now apologize. Right now! Go on. Apologize. I'm waiting."

Instead, the Headless Indian Brave stalked over to the Mirkin front door, opened a transparent version of the door while the real one remained closed, and made a sharp gesture, the meaning of which was impossible to misinterpret.

"You're throwing me out? *Me?* Who do you think you are, you uneducated beast? I'm the one settling for someone beneath me here, *way* beneath me!"

The Headless Indian Brave repeated his gesture, more forcefully.

"You think you can just have your fun with me and then chuck me out? Think again, you aboriginal moron."

The Headless Indian Brave walked over to Claudia, grabbed hold of her head, tore it off her neck again, walked back to the entryway, and threw her head through the door, so that it landed on the front walk.

"*How dare you?*" squawked Claudia's head from the front yard, "Who do you think you are? You're *nothing* without *me!* I gave you the best years of my death. I'm warning you; if my body has to come out here to retrieve me, I won't come back. I mean it. You'll be begging me to come back in an hour. In *half* an hour!" But the Headless Indian Brave just folded his arms and dematerialized. With no one left to shout at, Claudia's body came outside, picked up and reattached her head again, and floated off into the sky. The psychically attuned might have heard her snort with contempt, "*Men!* Can't live with them; can't not-live with them."

***

The Alta Caca jail was the most full it had ever been, even on the rowdiest 4th of July or New Year's Eve: fifteen Indians, speaking an unknown language, all accused of murder, nine bikers, accused of harassment, menacing, intent to do bodily harm, drug trafficking, and operating a car-washing business without a permit, Phil Rains, accused of murder, and Harry Mirkin, accused of manslaughter and reckless disregard in the death of Dick Rockwood.

Harry and Phil, by virtue of their social standing, got individual cells, so Phil was alone when his late wife materialized in his cell, holding her head in her hands. "Oh my God," said Phil, "Claudia? Are you really here? Or have I gone insane?"

"Does it make any difference, Phil? I'm here now, and I'll never leave you again. You've got me for eternity now."

"Well, if I'm not insane, that should do it."

"*Hey!*" yelled Deathspewer Jones from a cell down the hall, "Keep it down. We're trying to sleep in here."

"Well, Phil," said Claudia's head, "here's another nice mess you've gotten me into."

By midnight, Sheriff Hermosa had questioned and released most of the people in the auditorium. Harry Mirkin hadn't mentioned to Henry that his daughter had blackmailed him out of $10,000. Either some small shred of fatherly decency remained in him, or maybe he just didn't want to account for where exactly he'd laid hands on such a large lump of untraceable cash. All Harry had asked of Hermosa was that he put off questioning Fanny until the next day, to let her get some sleep.

It was an accommodation the Sheriff was glad to make. He had more than enough people to deal with that night. Somehow a simple theatrical opening had blossomed into an unprecedented crime wave. By a preliminary count, they had thirty-two severed heads to deal with, only one of whom they could identify. Frankly, with fifteen murder suspects with whom he could not communicate nor identify, Henry was at a loss to know how even to begin his investigation. Who were these people? Who were these victims? Where had they come from? So far, he knew only one thing about them; they all appeared to know Tallulah Morehead, and she apparently knew them. But when questioned, all she would say about them was that they were her devoted fans. Well, she did appear to be right about that. The Imawankah Indians had appeared quite literally to worship her.

But he had nothing to hold Tallulah on, so around midnight she was allowed to leave, though he informed her in no uncertain terms that *BJ!* would not be reopening. The theater was a crime scene, and one of the leads was dead. It was a disaster all around.

Rudy had been released earlier, and had left for The Mirkins'. Tallulah took a taxi to the house. When she got there, Rudy was out front, loading her luggage into the Rolls. Minge was standing on the porch. As Tallulah staggered up the walk, Minge came down to her. She had tears in her eyes.

"I'm sorry, Tallulah..."

"It's Miss Morehead, Mange."

"I'm sorry, Miss Morehead, but I have to ask you to leave."

"What on earth for, darling? With Merle banished and Harry in jail, there's *lots* more room."

"Tallulah..."

"Miss Morehead."

"Miss Morehead, I realize that you didn't drive Harry into that awful woman's perverted arms. It appears that that has been going on since long before you arrived in town. But your influence on my children has been, well, catastrophic. As much as I've enjoyed having you here, and I have actually enjoyed having you here, I have to ask you to leave, now, tonight, at once. I'm sorry. Goodbye." She turned to walk back inside.

"How about a quick one for the road, Mange?" Tallulah called after her.

Minge stepped inside without any more words, and closed the door.

***

(From the personal journal of Tallulah Morehead.)

How quickly Life wrings its changes. A few hours before I was opening as the star of a show, was semi-happily married, and was being quite literally worshiped. Now here I was, unemployed, dispossessed, and newly-widowed. The way things were going, any minute now something *bad* might even happen to me, knock on wood.

On top of all this, I couldn't get poked. I've long ago learned the not-hard way that dead husbands are no damn good in the sack (Count Vlad Tepes being the lone counter-example, and he was really only *undead*). Sir Ludwig had trailed off after his odious wife, terrified to have her see him give me even a glance, perhaps with good reason. Of course, even he could have had it worse. He could have been married to Odette Snype.

But then, to have Minge turn on me after all I'd never done for her, just a few scant hours after my husband's quasi-tragic death, well it was just plain unfeeling of her. She'd been like my own sister to me, that is to say, nonexistent. She is obviously an insensitive, self-centered, low type of woman. No wonder Harry cheated on her. I almost wished I could marry her myself just so I could cheat on her. Thank Heavens for alcohol, the lover that never rejects you.

Rudy came up to me with a travel martini. I asked him, "Did you retrieve the Headless Indian Brave's bone from the garden?"

"Yes. He's waiting in the car." I glanced in through the open car door. Sure enough, there he was, pouring firewater down his open neck stump.

"Brave," I asked, "where's your lady friend?" The Brave made the hand sign for "don't ask," and then poured another slug of firewater down his throat. I turned to Rudy and said, "Let that be a lesson to us all. A heart doesn't have to be beating to be broken. Dead women can be so fickle."

"So," said Rudy, "where are we off to? Back to the hotel to collect Iris and then home to Hollywood, or do you want to stay there for the night?"

"Tallulah?" asked a small, weepy voice. I turned, and there was little Fanny.

"What is it, dear? Oh, and by the way, you were *sensational* tonight. You were a panic. Talk about killing the audience. After you were done, there was what? Thirty-five dead people on stage? The most riveting theatrical debut I've ever witnessed, and I was there for Richard Burbage's debut, I think."

"Tallulah, it's Merle. Could you talk to him? He's so unhappy. His heart is broken."

"There's a lot of that going around tonight. And heads seem to be an endangered species around here, as well. But darling, I have no idea where he is."

"I can take you to him. I know where he's been staying. It was always our secret place."

"Well, get in the car and let's go. I've had more than enough of this dump anyway. Rudy, we're off."

At Fanny's direction, we drove over to The God Dam. The God Dam Hydroelectric plant was at the north end of the dam, but we parked outside the south end. There is a locked door there, at the base of the dam. Fanny the Junior Locksmith had a homemade key and let us in. We climbed a flight of stairs to another locked door. Fanny knocked at it, and said, "Merle, it's me."

The door opened, and there was Merle. "Merle darling," I said, "it's me!"

Merle, red-eyed, said, "Tallulah. What are you doing here? I thought you'd be at the opening night party."

"It was cancelled, along with the rest of the run and some of the cast. The evening took some novel turns. So I thought I'd come over and cheer you up. Care for a cocktail?"

"All I want is my Snake back."

"Well, we'll have a cocktail anyway. Rudy, this boy needs an Invigorator."

As Rudy was fetching Merle a drink, Fanny pulled me aside. "I think I know where Snake is. It's a couple hours' drive away. It's a place I heard him talking about at - well - at the motel, you know, when I was watching and taking pictures. It's where he said he liked to go to get away from the biker gang. If you'd loan me Rudy and the car for a few hours, I think we can find him."

"Why not? Just tell Rudy to leave me my overnight bag."

Soon Fanny and Rudy had driven off, and Merle and I were camped out in his little room, tucked away inside The God Dam. The room contained only an old mattress, an elderly, rickety end table, some ancient wooden crates being used as tables and shelves, and a sink. My overnight bag came complete with a small bar, some candles, and a nightgown. I set out my candles around the room, poured us some vodka, and squatted down on the mattress on the floor in a ladylike manner.

"So what is this place, darling? Your love nest?"

"No. When I was a kid, this was like my fort. Then, later, it became the place where I went to be alone with, well, these." And Merle lifted the corner of the mattress. There were muscle men magazines and copies of *Playgirl*.

"Oh, I see. A jack shack."

Merle blushed boyishly. "I used to keep these in the house, but I was afraid that if Dad found them that he'd, well, he'd react like you saw. And so now, here I am again. No one ever comes to this side of the dam interior."

"Language Merle. You don't want to end up as foul-mouthed as that shithole father of yours. Speaking of him, well, he's not going to be a problem anymore. Your mother is divorcing him, which is the smartest thing she's done since inviting me to stay with you and solve all your family's problems, which I've done. It turns out that while you were sweating up the sheets with Snake at Pay Ten Place, your father was just a couple rooms away, playing similar games with that Snype woman."

Merle's eyes grew wide, "Dad is having an affair with Odette Snype?"

"He was. I think I can safely say it's over now. The news has come out. And besides, I think your dad's next lover is liable to be named Guido."

"If there's one thing Dad is not, it's gay."

"I know. That's what will make it fun."

"You've always been so kind to me, Tallulah."

"Well, I'm kind only to be cruel. And if I want to be very rotten, I must be very kind."

"But the whole world isn't like you. I'm scared. It's not easy to be gay."

"Oh, I don't know. Many of my closest husbands found it effortless. Are you certain you're gay? Have you ever made love to a woman?"

"God no! *Ew!*"

"Well, maybe you should try it, just to be sure. Maybe you have an inner muff diver you've never tapped into."

"I suppose you could be right. But I don't know any girls who would sleep with me just to test myself. You know what girls are like."

"On occasion."

"They want lovers, not experimenters."

"Who said anything about girls? I said a *woman*. A woman like *me*."

"You?"

I lay back, shrugging off my blouse, and reeling out my breasts until they unrolled and flopped free. "Yes, me. Come here, my darling, and let me show you the beauties of heterosexual love."

As I pulled Merle's head down onto my chest, and flopped a tittie across his face, I said, "When you speak of this, years from now - and please do - be kind. By which I mean *exaggerate!*"

As Merle struggled to avoid being strangled by the breast wrapped around his throat I reached with all the grace and class of that whore Deborah Kerr for my overnight bag, pulled out my jackhammer-dildo-personal massager and asked, "Where can I plug this in?"

"Right here!" said Merle, pointing at an outlet above his head with his feet.

***

It was after 8 a.m. when Rudy and Fanny returned. When the knock came at the door, before answering it Merle said to me with great solemnity, "Tallulah, I want to thank you for last night."

"Really, darling? Because frankly, it wasn't my best work. And I think my vibrator may have damaged the floor."

"I've been sexually confused for so long, but now I know who I truly am."

I opened the door. A large, burly man was standing there. He said to Merle, "Hey, kid. I - well - I missed you."

Merle screamed, "***SNAKE!***" and rushed into his man's arms. "Snake, I know now for sure. Women repulse me." He shot me a loving glance, and added, "Boy, do they repulse me. Sweet bleeding Jesus, how they repulse me! I love *you!*"

Snake replied, "I realized while I was alone this week, I love you too, kid." Snake got down on one knee and asked, "Merle Mirkin, will you be my bitch?"

Merle jumped up and down. "Yes, Snake, yes. I was born to be your bitch." And Snake stood, and he and Merle kissed with as much passion as ever I've seen. I confess, this old romantic got misty-eyed.

Snake picked up Merle, slung him over his shoulder like a bag of trash, and walked out of the room. I could see Merle's blissful grin as he was hauled off. I picked up my overnight bag, stepped out of the room, and slammed the door firmly shut. I could hear something fall over inside, but I knew this room had served its purpose, so I just went down the stairs and out the outer door.

Merle was seated firmly behind Snake on Snake's motorcycle. "Where are you boys going?" I asked.

"Any place the men are men," said Snake.

"San Francisco," added Merle.

"Wait!" yelled Fanny, and she ran over to Merle and Snake. She handed Merle a thick envelope she pulled out of her blouse. "You'll need this more than me."

Merle asked, "What is it?"

Fanny looked down for a second, and then said, "Eleven thousand dollars in unmarked bills. One thousand of it is Snake's."

Merle's eyes bulged, but Snake grinned and said, "For a blackmailer, you're okay, kid. You need a lift?"

Rudy said, "We'll drop off Fanny."

"Goodbye!" was yelled by pretty much everyone, and Merle and Snake roared off down the highway towards whatever life awaited them.

Rudy drove Fanny and me over to The God Dam Hotel to collect Iris. When we got there, Rita Morecombe was also waiting for us with a packed bag. "Tallulah," she asked, "could you give me a lift to the bus stop out on the Coast Highway? I'm blowing this burg before Sheriff Hermosa figures out that I had Fanny working as a motel clerk, let alone finding out about my little secret room. I don't know just how many laws I've violated, but he'll figure it out. By then, I'd like to be in another jurisdiction."

"Hop in. It's a deceptively roomy Rolls."

"We're taking Fanny, too," said Iris.

"We are?"

"Yes. I'm going to take her to her Uncle's home in El Portal with me. I've cleared it with Minge. She needs some alone time now anyway. I've got a bag packed for Fanny in the trunk."

"We're going to El Portal?"

"No. *We're* going to Morehead Heights. I'll type up your last journal entries, pack up my things, and then I'm moving in with Hugh. He and I will take care of Fanny until Minge is able to deal with Life again."

"Seen the paper this morning?" asked Rita.

"No. How are my reviews?"

"Unforgettable." Rita handed me *The God Dam Gazette*. The headline was "MOREHEAD OPENING NIGHT A CRIME SCENE: 'Heads Will Roll' Promises The Arts Council."

"Hmmm," I said, "About average for me."

Below that was "MAYOR MIRKIN KILLS LOCAL ACTOR TO COVER UP AFFAIR." I quickly flipped past all these unnecessary, boring stories, and the lurid pictures of Indians and severed heads and Odette (Talk about grim: *Odette!*) to the theater page, where the headline "*BJ! BLOWS*" pretty much told me all I needed to know, although there was a charming photograph of me standing behind a pile of human heads and my husband's corpse, with the caption "Tallulah Morehead Slays 'Em." *[Note to Iris: Remind me to write to Hack to request a print of this picture.]*

"Well then, everyone, road trip it is. Cocktails?"

As we reached the point where the road crested the dam and reached the shores of Swan Song Lake, we saw Moondog and Sandcrab standing beside the road, their woody with their surfboards inside parked beside them. We pulled over.

"I am so glad we caught you," said Moondog.

"Did you catch me, darlings? I didn't realize I was contagious," I said.

"Well, we certainly caught something," said Sandcrab, scratching his crotch vigorously.

Moondog slapped Sandcrab's shoulder, and then said, "We just wanted to thank you. It's been a boss summer."

"Most righteously boss," added Sandcrab helpfully.

"My pleasure, and it often was," I said, "And boys, if you're ever in Malibu, come up and see me sometime."

A school bus roared past us on its way out of town. I asked, "Is there a school inland that serves this two-bit town?"

"Actually, Tallulah, that bus is yours and Rudy's doing," said Rita, "That was your underage cast of *The Boys in the Band*. The show was such a hit, they've been asked to perform it in Monterey, San Jose, and, of course, San Francisco. Those kids are off on tour playing a show they wouldn't be allowed to see."

"Amazing. Well, it's nice to know one of the shows I was involved with here is a hit. Goodbye, boys. Remember what Ben Franklin said: 'If we don't hang together, we will all hang ten.'"

"Gnarly," the boys said in unison, and we rolled off down the highway.

Fifteen minutes later we hit the turnoff for the Coast Highway south. As we were letting Rita out of the car, we heard a distant boom to the west. "What the hell was that?" I asked. "The only bomb I know of in that town closed in one night."

Rudy said, "Who cares? Tallulah, just forget about Alta Caca."

I thought this was a God Damn good idea, so as we headed off south, back to the welcoming dust of Morehead Heights, and I began my serious travel drinking, I did just exactly that.

Chapter 19
Bad Vibrations

When Tallulah slammed the door to the small room near the base of the south end of the God Dam, the rickety old end table inside fell over. There were three candles still burning on that table, and some of Merle's old beefcake magazines, which Tallulah had pulled out from under the mattress to thumb through, caught fire. Very shortly after that, the wooden crates caught fire, and soon afterward the mattress too was ablaze. By the time Tallulah's Rolls drove off from Moondog and Sandcrab, to cruise away from Alta Caca, the room was an inferno.

The highway they were driving along had been blasted out of the mountainside with tons of dynamite. But the Damfino Crime Family was an organization which believed that you could never have too much dynamite, a substance they felt came in handy for so many everyday household uses, from teaching reluctant extortion victims a lesson, to solving permanently domestic disputes, to taking care of folks who "looked funny." Therefore, they had taken advantage of the highway-building project to purchase and store roughly five-times as much dynamite as the project required, with the state of California footing the bill.

The leftover dynamite had been stored in a room in the dam itself, behind a disguised, hidden door, where they could avail themselves of their secret explosives supply whenever needed. It was a perfect arrangement except for one small problem. The Damfinos were murdered around the time the dam was completed, for reasons unrelated to that project but not unrelated to the adventures of Miss Morehead, as chronicled elsewhere, and so there was no one left who knew of the gigantic stash of old dynamite in the dam, aging and sweating and growing more unstable with each passing day.

As it happened, the secret room full of old, unstable explosives was directly below Merle's hideaway. Tallulah's industrial strength vibrator had indeed damaged the room's floor, which was further weakened by the fire, and before too long, it gave way, sending the fire plummeting into the room below, directly onto the enormous store of forgotten dynamite.

So the distant boom that Tallulah heard from some twenty miles away was actually tons of dynamite exploding, obliterating over half of The God Dam in a single second. The ensuing force of the water pouring through quickly tore away what little was left.

Swan Song Lake, held back no longer, gushed forward in a wave that would embarrass a Tsunami, thundering down on and over Alta Caca in a devastating, all-obliterating wave of destruction, as it headed for the sea five miles away.

Moondog and Sandcrab had been sitting on a rise above the highway, sharing a joint and relishing their view of the sea, when the explosion hit. As it happened, they were protected from the force of the blast, by the rugged tor they had selected as their spot for toking up. They stood and rushed down to the highway, where they saw a sight well worthy of that Celestial Call of God that they had heard (the last thing they would hear for some hours): the biggest, most humongous wave they had ever seen.

"Gnarly," said Moondog.

"Bitchin'," said Sandcrab, though neither heard the other speak. But they didn't need to speak to know what to do next. They ripped open the backend of Moondog's woody, took out their surfboards, and ran to the rapidly draining lake. Surf was definitely up.

The wealthiest of Alta Caca's residents lived in houses on the highest accessible points on the hills on either side of Beaver Valley. Safely above the flood devastation, thus, as it so often happens, the richest came through the catastrophe unscathed, while the less-affluent were wiped away. Some of those survivors later reported a sight so strange that they could never truly believe they had not hallucinated it from the shock of the horror they were beholding: two men actually surfing on the crest of the giant wave rolling over Beaver Valley, and washing Alta Caca away. The few nearest to these ultimate surfers even reported faintly hearing them crying "*Cowabunga!*" as they went by, lost in religious bliss.

But The God Dam Flood was not the last of the catastrophes to strike Alta Caca that morning. Deep beneath Swan Song Lake, far below the immediate land that formed the floor of that reservoir, lay Richard Nixon's Fault, the fault line created by the collision of the valley land with the continental shelf, of which the Gorge of Death had been the visible top.

The incalculable trillions of tons of water, which had made up Swan Song Lake, had, for fifty-four years, pressed down on Richard Nixon's Fault with an enormous pressure. But now that pressure was released, and released quite suddenly.

At the same time that weight was transferred to Beaver Valley, only delivered with a thundering force that hammered down on the valley, which more than trebled its pressure. And this redistribution of weight and force was completed in barely fifteen minutes, less than a nanosecond of geologic time.

The effect on the fault line was not unlike what you would get if you took a pair of scales with a brick on one end and nothing on the other, and suddenly took away the brick, and then smashed it down on the other end.

The fault, suddenly released from all that pressure, reacted with a massive earthquake. Were it not for the excellent suspension system on her Rolls, and her own always-somewhat shaky condition, even Tallulah, now almost forty miles away, might have felt the tremor.

The scales tipped violently. The shard of land that made up Beaver Valley, never truly a part of the continent it had invaded millions of years before, shook free, upended, and slid forever back under the churning waves of the ever-so-mis-named Pacific Ocean, carrying all of Alta Caca with it into the offshore depths. The sea roared in, again reclaiming the inlet of which it had been robbed so very long before, carrying on its surface two surfers in the throes of the greatest ecstasy they had ever known, riding the finest surf they had ever beheld.

And the waters came together, forever covering what had once been Beaver Valley and Alta Caca, all because Tallulah Morehead had left some candles burning and slammed a door.

And floating serenely above the drowned town, two surfers sat on their boards and spoke to the God of Surf, who had showed his hand so plainly that day. "Righteous, man," they both said, with true and deep reverence, and began paddling their way out to sea.

Chapter 20
I Am Become Drink,
The Destroyer of Memories

O n any almost other day in the 20th century, a dam breaking, a flood, and an earthquake combining to utterly annihilate an entire, if obscure, California coastal town would have been front page news all across the nation. Sympathy and aid for whatever survivors there were would have poured into California from all over the world.

But it was Alta Caca's further misfortune that it was abruptly snuffed out of existence on the 8th of August, 1974, which was, to put it mildly, not a slow news day.

Three thousand miles away, in Washington DC, and three days before, on August 5th, the so-called "Smoking Gun" White House tape had been released, on which Richard Nixon was heard to authorize hush money to Watergate burglar E. Howard Hunt, and had ordered administration officials to try to have the FBI investigation stopped. Shortly thereafter, a number of key Republican senators convinced Nixon that enough, indeed more than enough, votes existed for his impeachment to proceed, and to succeed.

And so, at 9 p.m. Eastern Daylight Time in Washington DC, 6 p.m. Pacific Daylight Time in California, on August 8th, Richard M. Nixon went on national television and announced that he would resign the Presidency of the United States of America, effective at noon the next day.

Earthquakes and floods were traditional news, and few was the number of people in the population who had ever heard of Alta Caca. But the resignation of a United States President caught neck-deep in high crimes and misdemeanors, essentially fleeing from the White House with Justice and Retribution snapping at his heels, with prison a very possible future (since no one yet knew that the fix was in with Gerald Ford), and a brand-new President who, in a tremendous irony, had been appointed by the very scoundrel he now replaced after the previous Vice President had also been forced out in a crime-ravaged scandal, trumped any imaginable news story short of a nuclear war. There had been nothing like it before in the whole history of the Republic. It would be almost thirty years before another administration as corrupt would pollute the White House, and even its fall would not be so spectacular.

Richard Nixon's resignation was front-page news. *Entire* front pages, and the second, third, and fourth pages as well. Whole editions of nothing but the sudden change of Presidents, and the endless rehashing of every known detail of the two-year scandal that had led to it, filled the papers. If Harry Mirkin hadn't already been dead, this would have killed him.

Vague reports of an earthquake and a flood somewhere in the middle of the California coast, which had resulted in some "damages," appeared buried in the second sections of a few California newspapers. It never made the national news at all.

Nor was there time to squeeze in any coverage of The God Dam Disaster (as it was known to those few who knew of it at all) in the non-stop barrage of White House coverage on television. Lost to the world, Alta Caca's demise was similarly lost to the news.

Even the Hollywood press, when, months later, the death of former film star Monica Montana was finally reported, the cause of death given was only "Natural Causes." "Act of Nature" might have been more accurate. An acute case of Tallulah Morehead might have been more accurate still.

But survivors there were. Fanny Mirkin was safe in Tallulah's Rolls when The God Dam Disaster hit, though as she grew, raised in the shadow of Yosemite by her Uncle Hugh Johnson and her Aunt Iris Johnson *nee* Cole, her own feelings of guilt over the role she had played in the dissolution of her family weighed on her. She resides today in San Francisco, near to her brother Merle with his partner and, as of June 2008, spouse, Daniel Bendix, formerly known as "Snake."

Rita Morecombe was last seen by Tallulah boarding a bus for points north. Nothing is known of her life thereafter, but she was certainly not in

Alta Caca when the catastrophe struck.

Nor were Darien Littlewood and Henrietta Shemp present for the cataclysm. They were in an airplane at the time of the explosion, flying to Las Vegas, where later that day they became man and wife. They watched Nixon's speech from the bed of their honeymoon suite at The Sands Hotel, laughed at the fall of the old fraud, and made love in anticipation of a better future for America. Sadly, Darien did not live quite long enough to see the election of Barack Obama, but Taonga did, and cried tears of joy and Black Pride.

At the time of the calamity, Floradora Windwillow was in the bus with the cast members of Rudy's junior production of *The Boys in the Band*, whom she was chaperoning on their tour, leading the boys in singing *Do You Know the Way to San Jose?* to a very annoyed bus driver, who did, in fact, know the way to San Jose, and who would have appreciated some peace and quiet along that way. Floradora only began to suspect something was wrong that evening, when none of her young charges could get through to home on the phone.

And as for Tallulah Morehead, her memories of Alta Caca were all spewed forth onto tape and duly typed up by Iris Cole as her last act in Tallulah's employ. The manuscript was placed in the box in which I found it, three decades on, apparently unread in all those years. By the time Tallulah woke up in her own well-used bed in Morehead Heights on August 9th, she had forgotten Alta Caca had ever existed. By the time I met her in 1990, she had forgotten the entire decade of the 1970s ever happened.

And so it was that Alta Caca, California, had obliteration visited upon it, and suffered The Greatest Plague of All: Oblivion.

- Douglas McEwan, Morehead Heights, December 2008.

Acknowledgments

This book was born when I read a book titled *Me and Jezebel* by Elizabeth Fuller. Her allegedly-nonfiction book related a story of when Bette Davis came to lunch in Fuller's lavish home one day in 1985 and stayed for a month, owing to a New York hotel strike. Fuller repeatedly states that she is a normal, average housewife, though every word tells you she's actually a privileged, over-monied upper-class housewife-and-writer from a highly upscale Connecticut enclave. Her tale of having her home basically commandeered by that irresistible steamroller Bette Davis promises more comic nuggets than what she delivers. The idea of taking Bette to McDonald's is rife with possibilities, but the payoff is: some folks asked for autographs and she was nice to them. The book's "dramatic" arc is Fuller's desperate desire to become Bette's chum, which she believes she achieved when Bette sat and watched her movie *Jezebel* on TV with Fuller, and didn't insult her.

But though the book is only mildly entertaining at best, it hit me as a really ripe story possibility for Tallulah, pulling a *Man Who Came to Dinner* on a normal, non-show business family. Kaufman & Hart's famous play has always held a special place in my life. But I also immediately realized that, since I wasn't writing small for the stage, why not extend it to an entire fictional community, have her come charging in, leaving unintended chaos and devastation in her wake. The thought of Meredith Wilson's *The Music Man*, a lifelong favorite musical to me, instantly presented himself.

Making Tallulah a reverse-Harold Hill, teaching "The Drink System" to teenage boys, came within minutes. The conclusion of this story, pretty much as is, was fully formed within half an hour of my first saying: "There's a book in this."

Other works I love soon wormed their way into the layers of parody. The beloved Ray Bradbury's (The first novelist I ever met, and a lifelong inspiration) *Something Wicked This Way Comes*, Charles G. Finney's mysterious and wonderful *The Circus of Doctor Lao* along with George Pal's delightful film derived from it, *7 Faces of Dr. Lao*, written by the wonderful Charles Beaumont, Stephen King's '*Salem's Lot*, and even *Mary Poppins*, were all strong influences on this book, along with, obviously, Henry Farrell's *Whatever Happened to Baby Jane* and Mart Crawley's important, seminal comedy-drama *The Boys in the Band*. My desire to try my hand at populating an entire fictional town also played a big hand. So my thanks to all these great authors for the inspirations they provided, along with so much reading pleasure.

I must thank my oldest friend (in the sense of having known him longer than any other non-relative), Will Wixon, for gifting me with the book's title after I had failed to invent any title that I liked.

I must thank the lovely Jayne Hamil, another long time friend, and an experienced network TV comedy writer, for reading the first draft and giving me pages and pages and pages of exact, specific, and helpful suggestions, corrections, and responses. Several scenes now live in the book's second act that didn't exist at all until Jayne said she felt she needed a bit more of this here, or that there. Her work on this book was of tremendous value, and done solely for friendship's sake.

You wouldn't be reading this book if it weren't for Lee Nordling & Adam Rosenblum's decision to publish here at Electric Noggin. I am most grateful for that.

My brothers Barry and Duncan see to it that I have a functional computer. Without them, I couldn't have written this book or any other. Oh, and their unconditional love for the past six decades has been an essential sustaining force in my life. My siblings are the best gifts my parents ever gave me.

Jeff Swanson listened to most of this work read aloud by me, serial fashion as written, which was a big help in discerning which jokes worked and which didn't. You can't write comedy in a vacuum.

About "Phil Rains": my old friends all know that I had a choir director in high school named Phil Haynes, and that the real Phil physically resembles the fictional Phil. He directed me in Concert Choir and Choraleers for four years, mentored me in many ways, a father-figure who was interested in the same stuff I was, unlike my real father, who was a fine man, but, well, Dad thought Math was "fun." Phil and I also appeared together onstage in *Camelot* away from school, as peers, not as student-and-teacher. Phil was that rarest and most valuable of things: a good influence. Sadly, I have not seen nor heard from him in forty years, and have not the slightest idea if he's still alive or not. Phil, if you're still out there, thanks again for 1964-68.

So let me be clear about this: the real Phil was a sunny, happy man with a rich sense of humor and a loud rolling laugh. Yes, he was the starting point for the book's Phil, but the real Phil when I knew him was in a very happy marriage, with a beautiful wife and lovely daughter. The darkness of "Phil Rains's" storyline in this book comes entirely from a weird, morbid nook in my imagination.

I happened to read Professor Richard Dawkins's book *The God Delusion* (my highest recommendation to all readers. This is a great book) while writing the first act of this novel. From its account of post-World War II Pacific Islander "Cargo Cults," sprang into my head the Imawankah Indians plotline, the only storyline born after I began writing the first draft, and one which pleases me a good deal. So my thanks to Professor Dawkins. Everyone, really, read his books.

Ken Levine's enthusiastic support for my work has bolstered my confidence and opened doors for me, particularly at *The Huffington Post*. I am most grateful for his support and friendship.

Many readers of this book's "prequel," *My Lush Life*, and/or of my now-defunct column on Ye Olde Huff Po, have written to me and demonstrated love and support for the work I was doing. That so many people, from as far away as England and Australia, made clear to me that they wanted "more Tallulah," was essential in motivating me to open the *Tallyho, Tallulah!* file each day and keep on writing it. You, my happy readers, make it worth the doing. Tallulah thanks you as well.

Lastly, an overdue thank you left over from *My Lush Life*. The Australian comic genius Barry Humphries, a man I feel to be every bit the equal in his unique ways to Chaplin, Keaton, Groucho, and W. C. Fields, was kind enough to read *My Lush Life* in manuscript form (when it was still titled *Miss Morehead, Please*) and to blurb it. I can not adequately express how proud it made me to have my first-born book go out into the world bearing the recommendation of one of the greatest comedy geniuses of the 20th (and now 21st) Century.

I set this book in 1974 for a variety of reasons (I wanted Nixon lurking in there, for one), but the biggest reason was that it was the happiest year of my life to date, and it was fun for me to return to that era. I truly hope that all of you reading this book get as much pleasure from reading it as I got from writing it. I hope to see all of you again, next book. Until then, happy reading.

About The Author

Douglas McEwan is the author of the books *My Lush Life* and *The Q Guide to Classic Monster Movies*, as well as the forthcoming *My Gruesome Life*, also from Electric Noggin. He contributed essays, TV scripts, and the forward to *Creatures of the Night That We Loved So Well: The Horror Hosts of Southern California*. As "Tallulah Morehead," he wrote comic essays and reviews in The *Huffington Post* for two and a half years. He has written comedy sketches and plays for stage, radio, and TV. As a radio personality in the 1970s, he interviewed such comedy giants as Groucho Marx and Bud Abbott. He lives in Reseda, California, with two cats who do not find him all that amusing.

www.ingramcontent.com/pod-product-compliance
Lightning Source LLC
Chambersburg PA
CBHW030520020726
47494CB00004B/1174